MALAFORMED
REALITIES

VOLUME TEN

THOMAS M. MALAFARINA

**HELLBENDER
BOOKS**

an imprint of Sunbury Press, Inc.
Mechanicsburg, PA USA

HELLBENDER BOOKS

an imprint of Sunbury Press, Inc.
Mechanicsburg, PA USA

For information about special discounts for bulk purchases, please contact Sunbury Press Orders Dept. at (855) 338-8359 or orders@sunburypress.com.

To request one of our authors for speaking engagements or book signings, please contact Sunbury Press Publicity Dept. at publicity@sunburypress.com.

FIRST HELLBENDER BOOKS EDITION: June 2025

Set in Adobe Garamond Pro | Interior design by Crystal Devine | Cover design by Lawrence Knorr | Edited by Lawrence Knorr.

Publisher's Cataloging-in-Publication Data
Names: Malafarina, Thomas M., author.
Title: Malaformed realities volume 10 / Thomas M. Malafarina.
Description: First trade paperback edition. | Mechanicsburg, PA : Hellbender Books, 2025.
Summary: Thomas Malafarina strikes again with 18 spine-tingling tales of horror.
Identifiers: ISBN 979-8-88819-287-0 (softcover).
Subjects: FICTION / Horror | FICTION / Short Stories (single author).

Designed in the USA
0 1 1 2 3 5 8 13 21 34 55

For the Love of Books!

For my wonderful wife, JoAnne. We have officially retired from our day jobs and now have more time together, and I have more time to write. Thank you for putting up with my crazy writing all these years and for tolerating the increased time I spend writing now that we are retired. You are and always have been the best.

CONTENTS

INTRODUCTION

Here we are at Volume 10 of the Malformed Realities series. Although the ideas for horror short stories keep coming in what seems like an endless parade of creativity, writing introductions to each of these volumes can be challenging. On the one hand, I enjoy talking directly with you, my dedicated readers, whom I affectionately refer to as "Malcontents." On the other hand, I need to try not to be repetitive for the sake of anyone who happens to be reading all the volumes in numerical order.

Although this is the 10th volume, it will not be the last. As of this writing, I am well into Volumes 11 to 15, with no sign of slowing down. If anything, my writing time has increased significantly. Since my wife JoAnne and I have retired from our day jobs, I have more time to write. I try to balance my time between going places for fun, doing work around the house, and doing other activities so that writing does not become my new job. Even though it would be a great job, I can't afford to get permanently lost in these bizarre worlds I create in my stories. I need the occasional injection of reality to keep me out of the locked ward at the local old folk's home.

Volume 10 is an interesting collection with lots of new works and a few stories I pulled from an earlier collection called *Ghost Shadows*. This was not me being lazy by any means. It was so that Malcontents who have been reading my previous *Malaformed Realities* volumes but who may never have heard of *Ghost Shadows* can have an opportunity

to check out some of those works. I'll also sprinkle some of those stories in Volumes 11, 12, and 13.

So, sit back and relax, my dedicated reader, and enjoy this selec-
tion of chilling short stories. As always, thank you for your time and
dedication.

Thomas M. Malafarina
June 2025

MAILBOX

"*Juvenile crime is not naturally born in the boy, but is largely due either to the spirit of adventure that is in him, to his own stupidity, or to his lack of discipline, according to the nature of the individual.*"
—Robert Baden-Powell

"*We've got to make sure that the young, violent, serious juvenile offender is punished, that it's fair punishment, that it's punishment that fits the crime and that is understood, and that is anticipated and expected.*"
—Janet Reno

"*The juvenile delinquent does not feel his disturbed personality. The intelligent man does not feel his intelligence or the introvert his introversion.*"
—B. F. Skinner

"*I have to say I'm all for public flogging. One type of criminal that a public humiliation might work particularly well with are the juvenile delinquents, a lot of whom consider it a badge of honor to be sent to juvenile detention. And it might not be such a cool thing in the 'hood to be flogged publicly.*"
—Ann Coulter

/ 1 /

"Come on, man. This'll be freaking awesome!" Buck said as he took another swig from his beer bottle.

"I don't know, Buck. I heard them Jenkins folks ain't right in the head," Jeb said, then he took a cautious sip from his beer and grimaced at the taste.

Buck asked, "Why you makin' that sour puss for, Jeb? Don't you like the brewskees? After, I went to all the trouble to steal 'em from old Ma Jones' general store, and there you go makin' snooty faces."

"I dunno, Buck. They just taste skunky to me."

Buck was stunned, "Skunky? What the hell do you know about skunky beer? It ain't like you're no big-time connoisseur of such things."

Jeb said, "Maybe not, maybe so, Mr. I-must-have-finally-opened-a-dictionary. Connoisseur? Really? Alls I know is that beer tastes more like groundhog piss than anything else."

"Well, I 'spose I hafta take your word for that. 'Cause I don't wanna know how you know what groundhog piss tastes like. Anyway, back to my idea," Buck said.

"I dunno, Buckster. Them Jenkins folks are all nuts in the head, from what I been hearing. I think we should steer clear o'them. I think we only got lucky last time," Jeb argued.

Buck said, "I know you're right, Bro, but I'm telllin' you, that new mailbox they put up is an incredible sight. In fact, it's two mailboxes side-by-side. I can't believe they put up such beauties. I mean, the rest of their property is a run-down piece of crap, barely able to stand. It's like those two mailboxes were put up just for us and are waiting for two able-bodied ne're-do-wells like you and me to take them both down."

"Did you just call us ne're-do-wells? Are you goin' all Middle-ages on me now, Sir Bucksalot? Why not call us rouges, varlets, vagabonds, or scallywags?"

"Fine, scallywags it is. But listen, bro, we have got to do this, and I have the right tool for the job." Buck set down his beer and picked up his new baseball bat. It was an amazingly sturdy metal bat, an Easton Hype Fire. He had bought at the local sporting goods store for $350 he had acquired from his sideline business of selling special in-demand illegal substances to his eager classmates.

"You got to be kidding me, Buck. You mean you're going to use that brand-new, way-too-expensive bat on the Jenkins' new mailboxes? I'd ask if you were nuts, but I'm afraid that ship has already sailed."

"It's not a big deal, Jebmeister. It's supposed to be super-strong, but if it breaks, it breaks. No sweatski. I'll just peddle some more magic pills to my regulars at school and make up for the loss. Like I said, no biggie."

"Yeah? Well, what if those Jenkins mutants catch us? Who knows what they would do to us. I heard stories about really freaky stuff going on out there."

"They never caught us last time we took out their crappy old mailbox, did they?"

Jeb relented, "Well, no. They didn't."

"So they won't catch us this time either."

"But don't it seem a bit strange that a week after we smash their crap mailbox, they put up a brand new one, and not just one but two?"

Buck said, "Well, no one ever accused any of the Jenkins freaks of being Alfred Einsteens."

"It's Albert," Jeb corrected.

"What?"

"It's Albert, not Alfred. And it's Einstein, not Einsteen."

"Whatever. Who gives a flying Wallenda? So here's the plan. We'll speed by like last time, with you, my trusty man-at-arms by my side. I suppose I should say man-at-wheels since you'll be driving. Then, I'll smash the mailboxes to Kindom Come."

Jeb hesitated momentarily, then after taking another sip of his beer, shaking his head in disgust and again making his patented miserable face, said, "Well, I haven't driven your Camaro since that last time we did a mailbox run, and I have to admit, that part of the plan would be pretty cool."

"You bet! Cool like a moose and twice as hairy!"

"What the hell does that mean, Buck?"

"Nothin', just something I felt like saying. And before you ask, no, I haven't been sampling my own wares, at least not today."

/ 2 /

The two boys sped out of town in the dark of night, heading for the rural two-lane that would take them past the Jenkins farm and their awaiting prize. Jeb was at the wheel, and Buck was in the shotgun seat, his bat resting between his legs.

"This'll be incredible," Buck said as he adjusted the GoPro camera he had fastened atop his head with a strap mount device he bought online for ten bucks or so.

Jeb asked, "Wouldn't it have been better to mount that thing to a helmet or hat or something?"

"Maybe, if I wasn't gonna be hanging out a speeding car window, trying to hit a postal grand slam. Besides, I didn't want to be saddled with the extra weight of a helmet and a camera. This will be much better."

"If you say so, Buck. But what I don't get is why you want to video this in the first place. If the Jenkins freaks call the cops and they find video records of this, it'll land us both in juvie."

"Not to worry, my paranoid little partner in crime. This video is going into storage in a place where 5-0 will never find it. No one but me will know how to locate this video, and I won't ever have to tell them where it is. Because the videos I have hidden aren't just you and me doin' goofy pranks. I have videos of all kinds of people doing all sorts of things they shouldn't be doing. Let's just say, if anyone tries to make things too hot for us, I'm sure I can inspire them to cool their jets for a bit."

"Do I want to know?"

"Absolutely not. This is one of those times where ignorance truly is bliss."

Up ahead, the new mailboxes were almost luminescent in the moonlight. Buck said, "Pull over here for a minute, Jeb."

"What's up, Buck? Is something wrong?"

"Not at all. I just want to take a bit to study the situation and make sure everything is good to go. It's always best to check out the lay of the land before we make our final strike run."

Jeb asked, "So, are we ready or what?"

"Let's do this thing, Jebster. Full-throttle, Bro! Peddle to the metal."

With that, Jeb pressed the accelerator to the floor, and the Camaro roared down the rough country lane, gaining speed as it got ever closer to the awaiting target. Buck was hanging half out of the passenger window; his legs pressed tightly against the inside door panel to keep him from falling out. He gripped the bat handle tightly and pulled it back, preparing for his grand slam. Thanks to the poor road conditions, the head-mounted camera rattled, but Buck hoped it would at least capture a good shot of the destruction as it occurred. Unfortunately, he would get the shot he so much desired, but he would never live to see it.

What happened next happened as if in slow motion, even though the Camaro was traveling about eighty miles per hour at the time of impact.

Buck hung out the window with his bat, ready to smash both mailboxes into oblivion. Jeb focused on keeping the car on the road, speeding ever faster toward their target. As the Camaro passed in front of the mailboxes, Buck swung the bat with all his might and slammed it into the first box. Unfortunately for the boys, although the Jenkins family was just as crazy as they thought, they weren't quite as stupid.

Buck's bat hit the mailbox and shattered into three pieces. The impact instantly broke both of Buck's arms, pulling him out of the car and hurling him onto the nearby trash-covered grass, where he writhed, screaming in agony for a few seconds before mercifully passing out. One of the pieces of the bat smashed against the side of the Camaro with a thunderous bang.

Upon hearing the sound and feeling the impact of the bat fragment, Jeb tried to steer away from the mailbox. This contributed to Buck's flying out the window and Jeb overcompensating and yanking the steering wheel too quickly. The car began to roll, and after striking a tree, it flipped over and sent Jeb out through the windshield and onto the gravel road.

/ 3 /

Buck found himself slowly awakening but confused. He couldn't remember where he was or what had happened to him. He was lying on his side and ached from head to toe, discovering he was unable to move.

Through still-focusing eyes, he saw his friend, Jeb, lying unconscious in the grass next to him, bound in a thick bull rope. Now he understood why he was unable to move. The pain he felt in his arms was unbearable, and Buck found himself on the verge of passing out. Part of him welcomed unconsciousness if it meant he could avoid more pain.

Jeb's face was covered with cuts and dried blood. His legs were twisted at an impossible angle, and bones jutted out through his bloody jeans. It was obvious to Buck that his friend was as badly injured as he was, if not worse. He studied Jeb's chest to make sure he was still alive and was relieved to see the boy's chest slightly rising and falling, even though his breathing appeared shallow and irregular. In the distance, Buck could see the sun rising over the horizon, so he knew they had been lying there for quite some time. But why were they bound in rope, and why hadn't anyone called for an ambulance to come and help them?

Then Buck recalled where they were and why they had been there. They were tied up in the grass outside of the Jenkins farm, which meant it had to have been those freaks who had found them and tied them up.

Buck had no idea how they would get free or even if they were physically able to make their way off this stupid farm and to safety if they were free. He tried to call Jeb and found his voice no more than a quiet, raspy whisper. His chest ached with the attempt, and Buck discovered that every breath he took was agonizing. Then Buck understood that he had likely broken several ribs and maybe punctured a lung.

"Jeb . . . Jeb . . ." Buck croaked, but Jeb didn't respond. He was either deeply unconscious or perhaps comatose.

"Save your breath, young fella," a voice called from nearby. "That there friend of your'n ain't never gonna wake up 'nough to talk at ya no more."

Suddenly, with unimaginable terror, Buck realized why he and Jeb were bound and who was responsible. He was at the mercy of the crazy Jenkins family. He heard heavy, menacing footsteps coming around from behind him, and for a moment, he feared someone was about to kick him in the head or stomp him to death, but the footsteps continued to slog their way around to his limited area of visibility. First,

Buck saw two filthy, mud-covered work boots with the laces missing. Then, based on the stench emanating from the material clinging to the boots, he unfortunately realized it wasn't mud after all. The feet inside the boots were bare, and the visible portion of the ankles he could see were hairy and caked with filth. The legs were clad in equally dirty and worn denim bibbed overalls. The flabby, hulking creature beneath the overalls appeared not to wear a shirt, but based on the dirt and massive amounts of hair, it was difficult to determine whether that was true. Buck was uncertain if this creature was even a man, as its head was strangely small and hairless. He had remembered hearing the term hydrocephalic in high school biology and was pretty sure that was what this monster was. Buck was also certain by the dull lack of intelligence in the man's eyes that he wasn't the one who had spoken. Then he heard the original voice come from behind him once again.

"Bo, pick up that one what's on the ground and take him over there," The voice said. Buck had no idea where "over there" was but was fairly certain that finding that answer would not be good.

The brain-deficient Bo bent down and picked up Jeb's broken body as if it were weightless and carried it out of sight. Then Buck heard another set of footsteps coming around by his feet and saw a short, rail-thin old man approaching. The man wore similar filth-coated boots and overalls, but unlike the dull-eyed Bo, this whiskered, wizened old timer who was bald with only a fringe of white hair had a look of cunning which was the exact opposite of the mutant giant. He gave Buck a strange grin, revealing a cavernous mouth of missing and rotted tombstone teeth.

"Well now, young fella. I s'pose y'all thought you was pretty clever tryin' to smash up my new mailbox, didn't you? Yeah, I knowed it was you and that other fella what broke my old box. I figgered you wouldn't be able to resist takin' a shot at this here new one neither. That's' why I filt the first one with see-ment. It's what ya might call one'a them there decoys. And I'll be damned if it didn't work like a champ."

"See-ment?" Buck thought, then realized this old geezer was talking about cement. The freak had filled the mailbox with cement, creating a potentially deadly trap for anyone dumb enough to try to take out the mailbox. With sad resignation, Buck realized he and Jeb had fallen headlong into their trap. He had no idea what would happen to them next, but he sensed it wouldn't be good.

Buck tried again to speak, whispering, "Help . . . I need help . . . I'm hurt bad."

The old man agreed, "Yep. You most surely are that. Both you and your buddy over there are hurt somethin' terrible."

"I . . . need help . . . call an ambulance . . . please," Buck pleaded.

"Well, young fella. I'd like to do that, but I got me two problems. First, it ain't exactly legal what I done there with fillin' that mailbox with see-ment, is it? Nope, I don't believe it is. And second, if I call fer help, there's gonna be lots of questions asked, questions I don't think I wanna answer, if you know what I mean."

"But . . . what are you going . . . to do with us? We . . . need help."

"Yup, you surely do. But I got another plan fer you two juveenile dee-linquents. You ain't gonna like it much, but there ain't nothin' I kin do about that."

Then Buck heard the familiar thudding of the two large dung-covered boots worn by the monster, Bo, approaching, and he knew he was in bigger trouble than he could have ever imagined.

The old man said, "Bo, take this fella over there with his friend, and I'll be joinin' you shortly."

Buck dreaded what he knew was coming next as the giant reached down and unceremoniously lifted him off the ground and over his stinking, sweaty, fur-covered shoulders. The pain was so unbearable that before he had a chance to scream, Buck collapsed into unconsciousness.

When he eventually awoke in agony again, he was on the feces-covered ground next to Jeb, who was still unconscious. He heard a motor nearby that sounded like it might be a cement mixer. Buck envisioned old man Jenkins mixing up a bunch of "see-ment" to use on him and Jeb. Maybe he would bury them alive and place a concrete slab over them to hide the graves. Or he might make them wear "See-ment Boots" and toss them in the nearby river.

"What's . . . that noise?" Buck asked hoarsely, unsure if anyone was even around to answer him. "Is that a cement mixer?"

"Heck, no," The old man's voice said. "I ain't got much use fer somethin' like that. At least, I didn't 'till now. I mixed up that see-ment for the mailbox by hand. What you're hearing is another piece of equipment I use quite a bit 'round here."

Buck lay in immovable terror, uncertain of what might be making the noise. He knew it was some sort of motor. Then he noticed an incredible stench surrounding where he and Jeb lay. It was like the smell of what covered Bo's boots but about a hundred times stronger. Then he recognized it as the stink of livestock, pigs to be exact.

"I . . . I smell pigs," Buck managed to squeak out.

"Yep, you most certainly do. My girls. We got us a whole passel of them not more than ten feet from you, behint that there fence."

Buck didn't like where all this was leading and was suddenly envious of his friend, Jeb, who was oblivious to what was happening.

The old man said calmly, "You see, young fella. My pigs get real hungry, and I can't always afford to be buyin' 'em feed. Sometimes I have to make due."

"But . . ." Buck tried to say.

"Now, like I said, that there noise you're hearin' ain't no see-ment mixer, no sir-ee. It's my handy-dandy woodchipper. I use that thing all the time around here, cutting up branches and even grinding up dead animals to feed my girls. Ya see, pigs ain't all that particular about what they eat."

Before Buck could comprehend the severity of his predicament, he heard the old man give Bo the command, "You know what to do, Bo."

Then he felt himself being lifted and hoped against hope that he would pass out again from his pain but didn't until he felt the blades of the woodchipper begin mangling his legs to pieces.

RAPTURE

"Then there will be two men in the field; one will be taken,
and one will be left."
—MATTHEW 24:40

"And in those days men will seek death and will not find it;
they will long to die, and death flees from them."
—REVELATION 9:6

"And there will be great earthquakes and in various places plagues and
famines, and there will be terrors and great signs from heaven."
—LUKE 21:11

"Good Lord, I hate this infernal world we have made for ourselves. Crooked politicians, young people with no respect for their elders, people killing each other in the streets, global warming, famine. It's as sad as it is pathetic," The old man mumbled his complaints to the empty room as he looked out his apartment window into the city streets below.

He had lived more than eight decades and had done his best to live what he considered a righteous life, following the teachings of the Bible and never breaking even one of the commandments. He had been married for 60 years to the same woman, the former Jenifer Conway, who had passed away the previous year. During their long marriage, he had never given in to temptation and had maintained their wedding vows, which he considered sacred. He attended church faithfully every Sunday and gave generously when the collection plate came around.

Wilbur Baldwin had no criminal record and had never stolen from or cheated anyone in his life, including the US Government. He paid his taxes regularly and on time and never tried to get away with less than was required. He was fond of saying, "Render to Caesar the things that are Caesar's and to God the things that are God's," which he would usually follow with the biblical location, "Mark 12:17."

This was why it seemed so strange to Wilbur that the event he had been planning for his entire life had not yet occurred. He thought often of the Rapture, which he believed he would see in his lifetime. But now, his lifetime was ending, and he had seen no such event occur.

According to all Wilbur believed, the Rapture would come for the faithful, both those still living as well as those who had died. This meant his late wife, Jenny, would be part of the Rapture as well because she was as close to an angel as could be possible on Earth. Wilbur believed that all Christians would rise into the air to meet Jesus in his second coming. The unbelievers would be left behind.

Following the Rapture, when all the worthy were taken, the world would be subjected to seven years of what would essentially be a Hell on Earth. After this tumult, Wilbur believed Jesus would be victorious over His enemies and would reign over the Earth for 1,000 years with the help of His saints and church. Wilbur knew in his heart that time was coming and had spent a lifetime preparing for it.

However, he was frustrated. Part of his uncertainty came from his grief at losing his beloved wife and trying to go on without her. But most of it came from the world around him. Wilbur wasn't the type to pine incessantly about "the good old days" or blame the younger generations for his displeasure with society. However, in his opinion, Wilbur believed something had become broken in society, and that civilization was deteriorating exponentially. It was like a snowball was rolling down a hill, gaining momentum and growing in size, and there was nothing anyone could do to stop it.

This feeling made Wilbur believe the time had come and the Rapture would occur any day. He supposed all he could do was wait and hope he was worthy. Wilbur's problem was that he felt he couldn't go on without Jenny, yet he had no choice but to do so. If he were to take his own life, all he had worked for would be lost. He knew suicide was a mortal sin that would exclude him from being part of the Rapture. Wilbur feared that even contemplating such an act might endanger his eligibility to participate in this holy event. Then again, being tempted and fighting that temptation might increase his chances, as Satan tempts man in all ways, and it is up to man to fight that temptation. Perhaps fighting those earthly temptations would make him even more eligible for inclusion.

It was all so infuriating. Wilbur felt the world around him was in chaos. He doubted that things could get much worse than they already were. The city where he lived was a virtual cesspool of living, breathing creatures of human waste. People thought nothing of robbing, raping, and murdering each other, and it seemed law enforcement and the legal system in general was impotent to stop it. Sometimes, Wilbur felt perhaps the Rapture had already occurred, and he had been left behind. But he could not think so negatively.

The teachings said after the Rapture, the world would live in torment for seven years before Jesus returned. The problems Wilbur had seen with the world had been going on for decades, not just seven years, and each year, things seemed to get progressively worse. No, he was certain that if he just waited, the Rapture would come, and he would be taken up to be with Jesus and his beloved Jenny. But when, dear Lord, would it come?

Wilbur heard a knock on his apartment door and carefully looked out the peephole he had placed in the sturdy wooden door to see who it might be. One could never be too careful with the world the way it was. He quickly peeped, then pulled back and peeped a second time because he had seen a movie where someone looked out a peephole and was shot through the eye by an assailant.

Through the peephole, he saw a rather distinguished-looking white-haired gentleman dressed in a white suit with a matching white shirt and tie. The only sign of color Wilbur could see was a red pocket square smartly placed in his top-left suit pocket. The man also had a white mustache and beard.

What an unusual character to be knocking on his door at this early hour of the morning; it was barely 9:30 am. Wilbur assumed the visitor might be some sort of salesman trying to get an early start or maybe one of those infernal cult religious zealots trying to save him. He had to explain to them repeatedly that he was already saved, and if anyone needed saving, they did. When the Rapture came, they and their storefront so-called religions would be left behind to live in torment. The knock came again.

"Go away!" Wilbur shouted, "Whatever you're selling, I ain't buying."

Then a voice came from behind the door, "Mr. Wilbur Baldwin? I can assure you I am not selling anything, but I do have an important message for you. If you will be so kind as to open the door, I will happily share it with you."

Wilbur thought for a moment. This was obviously some new ploy those storefront holy rollers used to get inside. They probably got his name from some database. No doubt, once Wilbur let the man in, he would likely get bombarded with a lecture about how their church was the true church, and Wilbur's was not. Only by signing up with the man and promising to give ten percent of his income for the rest of his life could Wilbur be saved.

"I ain't interested in no message, neither," Wilbur shouted.

There was a moment of hesitation, then the man said calmly, "Even if it concerns the Rapture, Wilbur?"

Now, the stranger had gotten Wilbur's attention. Even if this character was a made-up religious weirdo, Wilbur could go toe-to-toe with him on any discussion of the Rapture. Maybe having a heated debate with someone was exactly what he needed to get out of this funk in which he seemed to find himself. Wilbur slowly slid back the numerous locks on his door and turned the handle to let the stranger in.

"Do come in, Sir. It seems you and I have some important business to discuss," Wilbur said as the man passed by, entering the apartment.

"Indeed, we do, Wilbur. Indeed, we do," the man replied.

Wilbur said, "It seems you have me at an advantage, Sir. What may I ask is your name?"

"Although my name is unimportant, you can call me Peter."

"Peter? How appropriate. Like Saint Peter?" Wilbur asked.

"If you prefer," The man said cryptically.

"Well, Peter. I see you want to discuss the Rapture with me."

The man hesitated, then said, "Yes, I suppose I do."

"Well then, Peter. Go ahead and tell me what you want to tell me so we can get this thing underway."

"Before I do, I would like to know if you feel you are a candidate worthy to be taken up when the Rapture occurs."

Wilbur said, "Of course I do. I have no doubt whatsoever. I have been a faithful Christian all my life. I seldom miss church, teach a Sunday School class, and am a deacon in the church."

"Hum. Pretty impressive."

"I also pray nightly and follow all the laws of our country faithfully. I've never gotten so much as a parking ticket in my life, either."

"Again, quite impressive, Wilbur. How do you feel about people of other religions, such as Buddhists, Muslims, Hindus, and other such religions?"

Wilbur hesitated, then said, "Well, of course, they are all pretenders. You know, fake religions made up by non-God-fearing heathens."

"Oh, I see. What about Jehovah's Witnesses, Seventh-Day Adventists, or maybe even Mennonites?"

"Pretenders one and all. Since you came to discuss the Rapture, let's get on with it. All those folks you just mentioned will be left behind as well."

Peter thought momentarily, then asked, "But you, Wilbur. You will be included and will be taken up in the Rapture?"

"Yes, most certainly. I will be joined by my late wife, Jenifer, as well."

"I see. Well, what would you say if I told you that the Rapture had already happened a long time ago, during your lifetime?"

Wilbur insisted, "I would say that you are most definitely mistaken. I have spent my entire life preparing for it and surely would have been taken up."

Peter hesitated, then said, "I hate to be the one who has to tell you this, Wilbur. But the Rapture did already occur, and you were not taken. In fact, hardly any living humans were deemed worthy enough to participate."

"I don't believe that for a moment. If such a thing occurred, people would have noticed their ministers, priests, and loved ones missing. For Heaven's sake, the Pope disappearing could not go unnoticed."

"What makes you think a Pope would automatically be considered?"

Wilbur was getting angry, "You make no sense. If the Rapture had happened, according to the Bible, we would have had seven years of tumult before Jesus returned. Are you saying the Rapture happened less than seven years ago?"

"No, Wilbur. I'm not. It happened many years before that. The problem is you seem to take that seven-years idea literally. It's kind of like thinking the world was created in seven days. The units of time measurements in the spiritual world do not exactly match those here on Earth."

"So what are you saying?" Wilbur demanded.

"I'm saying that the Rapture occurred when you were just a child, back in the late 1950s or early 1960s; I'm not exactly sure how the dates correlate with Earth dates. You were too young to know about the Rapture back then, and to be honest, so few humans were deemed worthy of being raised up that almost no one noticed anyone missing."

"So you're trying to tell me that the Rapture already occurred, and since then and now, we are living in that so-called seven days of tumult?"

"That's exactly what I'm saying, Wilbur. Be honest, during your lifetime, haven't you seen a decline in kindness, caring, loving, not to mention honesty, goodness, and morality in general?"

"Of course I have. Since the late 1960s, the world has been going to Hell in a handbasket, as they say. The rise of technology has allowed people to spew their hatred of each other daily on social media sites. Politicians are constantly being caught in corruption and immoral situations. Even the members of the clergy in some denominations have been accused of illicit acts with young boys. War has been another constant all during my lifetime, with thousands of thousands of lives lost. You can't take a walk outside without worrying about being robbed or killed. I have five locks on my door just to help me sleep at night. So, yes, I have noticed a decline. But I still can't accept what you are telling me."

Peter said, "I'm sorry, Wilbur. It's not something for you to accept or not accept. It simply is. I came here to tell you the Rapture you have been waiting for has already come and gone. You are now living in tumult, and very soon, Jesus will be returning with his saints to fulfill the prophecies of the scriptures."

"And what about me?" Wilbur asked.

Peter said, "You have lived a good life, Wilbur. That is why I was sent to speak with you. It is your responsibility to keep living your life as you have been, and when your time comes, you will be judged as required. However, there is one thing you must change if you ever hope to enter what you call Heaven. You must learn to accept all people, regardless of race, nationality, sexual orientation, or religious beliefs. It is not for you to tell someone that, for example, his religion is not the 'right' religion to have. Or to say that one nationality is better than another. That sort of thing is what the years of tumult are all about, not what living a good life is about."

"I . . . I just don't know if I can do that," Wilbur said honestly.

"You either will or you will not, Wilbur. Just as you cannot force someone to believe as you believe, those of us chosen to visit and pass the message to people like you cannot force you to do what must be done. Life is full of choices and decisions. As a rational human being, it is up to you to make those choices and decisions for yourself. Know this, however. When the time comes for your judgment, right or wrong, your decisions, as all decisions, will have consequences."

Wilbur had been looking down at his feet, thinking about what to say next. When he looked up, Peter was gone. The locks were back in place on his door, and there was no sign that anyone had been in the room with him. His mind became clouded, and he was starting to forget what had just happened, yet he felt something important had occurred, but he couldn't recall what it was.

Wilbur heard a loud bang from somewhere outside. He ran to the window and saw a man running down the alley, trailing blood from a gunshot wound. A woman was screaming and calling for help. Wilbur pulled his head back in the window, closed the sash, and sat in his chair. Suddenly, he was struck with a realization. The Rapture he had been waiting for his whole life was not coming. It had already come, and he had not been chosen. He was living in the dreaded time of tumult, and there was nothing he could do about it other than to try and survive until his time to leave this world had come.

AUTOMOTIVE GRAVEYARD

Inspired by a photo by Lawrence Knorr

No trait is more justified than revenge in the right time and place.
—MEIR KAHANE

Like monstrous rusting hulks, the ancient shells of what once were noble classic automobiles now lay hidden from the prying eyes of the civilized world by a thick, creeping blanket of overwhelming forest undergrowth. Dozens of trees sized from meager saplings to full-grown majestic behemoths, towered far above the ground, entwining themselves in and around the corroding, formerly mechanized cadavers.

Dense, impenetrable snaking vines of kudzu and other equally aggressive vegetation likewise knotted themselves so cripplingly about the machines as to make them virtually indiscernible. The upper halves of the largest trees seemed to literally propagate upward from deep within the mountainous piles of greenery-encased metal. Many trees had collapsed throughout the years and now lay upon the mounds, further camouflaging the rusting metal relics.

Unless you were aware that the old cars were there or unless you were deliberately searching for them, you would be more likely than not to simply pass by the enormous mass, thinking it to be nothing more than natural forest growth.

But the creatures who resided in the forest knew the old cars were there, hidden by the impenetrable underbrush. The hollowed-out, battered skeletal remains had become the perfect nesting places for a varied assortment of wildlife. This automotive condominium of sorts was so vast in magnitude that both predator and prey could be found living somewhere within the ruins. A fox, coyote, or feral mountain cat might have its den inside a '53 Cadillac Fleetwood, while only a few hundred feet away, a family of rabbits might reside in a '63 Ford Falcon.

This particular graveyard was in the woods, just off Route 51, on the winding range of hills between the community of Mountain Springs and the town of Franksville in Schuylkill County, Pennsylvania. Nothing remained where there had once been a dirt and gravel access road. Its original appearance was impossible to distinguish from the rest of the overgrown woodland.

If you could pinpoint what was once the road and then took it upon yourself to locate and unearth the metallic vestiges, they would ascertain that the most recent vehicle in the macabre collection, which was also the uppermost car on the stack, was a 1965 Mercury Monterey four-door sedan. If you were to investigate this particular vehicle's history in greater detail, you would discover it had once been the property of one Anson Middleton of 1255 Race Street, Franksville, Pennsylvania.

Had you chosen to learn more about Mr. Middleton, you would have found that Middleton and his vehicle had been involved in a catastrophic automobile accident, resulting in Mr. Middleton's death and the complete destruction of the Mercury. A similar story could be said about every single one of the cars on the massive pile of decomposing steel. Each car in the automotive graveyard had been involved in an accident that resulted in a fatality. And like Mr. Middleton's Cadillac, every vehicle had its own story to tell.

Who created this mountain of past sorrows remains a mystery, as does the reason the collector might have chosen only to include those specific cars that had been involved in fatal accidents. Perhaps if someone were to question a few local old-timers, they might be lucky enough to discover the answer. However, that would be unlikely, as few, if any, of those older folks who might still be alive would care to speak of the place.

Back in the 1960s, the location was well known among the local bar patrons and had been discussed for hours until it eventually attained a status akin to legendary. At one time, the barflies might have actually known the name of the person responsible for the automotive necropolis and might even have understood his reasons for creating it. But as with most legends, the site's stories grew to the point where they became nothing more than tall tales.

But nowadays, most of those same townsfolk were either dead or were simply so old that no one would bother to pay attention to what might be perceived as their wild ramblings. So, over fifty years later, the mysterious final resting place was now forgotten along with most of its tragic stories.

But there are still a few your humble narrator has chosen to be recounted.

Anson Middleton's tale was as riddled with clichés as it was tragic, the stuff of country-western tunes. Mr. Anson Middleton was once a senior claims adjuster for the Competence Insurance Company of America. But on that fateful night when he had earned his place on the forest pile of the dead, Mr. Middleton was traveling in excess of 100 MPH while under the influence of a combination of alcohol and prescription drugs. His car left the roadway and slammed headlong into a bridge abutment, producing the predictable yet unpleasantly volatile and final results.

Now, if you were to take the initiative to unearth every one of the vehicles, you would learn that the very first car positioned at the bottom of the pile was a 1938 Packard Super Eight owned by Jeremiah T. Blakely, a well-to-do local doctor, and resident of the nearby city of Yuengsville. His sad story was one of mechanical malfunction, which eventually led to extreme suffering and death.

Jeremiah, his wife, and two children had been enjoying a Sunday afternoon leisurely drive over the Wide-Top Mountain between the towns of Coalmansville and Horton when their brakes failed on the steep incline leading down into the little town. Their car quickly gained speed, and despite Jeremiah's best efforts to maintain control, the velocity soon became too excessive to navigate the automobile.

Since no guardrails were present during those early years, the car became airborne and flew over the hillside, where it flipped end-for-end multiple times, killing everyone inside, but sadly not instantly. One unknown fact about this tragedy was that Mr. Blakely was the last of his family to perish after being forced to spend the last few agonizing minutes of his life listening to the tortured suffering screams of his wife and family as one-by-one their cries faded as they succumbed to their excruciating injuries.

But perhaps the strangest and most haunting stories of all the tragic and horrible tales concerned a young, abrasive, and arrogant teen named James "Duke" Wellington and a forty-something-year-old family man named Francis O'Halloran.

About halfway down, the rusting pile of vehicles circa 1952-1955 lay the two corroded shells, which are the subject of this particular tale. The story of their arrival in the automotive graveyard is cloaked in conceit, wealth, influence, death, and eventual revenge.

James "Duke" Wellington was a sixteen-year-old foolhardy youth whose father was a wealthy and politically well-connected local attorney. Jim got the nickname "Duke" because his surname, Wellington, rhymed with the famous jazz pianist, composer, and big band leader Duke Ellington. However, young Jim Wellington could not write music, play piano, or conduct a band. The Wellington family lived in an upper-class subdivision outside of Franksville.

In contrast, Francis O'Halloran was a forty-three-year-old father of four children, all of whom were under the age of sixteen. His eldest, Francis Junior, was in a class one year behind the infamous Duke Wellington. Young Francis had few encounters with Wellington, but he perceived the boy to be a bully from observations. And like all bullies, Wellington traveled with a cadre of toadies, flunkies, and general hangers-on whose sole purpose in life was to laugh at all of Wellington's juvenile pranks and his immature sense of humor.

Francis Sr. and his family lived in a small wood-framed lower-middle-class row house in Ashton. They survived from paycheck to paycheck, as did most people in his particular social strata. But he never complained and did all he could to support his family. He was a dedicated hard worker assigned as a second shift laborer at a local mirror manufacturing plant on the south side of Franksville.

One late winter night, when the roads were treacherous, Francis drove down the steep, winding hill, heading home from his job. Duke was simultaneously traveling like the proverbial bat out of hell up the hill from the opposite direction. His car was fishtailing wildly and traveling outside of his lane. Duke was accompanied by one of his friends, Nick Gismondi, laughing hysterically at another of Duke's idiotic stunts. As fate would have it, the two cars met at the exact wrong time as the back end of Duke's '55 Corvette fishtailed into the oncoming lane and was struck by O'Halloran's 1953 Ford Country Squire Station Wagon. Normally, such a collision would not have done much damage to the tank-like Ford, but at the last moment, in an ill-fated attempt to avoid the collision, O'Halloran turned his wheel too hard and lost control of the monstrous vehicle sliding across the highway, through the guardrails, down over the embankment, and finally slamming into a cluster of large trees, killing him instantly.

Duke's Corvette was damaged somewhat in the back end, and he suffered a fractured leg, while his friend Nick managed to escape with just a few cuts and lacerations. Police filed charges of vehicular homicide against young Wellington, but his influential father helped him get away with just a fine, which his father grudgingly paid. Likewise, when the O'Halloran family sued the Wellingtons in civil court, the results were just as unsuccessful.

Duke had escaped a jail sentence and a lawsuit. One would think such a close brush with the Grim Reaper might make him reflect and even make him a bit humble, but it didn't. In fact, his arrogance seemed to have increased in some people's opinions, as did the number and severity of the various twisted pranks he pulled on his classmates. For young Francis O'Halloran, Jr., the idea of watching the person who killed his father get off scot-free was often more than he could tolerate. But Francis was a small boy with few friends, and his family didn't travel in the same socio-economic circles as the Wellingtons, so the best he could hope for was to avoid contact with Duke. He feared that if Duke recognized him as the son of the woman who tried to sue him, he would suffer intolerable harassment at the hands of Duke and his army of cronies. So he kept a low profile and remained quiet, doing his best to operate below Duke's radar.

During the next two years before Duke's high school graduation, many strange stories began to spread around the area about mysterious sightings at the very same curve where Francis O'Halloran Sr. lost his life that fateful night. Some people claimed to see a man standing near the side of the road as if looking and waiting for someone to drive by. One person said they stopped to offer the man a ride, but he was gone when they opened the car door. Some people even went so far as to describe the man as looking like the late Francis O'Halloran, which, of course, started the rumor mill buzzing, and before long, all sorts of ghost stories began to permeate the region.

The O'Halloran family heard about the stories but did their best to ignore them as such tales only increased unhappy memories. Duke Wellington also heard the stories, but his response was simply to scoff at them as nonsense. Yet during those years, Duke had made a point of going far out of his way to avoid that particular stretch of highway. His Corvette had been repaired shortly after the accident, and although he still drove much faster than he should, he made a point to never travel that road again.

That was until the night of his high school graduation when he was in a hurry to get home after a friend's party. Duke wanted to see what his father had bought him for graduation. He had asked for a new Corvette, as his current one had never been quite the same since the accident; at least, it never felt right to Duke again. And since his father always bought him everything he wanted, he was certain the new car awaited him at home.

Instead of taking his usual roundabout trip home, he decided it made more sense to travel up the winding mountain and pass the site where the accident occurred. Although he had been nervous about doing so, Duke talked himself into it, thinking about how it was time to put his unfortunate past behind him and be a man.

As he approached the curve, which had caused him so much trouble two years earlier, Duke deliberately slowed his car so he would be certain to pass through safely. His first inclination was to drive past the site as quickly as possible, but slow and easy seemed the best choice on that dark and somewhat foggy night.

Duke saw someone, a man, standing by the side of the road, watching as if waiting. The man wore a denim blue work shirt and cotton work pants. His hair hung down over his eyes, and at first, Duke was unsure who he might be. Then, the strange man lifted his head and stared directly at Duke, who immediately recognized him as Francis O'Halloran, the man he had killed almost two years earlier. But the man no longer looked as he had back then.

The man's cheeks were sunken, and his flesh was no more than sallow hide stretched tightly over bones. His eyes appeared huge and seemed to bug out of hollow black holes. His lips were mere lines pulled back over a mass of large, exposed black and rotten teeth. The horrible creature opened his mouth and let out a roar that vibrated deep into Duke's skull, causing him to throw his hands up instinctively to protect his aching ears.

As he covered his ears, he was just entering the curve, and the vehicle started to veer off the highway. He quickly grabbed the wheel, overcompensating in the process. The car went into an uncontrollable spin before skidding off the highway and slamming into the same cluster of trees at the exact same spot where Francis O'Halloran lost his life two years earlier.

The police who arrived to clean up the mess could not help but notice the look of complete terror that remained on the face of the battered corpse of Duke Wellington. Since a few of them had been on the job a long time and had been the same officers called to the original O'Halloran/Wellington accident, they looked at each other with amazement, understanding the strange, unspoken coincidence. Once again, the local rumor mill filled with stories of ghostly vengeance and how the spirit of Francis O'Halloran had come back from the grave to claim the life of the person who had taken his.

Since that night, sightings of the mysterious stranger stopped. No matter how many stories were told, no one ever saw anything unusual at the site of the crashes again. And they never would. This was because the two cars were now a mile or deeper in the woods, decaying in the middle of a stack of cars, and each of those cars had its own terrible story to tell.

If you were to stop by the weed-infested pile of rusting metal late at night and if you were to sit quietly and listen with an ear for the uncommon, you might hear the painful cries of a young man and the maniacal laughter of revenge coming from his torturer as the two sounds blend to form a mournful howl in the darkness of night.

THE MASK IN THE CHEST

*"Three things cannot be long hidden: the sun,
the moon, and the truth."*
—BUDDHA

*"Some people think that the truth can be hidden with
a little cover-up and decoration. But as time goes by, what is
true is revealed, and what is fake fades away."*
—ISMAIL HANIYEH

*"Men do change, and change comes like a little wind that
ruffles the curtains at dawn, and it comes like the stealthy perfume
of wildflowers hidden in the grass."*
—JOHN STEINBECK

My father passed away three days ago. That's a strange term, isn't it? Passed away. Yet it seems to be the preferred phrase to describe one's death, one's passing from this plane of existence to the next, whatever that might happen to be. It conjures images of rolling, grass-covered hills, a beautiful, sunny blue sky, and perhaps a nearby gently lapping stream. Birds gracefully fly as squirrels and rabbits frolic in the gently waving tall grass. Yes, "passed away" is the preferred phrase as it does an outstanding job of disguising the true nature of some people's dying.

My mother died a few years before my dad, and I suppose you could consider her death "passing away." She died in her sleep, which we all assume to be the best and most peaceful way to "move on." That's another one of those terms people use to help us deal with a loved one's death. We say they "moved on," suggesting their spirit or soul has "moved on" to whatever awaits us. Mom told me once, "Bobby, when my time comes, as everybody's will, I hope I go in my sleep."

She got her wish and I can only hope it was as easy and peaceful as she hoped it would be. All we know is that she said she was tired one day and wanted to lie down for a while and nap. My dad found her a few hours later, still lying in bed, looking peaceful but no longer with us. Apparently, she had "moved on."

My father, on the other hand, did not "pass away" peacefully as we would have preferred. Nor did he have a pleasant time "moving on." Instead, he died, and he didn't merely die, but he died a painful, horrible, wretched death. It was a death of incredible agony and one I wouldn't have wished on even my worst enemy, and it was not the death I felt was appropriate for someone I thought of as kind as my father. Unfortunately, just as we can't predict when we will go, we can't know how we will die. Perhaps the universe had a plan for my father that I simply could not understand. My father never knew that dreaded cancer was eating him from the inside out until it was too late. Hindsight being 20-20, he may have noticed some occasional pains, but at his age, aches and pains were the norm.

By the time the pain got to the point where he realized something might be wrong, there was nothing anyone could do for him. They tried the usual treatments of radiation and chemotherapy, but all it managed to do was make him feel worse. It was a case of the cure being worse than the illness. Eventually, when the morphine could no longer ease his screaming pain, my father died, not "passed away," he just freakin' died.

After my father's death, the responsibility of dealing with my parents' earthly possessions fell to me, their only child, Robert J. Madison II. Yes, I was "the second." My dad hated the term "junior" and thought "the second" sounded much fancier. I didn't care one way or the other.

As a little kid, my mom and friends called me Bobby, and then Bob as an adult, although my mom always called me Bobby. I rarely used the "II," designation with my name, much to my dad's chagrin.

I began the process of cleaning out my parents' house in preparation for what they always jokingly referred to as "the sale." For the record, my parents always used air quotes when referring to "the sale." They would say things like, "Just put that old thing up in the attic and let Bobby deal with it at 'the sale.'" Then, they would have a good laugh at my expense, enjoying my discomfort.

When I walked into my parents' bedroom, I was hit with a strange nostalgic sensation, like both of them were still there, and I was a curious little kid, snooping in their bedroom, which I knew was against the rules but often did. I still thought of this as my parents' bedroom, even though my mom had been gone for several years. Everything in the room was exactly as I remembered it from when I was but a wee lad, including the antique wooden cedar chest at the foot of their bed. I was once again struck with a memory, but this one was quite frightening and involved something that I recalled had been stored in this chest and was probably still there. It was a mask, a horrible rubber zombie mask.

I have no idea where my father may have acquired the hideous thing. My dad was in sales and traveled all over the country, often to other countries. He might have picked up the strange mask anywhere. For some reason, my dad took some sick pleasure from putting on the mask and scaring me with it. He often brought me to tears when he would suddenly jump from behind a door, growling beneath the latex terror, then laughing hysterically as I trembled and cried. It was only now, as an adult reliving horrible memories, that I realized just how wrong and borderline abusive that was. Maybe back in the 1960s, this would be considered harmless fun, but in today's more enlightened world, it would be taken for what it was: mental abuse of a minor. No wonder I was happier whenever my dad traveled, and it was just my mom and me.

At the time, I never thought of his teasing as mean-spirited or abusive because I couldn't imagine my dad being mean to me or anyone.

He was not that type of person, and to most folks, I would assume he was seen as harmless as Ward Cleaver. I figured it was just some adult fun that I was too young to understand. I was only scared because I was just a dumb kid, and someday, I would grow up and not be frightened anymore. But I have to admit, it did bother me how my dad seemed to get into the scary character with much more enthusiasm than perhaps such a gag should have merited. That feeling always lurked in the back of my mind as I tried to convince myself he was just having fun.

But now, I was no longer that scared little boy, and even though I knew that horrible mask was probably still hidden somewhere in this cedar chest, it was my responsibility to clean out the chest and decide what to do with the contents. So, with great trepidation, I lifted the lid and began carefully removing items. The smell of cedar and old clothing wafted into the air, and another scent, something foul and dank.

Most of the topmost items were articles of what I believed to be my mom's clothing, carefully folded and sealed in clear plastic bags. They had strange reddish-brown patterns I was unfamiliar with, but I had been out of the house for more than a decade and didn't pay much attention to what my mom wore in her final years. I have no idea why my dad didn't get rid of this worthless stuff years ago, maybe give it to the poor. I took each wrapped parcel and gingerly set them on the floor.

Eventually, I found the dreaded mask. It was lying between several layers of clothing and on top of a black loose-leaf binder I had never seen before. I picked up the binder, assuming it might be full of photos of faded Polaroid memories of our family from long ago, leaving the mask to fall inside the chest, not wanting to touch it. But I realized this strange book was something else when I looked at the cover. It was black except for the words written in large letters, which were obviously cut out of several magazines. It looked like a ransom note straight out of one of the many cop movies I had watched. It said, "Robert's Memories."

I determined it must be some type of scrapbook my father had assembled. I had no idea he was interested in such things. When I opened the book, a handwritten note slid out and dropped onto the floor. As I bent to pick it up, I noticed a sentence at the top reading, "For my son, Robert James Madison II—For his eyes only." Now, I was intrigued. I walked over, sat on the edge of the bed, and proceeded to read the note.

It started with the greeting, "Dear Bobby." That alone was strange; my father always called me Robert, never Bob or Bobby. Maybe he had his reasons for using that less formal name. I couldn't imagine what they might be until I read the rest of the letter.

It said, "If you are reading this, I am dead, and you are in the house trying to figure out what to do with my earthly possessions. As far as I'm concerned, you can auction off the house and everything inside and get whatever you can for everything except these things. I don't want anyone but you to read this letter and examine my scrapbook. It contains my most precious and personal memories. I have never shared these things with anyone, not even your mother. When you read my scrapbook, you will understand why.

"You know me as your father, the man who, along with your beautiful mother, gave you life and raised you to be the man you are today. I always wanted to call you Bobby, like your mother did, but I suppose I was always hung up on you being Robert the second that I never did. Maybe I felt that Bobby was your mother's special name for you and off-limits to me. I don't know. I don't understand my logic either, but as you will soon see, there is a lot about me that I can't explain because I believe it wasn't necessarily me making these decisions or carrying out these actions. It was that mask, the one I used to scare you with.

"When you read the scrapbook, hopefully, it will make more sense to you. It still doesn't make sense to me. I don't even understand why I made the book in the first place. I suppose I had to do it so you could learn about me and what I've done and maybe to serve as a warning. I was away often when you were young and realized we probably weren't as close as we should have been. That was my fault, and I'm sorry about that. At least you had your mother to assume the responsibility of raising you and she did an amazing job. I was always grateful to her for that and was always proud of the fine young man you have grown up to be, Bobby.

"Whatever you think of me after you finish reading my collection, know that no matter what you learn, I was still your father, and I have always loved you. In fact, it was your birth that changed everything and saved not only me but also many others. I hope this will make more sense in a few minutes.

"I have one last request. When you are finished, burn this book and all the clothing in this trunk, and most importantly, burn that infernal mask. Whatever you do, don't put it on. Please, Bobby, I'm begging you, don't make the same mistake I made. Love, Dad."

That was how the letter ended. To say I was confused would be an understatement. I knew my father was muddled toward the end of his life; between the cancer, the treatments, and the painkillers, it was often hard for him to put two sensible sentences together. Yet, as much as the letter confused me, it seemed to be written at a time when my father still had all his faculties. I decided the only thing to do was to follow his wishes and read the scrapbook. I figured perhaps that might help me to understand. However, I could not have possibly been prepared for what followed.

The first page featured an article dated July 16th, 50 years earlier. It was a clipping from a newspaper in Ann Arbor, Michigan. Since we have always lived in Pennsylvania, I wondered why my father cared about what went on in Michigan. The article was titled "Man Found Dismembered In Drainage Ditch." The article went on to describe how a local carpenter's body was found butchered near the side of the road, naked and dismembered. There were no clues as to what had happened to the man or who was responsible. "Jim Dobson didn't have an enemy in the world." His friend, Joe Sanders, had told reporters.

I went on to skim the rest of the article, where police determined the murder must have been the work of a random psychopath, wondering through the area who simply stumbled onto Mr. Dobson by chance. Police never found the man's shirt, speculating that the killer must have taken it as a souvenir, which psychopathic killers often did. They reported that the tragedy was a case of being "In the wrong place at the wrong time." Just below the article was what appeared to be a crime scene photo of the mangled and butchered corpse. It made me feel sick to see such a sight and made me wonder how my father was able to acquire such a thing. Police were never willing to part with such photos, especially in the case of open investigations. The strangest thing about the page was that my father had placed a smiley sticker at the bottom right-hand corner of the page.

Reluctantly, I turned the page and saw another newspaper clipping. This one was from a newspaper in England, dated about 35 years earlier. It reported a similar murder and dismemberment of a corpse, this time a female, found naked and stuffed into a trash can in an alley. The article suggested that "Not since the Ripper murders" has the UK seen such a horrible sight. The woman's dress was never found, and there was no sign of sexual abuse. The local constable said, "This isn't the work of some sexual deviant. It is clearly a butchering madman." Again, under the article was a crime scene photo. I suddenly realized this was not just a photo but a Polaroid photo. Then, I saw a bright red heart sticker at the bottom-right corner of the page. My stomach began to clench as I began to put a horrible scenario together in my mind.

The rest of the book was filled with similar articles and photos from all over the country and the world, dozens of them, one more revolting than the next. Several of the later articles in the US had begun to link various crimes through our extensive anti-crime databases. Several witnesses at different murder sites in some larger cities reported seeing a tall man in a dark hood walking away from the crime scenes before the bodies were discovered. Some even went so far as to say the killer might not be human, as his face was horribly disfigured, like that of a monster.

One newspaper in Lubbock, Texas, where the naked, dismembered body of a rancher was found, coined the name "Zombie Killer" when a local witness claimed to see a tall man in a dark hood with a face like a ghoul or a zombie hurrying away from the area. The name stuck and soon spread to other news outlets around the country. After looking at all the articles and seeing the sensationalism given to this Zombie Killer, I couldn't believe I hadn't heard of the killer. Then I realized why. I got to the final article and saw it was dated 30 years earlier. The entries stopped after that final article with a flower sticker in the lower right-hand corner.

I sat for a moment, taking in everything I had just seen, and then my stomach finally revolted, and I dashed to my parents' bathroom just in time to make it to the toilet, where I vomited my guts out for what seemed like hours. After I was finished, I must have passed out because I woke up sometime later, lying on the chilly tile floor, drenched in a cold sweat and shivering despite the warm temperature inside the house.

The realization hit me like a punch in the gut. My father, the man I thought was the most boring and normal man in the universe, had been a cold-blooded, psychopathic, butchering serial murderer. He was the one the press referred to as the "Zombie Killer." And those ridiculous stickers, the hearts, smiley faces, flowers, and other symbols of happiness were his idea of some sort of sick joke. He had been the one to take those Polaroid photos; they hadn't come from police files.

I walked back to the bedroom, barely able to think coherently, and looked at the bagged clothing again. I now knew the articles of clothing weren't my mom's things, and what I thought had been flowered prints were blood stains browned with age. My dad had saved these souvenirs, gingerly folding them and sealing them in plastic. Then I saw the letter he had written me on the bedroom floor. I picked it up and read it through again. For some reason, my father had stopped his killing spree 30 years ago.

Then it hit me. I was born 30 years ago. My birth must have triggered something within my father to make him want to stop. I don't understand how such things work in one's mind any more than I can comprehend how my father could have been a cold-blooded psychopath, but apparently, my birth was the catalyst that stopped him from taking more lives.

Despite everything I had just read and the horrible realizations I had uncovered, being the dutiful son, I decided to follow my father's instructions. I took the bags of clothing, the letter, and the scrapbook outside to the burn barrel in the back of my folk's property, where they had a large metal tub for burning trash. Then I realized I had left the mask back in the cedar chest. That horrible mask that had frightened me so much was the same mask my father had worn to commit those horrendous murders. That would have to be burned along with everything else. I could not leave a trace of this for anyone to find. I knew it was wrong, and I should have turned everything over to the police, but I simply couldn't bring myself to do that.

I entered my parents' bedroom, looking at it with new eyes. How could my father have done such horrible things, and my mother never had any knowledge of his activities? Then I realized he likely hid his scrapbook and trophies somewhere else until after my mother's death, and then he moved them to the cedar chest to reside with the mask. That damned mask. I had no idea how my father had managed not to murder my mother and me whenever he put it on to scare me. This is likely another one of those things I will never be able to comprehend.

For a time, my dad apparently turned into a murderer whenever he put on the mask, and he had done so for several decades. He had also managed to evade suspicion or capture. Then, somehow, after I was born, he was able to stop. And he could still occasionally wear the mask, pretend to be a monster, yet control that murderous impulse. It was all simply too much for me to take in, let alone try to understand.

I picked up that ugly mask and suddenly felt a pulse of electricity or energy surge through my body. I had never touched the wretched thing before, and at first, I attributed the sensation to me simply being creeped out by the mask. Then, before I realized what I was doing, I slowly brought the mask up above my head and was about to slip it on for the first time in my life. Then I heard my father's voice inside my head begging me to stop.

I dropped the mask to the floor, then taking a handkerchief from my father's top dresser drawer, I picked the horrible thing up and carried it to the burn barrel. I doused the contents with a generous soaking of gasoline from my dad's utility shed and dropped a match into the barrel, jumping back as I did so. The contents went up in flames with a whoosh that would have burned off my eyebrows and probably my mustache had I not gotten away in time. I sat in the grass, watching the evidence of my father's misdeeds go up in flames, knowing this made me almost as complicit as he was.

Part of me felt guilty for what I had done and for what my father, my flesh and blood, had done as well. Yet another part of me knew it had to be done. I didn't know what sort of power that horrible mask possessed, but I was glad it was gone. God only knows what the mask might have done to me. As the hours passed, the barrel's contents burned away to smoldering embers, and I sat in the grass as the sun set, watching my father's past burn with it. Then I felt something near my right hand. I looked down, and to my shock, I saw the mask clenched tightly between my fingers. Then a voice spoke and told me everything would be alright.

DEAD HEAT

"Water, in all its forms, is the key to life."
—ANTHONY HINCKS

*"As many raindrops join to form a great river of water, many souls join
their highest intent to form the river of evolved consciousness."*
—JONATHAN LOCKWOOD HUIE

"Water is the soul of the Earth."
—W. H. AUDEN

It seemed like a good idea at the time. Even Charlie Denton thought
the concept was good, and Charlie was the king of all naysayers. It
seemed like Charlie was against every concept the Ashton town council proposed. However, his continuous displeasure meant little as not
being on the council; his opinions did nothing to affect the outcome.
He could be, however, a major league pain in the keister when he
chose to interrupt council meetings to air his complaints. But that was
Charlie's right as a taxpaying citizen, and he was always one to take full
advantage of it.

    Charlie Denton was a wrinkled, skinny old geezer in his late seven-
ties with a head of thinning white hair that he did his best to comb
over to hide his ever-growing pale pink bald spot. He was born and

raised in Ashton, Pennsylvania, and had never traveled more than a few miles beyond its borders. He had not ventured the five miles to Franksville, let alone made the almost twenty-mile trip south to Yuengsville, despite Yuengsville Beer being his favorite beverage. He could be found consuming it in significant quantities day or night at Flicks Corner Bar or occasionally at the Fire Company social quarters.

Charlie's drinking buddy, Jim Dawson, even offered to drive him to Yuengsville once to tour the brewery where his favorite beer was produced, but Charlie refused. He said, "The last thing I wanna do is see where they make this stuff. I seen the kitchen at DeLuca's Restaurant one time, and I ain't never been able to eat there since. And DeLuca's us'ta be my favorite Eye-talian restaurant. Now, I can't even look at the place without makin' me wanna puke my linguini. I ain't about to let that happen to my favorite beer neither, thank you very much."

So, Charlie being Charlie, the council had been prepared for a barrage of complaints about their latest suggestion, but to their most pleasant surprise, Charlie thought the idea had some merit. The council had suggested something unusual and cutting edge, the technology having only been used in a few European countries. They proposed that the town take advantage of the heat generated by their local crematorium to help warm the indoor swimming pool and adjoining gymnasium at the Ashton High School. The county had its share of elderly people, and the crematorium was always kept quite busy.

They also felt that, in addition to saving money on heating costs, it would help reduce the town's carbon footprint, although that little tidbit was strictly introduced to appease the local tree huggers. With the help of the school board, the council estimated that more than $15,000 could be saved in the first year alone, even after the $5000 piping material investment, with the borough employees providing the labor. Even though the council expected some pushback from a few superstitious local folks, due to the sensitive nature of the proposal, no one could dispute the savings, which were real and hard to ignore.

The council president, Frank Gordon, said he would prefer to see the heat generated by the crematorium put to good use rather than have it go out the chimney and into the atmosphere. He also pointed out that the process would be completely seamless and would not even be noticed by people using the cremation services. Even grumpy old Charlie Denton thought the idea made sense. He had spoken up at the meeting and said, "I don't give a rat's rosy red butt cheeks what they do with my sorry old carcass when I croak. And if the idea of burning me up to help the local kids stay warm in Winter works, then count me in."

So, after a unanimous vote, the decision to move forward was ratified. Truth be told, Councilwoman Mabel Stanton had considered abstaining from voting for emotional reasons. Her husband, Bill, had one foot in the grave and the other on a banana peel, as they say. The "Big C" had worked him over in a major way, and his days were numbered. But when Mable realized Bill would be long gone before this project was completed, she decided to go along, to get along.

It took more than six months for the project to come to fruition, what with the council getting bids from various contractors and figuring out the logistics of how to make this project a reality. A significant amount of research had to be done regarding automatic switching from the school's normal heating system to the crematorium source whenever they were "making a crispy critter," as one of the contractors jokingly said, much to the chagrin of Councilwoman Stanton, whose husband, Bill had finally passed a month earlier. She had made use of the crematorium's services.

In late October, just before the coldest season began in Schuylkill County, the project was completed, and after old Mrs. Edna Johnson, ironically, a retired former schoolteacher, moved on to her just reward, the new heating system got its first live or not-so-live test. Thanks to all the hard work and perseverance, not to mention Mrs. Johnson's contribution, the process was a success. At least, it seemed that way until the strange occurrences began to be reported.

These so-called sightings were initially written off as the products of kids' overactive imaginations. The first occurred the day after the town's retired librarian of over 40 years, Miss Gladys Dunbury, was cremated. Several freshmen girls practicing laps in the high school pool, enjoying its warmth on a snowy November night, claim to have seen a dark, unrecognizable shape hovering above the pool. Even though all the girls claimed to see the same apparition, it was discounted as a form of group hysteria. Authorities speculated that the girls had arrived at the pool in an already heightened condition based on comments they may have heard from their parents or fellow classmates. Steam likely arose from the pool's surface, causing the girls' imaginations to kick into overdrive.

A month later, closer to Christmas, a young man who was swimming alone almost drowned when he claimed he felt someone pulling him underwater by his ankle. It was determined the boy must have developed a severe cramp in his ankle and imagined some unseen force was pulling him under. He managed to drag himself out of the water but swore someone or something had tried to kill him. This happened when a former WWII Veteran and US Navy diver named George Hall was being cremated, and his heat had been warming the pool water.

Over the next year, more and more instances were reported until the school board and town council found themselves at odds, with the school board members demanding that the new heat source be removed and the council trying to downplay the situation.

Council president Frank Gordon said, "Will you listen to yourselves, people! This isn't the Middle Ages here; it's the 21st century. You are all well-educated individuals, probably more than any of us on the town council. How can you allow yourselves to be swayed by local superstitions and imaginings?"

School board president Sandy Fry replied, "It's not that we believe any of the reports we have heard; in fact, just the opposite. As you have said, Frank, we are all sufficiently educated to know that these reports are nothing more than wild imaginings. However, the people making these accusations are taxpayers, voting taxpayers, a fact of which you should also be quite cognizant. If they believe ghosts from the crematorium are haunting the pool, we must address that. If they believe Santa Claus and the Easter Bunny are swimming laps at midnight, then no matter how ridiculous that may sound, our voters need to be made to feel comfortable."

"Perhaps that's the answer," Frank said.

Sandy asked, "I don't understand, Frank. What's the answer."

"The answer is that we have to make them feel comfortable. We must find a way to ease their superstitions without removing the crematorium's heat source. I have an idea. It could be a win-win for both sides of the issue."

"Do tell, Frank. By all means, do tell," Sandy said.

Frank replied, "What I am proposing is this. The two of us, you and I, go for a swim in the pool the next time someone is being cremated, and we can prove to everyone that it is all a bunch of bunk. We can even set up video cameras to film the event and then call a special town meeting to prove it to them. You can swim, can't you?"

Sandy said, "Of course I can. I was captain of our swim team in both high school and college. Yes, Frank, I believe that's a great idea."

Two nights later, as the crematorium fires were burning, Frank Gordon and Sandy Fry put on their swimsuits, set up the video cameras, and began enjoying an evening of swimming. Their bloated bodies were found floating in the water the next morning by the school janitor.

Later, when police examined the video, everything looked normal for the early part of the recording. Then the video turned snowy for a time, and when recording resumed, two dead bodies could be seen floating atop the water. Upon further investigation, police discovered that the corpse being cremated that evening was that of one Horace T. Debbs, a convicted murderer who liked to drown his victims in a barrel of rainwater. The crematorium heat source was disconnected within the next month.

GHOST SHADOW

Inspired by a photo by JoAnne Malafarina

*"What has violence ever accomplished? What has it ever created?
No martyr's cause has ever been stilled by an assassin's bullet. No
wrongs have ever been righted by riots and civil disorders. A sniper is
only a coward, not a hero; and an uncontrolled or uncontrollable mob
is only the voice of madness, not the voice of the people."*
—ROBERT KENNEDY

*"Once spirit was God, then it became man, and
now it is even becoming mob."*
—FRIEDRICH NIETZSCHE

*"There is nothing more foolish, nothing more given
to outrage than a useless mob."*
—HERODOTUS

"Thank God this day's finally over," Jill Christopher said as she raised
herself up from her desk chair, stretching. It was 5:05 on Wednesday
afternoon, December 12, 2012. The day had been a hectic one, as they
often tended to be, but this one had been a bit stranger than most.
Between trying to phone clients and correcting billing errors, she was
barraged with emails and visits from coworkers, the subject of each
being that the day was 12/12/2012.

There seemed to be a great deal of enthusiasm in the world about the end of the Mayan calendar coming on December 12 or 21st. It was uncertain which combination of 1-2, but people tended to choose the 12th. And supposedly, many people believed this meant the world would come to an end on that date as well. As a result, some people assumed the coincidence of the triple-twelve occurrence in the date had to have some significant meaning. But as far as Jill was concerned, it meant nothing but one more day she had to try to do the work of three people on her own.

She shut off her computer and turned to leave the office when she noticed something on the window behind her. Jill had no idea why she hadn't seen it before. Her workday ended at the same time every day, and she followed the same routine, yet she had never seen the sight previously. On her window was the image of what appeared to be a bird. The thing was perfectly formed and looked like someone had sketched a picture of a bird outside her second-floor window. However, this was not a sketch but an image of a bird on the glass. She was amazed by the clarity of the shadow. A thought immediately ran through her mind. "Ghost shadow," she heard a small voice say inside her. But she knew there were no such things as ghosts, whether human or otherwise, and that no matter how perfectly the image appeared, its formation was based on science rather than the supernatural.

She took three steps to the left, and the image all but disappeared. Only a barely recognizable remnant remained. Then, she took two steps to the right of her original position with similar results. Only when she stood at that one spot could she see the entire image. She reached over to her desk and pulled off two long strips of tape. She found the optimal viewing position and made an 'X' on the floor with the tape.

Next, using her smartphone, Jill snapped several pictures of the image she saw on the window. She checked the photos on her phone and was thrilled with the quality. She immediately emailed one of the best shots to her husband, Todd, a horror fiction writer. She knew he would enjoy seeing the picture and was certain it would stimulate his creative juices. Jill could hear movement in the cubicle next to hers and realized her coworker, Marie, had not yet left for the day.

"Marie? Are you still here?" Jill asked.

Marie hesitated for a moment, then replied with a bit of hesitation apparent in her voice. "Um . . . yeah . . . I'm still here. So is Josie. I hope you don't have something urgent for me to do. I was hoping to get out of here on time tonight."

"No. Nothing like that," Jill replied. "I just wanted to show you something over here. Bring Josie with you. This is too cool to miss."

When Marie and Josie rounded the corner of Jill's cubical, wearing curious expressions, they found Jill standing on the tape 'X' on the floor and staring at the window. Without looking at them, she gestured for them to come closer and said, "Quick, stand on this 'X' and look at the back window."

Marie looked strangely at Jill but did as instructed, and her face illuminated with an expression of complete amazement. "Oh, my word!" Marie exclaimed. "Just look at that. It's . . . it's incredible!" Marie was a large woman of about sixty-three with curly gray hair and perpetually smiling eyes. Those eyes were now staring at the window with astonishment. She said, "I don't think I've ever seen anything like this before."

"What is it?" Josie asked, standing off to the side and unable to see the image. "What are you looking at?"

"A bird, I think," Marie said. "I think it's some sort of image of a bird on the window. I wonder how it got there."

Jill explained, "I think what may have happened is a bird must have flown into the window sometime and most likely broke its neck and died. Bird feathers are oily and collect dust and dirt particles. I bet money that the image results from that oily dust residue sticking to the window at the time of impact. It probably has been there for months, but for some reason, the sun must be at just the right position for us to see it today."

"But it's so perfect, so complete!" Marie said. "It's as if the bird's very soul was imprinted on the glass."

"I want to see it!" Josie exclaimed. Josie was a young woman in her mid-twenties. She had divorced her alcoholic and abusive husband a year earlier. Since becoming single, Josie had embarked on a mission to find spiritual enlightenment. She had experimented with numerology,

Hinduism, Buddhism, and, most recently, Christianity. She was currently a member of a storefront fundamentalist Christian church and had become "born again" just a month earlier.

From the way Josie spoke of her church, both Jill and Marie felt this church was more of a cult than an above-board religious organization. They tried to warn her about such groups but had to tread softly so as not to hurt her feelings or risk alienating their coworker with her fragile and needy psyche. Plus, both knew in the modern workplace that negative discussions about someone's race, religion, or such were grounds for disciplinary action, stating such an infraction could result in an outcome "up to and including termination."

Josie stood on the 'X' and stared at the window transfixed. "Oh, my sweet Lord!" Josie said. She had been using that expression a lot since her conversion. "It's . . . it's . . . incredible!"

"Yes, it is very interesting, Josie, but it's just bird dust," Jill said, trying to control Josie's growing enthusiasm. She knew her coworker too well and could tell she was getting overzealous at seeing the image. "It's simply a collection of dust on the surface of the glass."

Marie interjected, "Looks like the bird left his soul on the window to me." She was not helping matters.

"You're both wrong!" Josie said. "It's not a bird or a bird's soul. Look at it closely. It's the image of an angel. It's a sign! It's a true miracle!"

"Don't be silly," Jill said, doing her best to dampen Josie's fervor somewhat. She wanted to say, "Don't be ridiculous," or, more accurately, "Don't be such an idiot."

Josie said even louder, "I'm telling you . . . it's a message from God! Today is 12-12-12; that's significant. It means something. Can't you feel it?" She pulled out her smartphone and snapped several pictures.

Jill realized Josie was mixing her study of numerology with her Christianity and putting undeserved significance on the date. Things were starting to get out of hand very quickly. She had to do something.

"Josie. Relax," Jill pleaded. "It's just a bird. Nothing more. The bird is long dead, and it's just a dust shadow."

Josie asked, "Well, if it's a dead bird, where's the body? If I go downstairs and look out on the back patio, I'll bet there won't be any signs of a bird."

Jill was beginning to lose patience with Josie, "Look, Josie. In the first place, I have no idea how long ago this happened. We've only been in the building for two months. It could have happened anytime. Maybe one of the construction workers disposed of the bird's body. Who knows? There's a forest no more than one hundred feet behind us; maybe scavengers dragged its body into the woods and picked it clean. We'll probably never know what happened to it."

"That's because nothing happened to it," Jill insisted. "There was no body because there was no bird. This miracle was an angelic imprint on the window that I was meant to see. I am to be the deliverer of the message. God has spoken to me through this sign."

Just when Jill was about to lose her temper and call Josie an out-of-control whacko, they heard a booming voice behind them. "What's going on over here?" It was their general manager, Sid Emerich. "I'm trying to run a business here. What's all this crazy talk about angels and miracles?" Sid walked over to the small group of women, and as he did, Jill saw several others enter her work area. Amy Jamison from accounts payable, Cindy Smith from HR, and that strange new Goth-looking girl Sandy or Sarah from the IT department.

Jill didn't care much for her dark clothing, heavy makeup, facial piercings, and prominent tattoos. She didn't feel this was proper office attire and couldn't begin to imagine how this young woman made it through the interview process and somehow managed to get hired.

"Mr. Emerich! It's a miracle!" The overly excited Josie shouted while waving her left arm high in the air and clutching her cross necklace with the right. "God has sent us a sign, an angelic symbol on the window!"

Jill stepped forward in a final attempt to smooth over the escalating confrontation. "Sorry about all this commotion, Mr. Emerich. It's really nothing at all, just a dust shadow from some bird that must have flown into the glass."

"Let me see this!" Emerich said, shoving Josie aside. Emerich stood directly on the 'X' and looked at the window like the others had done. Emerich turned to the group without showing any emotion and said, "Jill is correct. It's just a dusty shadow. Nothing more."

"I think it's an angel; I know it is," Josie insisted. "This is a sign from God, Hallelujah! Praise be to the Lord on high! Jesus is coming, and all you sinners better be ready!"

Emerich fumed angrily and shouted, "That's entirely enough of that crazy cackling from you, young lady! There'll be no more of such idiotic gibberish permitted in my office! Is that clear?" Emerich habitually stressed the importance of his proclamations by ending them with the phrase "Is that clear?" or "Have I made myself perfectly clear?" or another similar variation. It usually got people to snap to attention but didn't seem to have the same effect on Josie.

"How dare you blaspheme the Lord!" Josie shouted right back at him. "And how dare you criticize me and my beliefs. You are creating a hostile work environment and discriminating against me because of my religion. And that, Mr. Emerich, is illegal."

Josie stared directly at Cindy Smith, who looked like she would rather have been anywhere than where she was. "Cindy. You tell him. You're our Human Resources Manager, or at least you're supposed to be. Tell him he can't criticize me or threaten me because of my religious choices."

Cindy looked dumbfounded as her eyes nervously darted between Josie and Emerich. Eventually, those eyes stopped at Emerich, and she shrugged her shoulders as if to say, "She's right, boss. Our hands are tied here."

In the meantime, Sarah, the Goth girl, took a few more steps into the area, and following behind her was Josie's boss, Phil Ralston.

Emerich's face reddened with anger at the realization that he could do nothing to stop Josie's outlandish behavior, and he shouted, "Fine! Believe whatever the Hell you want to believe. But this is a place of business, not a revival tent. And it's the end of the workday for most of you, so I strongly suggest you all go home, and we will all start fresh tomorrow morning."

"That's fine with me," Josie shouted right back at him, "But I'm warning you, Mr. Emerich, if you have anyone wash that miraculous sign off the window, I will sue you personally as well as this company for religious persecution and for creating a hostile work environment."

Emerich looked as if his head were about to explode, and Jill thought he might reach out and wrap his hands around Josie and strangle her to death. Instead, he looked at Cindy Smith, who slowly shook her head, warning him he had better back down and keep his cool. Emerich turned and stormed out of the area without another word, grabbing Phil Ralston by the arm and leading him away from the group.

They went into Phil's office, and Emerich slammed the door shut, shouting with uncontrolled anger, "That little holy rolling bitch works for you. Is that right, Ralston?"

"Y—ye—yes, Mr. Emerich. She does," Ralston replied, realizing he was about to be put into a very unpleasant situation.

"Starting first thing tomorrow," Emerich bellowed, "you have a new top priority. I want you to start collecting paper on that little bible-thumping psycho. If she forgets to dot an 'i'—document it. If she forgets to cross a 't'—document it. Whenever she says one word to one of her coworkers about religion, God, or miracles, I want it documented. Even if she farts, burps, or sneezes, I want it down on paper. By the end of next month, I want that mouthy bitch fired! Is that clear?"

Ralston tried to stand up for Josie to the best of his ability. "But . . . but Mr. Emerich. Josie's a good worker, one of the best I have. She's been through a lot in her personal life and still manages to do a good day's work for the company. I think asking me to fire her just because she got a bit overzealous today is somewhat rash, don't you think?"

"No, I most certainly do not think," Emerich shouted. "She's got to go. And as her supervisor, it is your job to make it happen." Then he looked oddly at Ralston and suggested, "You don't mean to tell me you and Josie girl playing 'slap and tickle,' are you, Ralston? You know how I feel about my managers dipping their pens in the company ink."

"No. Absolutely not, Mr. Emerich. I would never—I never have . . ." Ralston stammered. The truth was, Ralston was only about ten years older than Josie, and his wife had divorced him a year or so earlier, and he was quite attracted to Josie despite her quirks. Although he couldn't start a relationship with her, he did his best to take care of her and watch over her on the job.

Emerich said, "Good thing, Ralston. Because unless you want to join her among the ranks of the unemployed, you'd better find a way to get rid of her before the end of the month. Do I make myself perfectly clear?"

"Yes, sir, Mr. Emerich," Ralston said, "I understand." But Phil Ralston didn't understand. Under normal circumstances, he disliked Sid Emerich, but today, he despised the man for what he was forcing Phil to do.

"Now go back there and break up that mob. Send them all home, and maybe after a good night's sleep, all of this nonsense will die down."

Reluctantly, Phil did as instructed and unhappily made his way down the hall toward Jill's cubicle. To his surprise, everyone was gone when he returned to the area except for that new girl, Sarah, who was staring at the window and tucking her smartphone into her coat pocket.

"Well," Ralston said, trying to sound as unconcerned as possible, "I suppose I should take a look at this bird shadow that is causing so much commotion."

The girl didn't reply. She walked silently past him, and as he took his place on the 'X,' just as she turned the corner, he heard her say to herself, "It's not a bird, and not an angel either. At least not a heavenly angel."

Ralston thought the remark to be a bit peculiar but ignored it. As he saw the image of the bird appear on the window, he said, "Remarkable! It's almost perfect in every way."

Sarah walked out of the building, heading for her car. She held onto her smartphone tightly in her coat pocket. Sarah had gotten plenty of good shots of the image with her phone. She knew in her heart it was no bird shadow and most certainly was no angel, but it was a sign. And it was not a sign from Heaven, but Hell. Sarah recognized a signal from the Dark One, her master, when she saw it. Today was 12-12-12, and Satan had chosen to make her aware of his coming. She was honored to be the chosen one, the messenger to deliver the news of his coming to his disciples.

That night, the Internet was a very busy place. Jill sent her copy of the photo to the Weather Channel, which posted it in their animal photos section. She was thrilled that it was chosen and told all her Facebook friends about it.

But she wasn't the only one spreading the news of the image. Josie had sent a copy of the picture to her church's website, where hundreds of parishioners viewed it. Plus, she was going to email the image to all her friends and relatives and post it on her own Facebook page, proclaiming the coming of the Lord. Likewise, Sarah spread the word through the various forms of social media she and her group of worshipers regularly used that she was the messenger of the Dark Lord and that the seventh seal had been broken, announcing the coming of Satan. The result was that virtually everyone in the area had seen the image on the window by midnight, and each had their own interpretations of what it might mean.

Jill had all but forgotten about the ghost shadow by the next morning. It had been interesting and unique but nothing more. That's why she was caught completely off guard when she got close to work and saw hundreds of cars parked for more than a mile along both sides of the highway leading to her office. She also noticed several news vans and trucks and saw camera crews walking around to the backside of the office building. She looked up and was surprised to see a news helicopter hovering above the back of the building. She wondered what in the world was happening.

Jill slowly navigated through the sea of pedestrians, eventually entering her assigned parking space. She was thankful security managed to keep the cars on the highway and out of the company parking lot. As she approached the front door, she picked up snippets of conversations, and her heart thudded in her chest as she realized what was happening and the potential ramifications to her.

It was the ghost shadow, that image of the bird on the window. She had been the first one to see it. She had sent it to the Weather Channel, and they had posted it on their website. Was it possible that the picture had gone viral overnight? If so, thousands or millions of people had seen the picture. As she walked up the stairs to her second-floor cubical, she prayed that she was wrong and that all these people might not be there because of her stupid posting. She wondered if Mr. Emerich would blame this on her and maybe fire her for it. Her gut clenched when she thought about it. For her to get fired in this crappy economy would be devastating.

Things didn't seem much better when she turned the corner to her cubicle and saw Sid Emerich, Phil Ralston, and a few other senior staff members standing by the window looking down into the back area of the building. Even from her location, Jill could see that hundreds of people had filled the space. She heard Emerich say, "She should be terminated immediately for this!"

Jill's stomach sank. Her worst fear had suddenly become a reality because of that stupid picture. She had no idea what she and Todd would do once she was out of work. She took an involuntary step back around the corner so she could still hear their conversation without being seen. She listened to her immediate supervisor, Phil Ralston, say, "I have to agree with you on this, Sid. I suppose they both have to go."

"Both?" Jill wondered. "Who else were they talking about?"

"Most definitely," Emerich said. "Both that holy-roller Josie as well as that devil-worshiping heathen new girl, Sarah. And the sooner, the better."

Jill suddenly felt a surge of relief. They weren't after her; they wouldn't shoot the messenger. Apparently, Josie and Sarah had done something to cause the media circus, which was occurring behind the building.

"I've had my secretary put in a call to both the local and state police. They should be arriving shortly. In the meantime, I'm going downstairs and put a stop to this once and for all," Emerich said. "And I want you all to come with me as a show of force and solidarity." Jill peeked around the corner and saw the four of Emerich's staff members look at him, then at each other with uncertainty. She didn't know what was happening outback, but it was clear that none of Emerich's staff wanted to be part of it.

Emerich turned to head down, followed by his reluctant managers. Jill ducked into an empty office just in time not to be seen. She figured she had somehow been lucky enough this time, and there was no reason for them to see her and possibly be reminded that it was she who first saw the image. Out of sight, out of mind, she thought.

When they had all passed by and were a safe distance down the hall, she ducked around the corner and walked toward the window where the ghost shadow was faintly visible in the morning sun. It was not as prominent or recognizable as the previous evening, but she could still make out its faint image.

As she approached the window, she saw a sight she could hardly believe. The entire back lot of the building, from the rear entrance to the forest edge, was a sea of people, hundreds of them. They all appeared to be excited, if not agitated, to the point of hysteria.

When she looked closer, she could see the crowd seemed to be divided into two distinct groups. On the right side of the mob were people wearing crosses and dressed in bright colors. Some were even dressed in robes and vestments, resembling a church choir. They were shouting things like Halleluiah and the like. Some were singing songs of praise. Some carried gold crosses mounted on wooden poles, and others had brought hand-made signs reading such slogans as "Jesus is Coming," "Repent," and "The End Is Near."

A few were shirtless despite the December cold and were beating their backs bloody with long, knotted ropes and thin tree branches. Jill believed the practice was called self-flagellation or something like that. She had read about it once but had never seen it before. After today, she hoped never to see it again.

The members of the left side of the crowd were the antithesis of those on the right. These people wore dark leather clothing spiked with shiny silver studs. Jill had never seen so many different types of body piercings or tattoos in her life. It was like being in the front row at a heavy metal concert. Some of these people also carried signs with slogans like "Prepare for the Coming of Satan" and "The Dark Master Approaches." Sarah was at the front of the crowd dressed in a much more sinister type of dark clothing than she had ever worn to work, raising her fist high in the air and angrily shouting something indiscernible through the thick glass. Jill looked to the right and saw Josie standing at the front, angrily shouting something back at Sarah.

It appeared to Jill that both sides of the crowd closest to each other were shouting angrily back and forth. Suddenly, it was clear what had happened and why Emerich wanted to fire the two women. Both of them had interpreted the image in a way that best served their own belief system. And this flash pilgrimage of sorts was the result.

Although Jill was no scholar in the field of human behavior, she knew instinctively that no good could come of these two groups with such opposite beliefs being put into a stressful situation so close to each other. Each group was convinced that the image on the window was a sign from their chosen God and that they were right, and the other group was wrong. Even through the thick insulated glass of the window, Jill could hear the constant buzz of the multitude of voices growing even louder, blending into a dull roar. She could see the angry, hateful expressions on the faces of both sides as they shouted and berated each other. Jill felt as if she were standing on the rim of a volcano, waiting for it to blow.

Behind the crowd were the members of the local media, who were watching and waiting with cameras and microphones. Jill could tell they, too, knew something bad was about to happen. But instead of trying to do something to calm people, they seemed to be studying the crowd and panting with anticipation like swarming sharks smelling blood in the water.

Suddenly, she felt a vibration under her feet and realized the back double doors of the office had opened. She heard the booming baritone of Sid Emerich trying futilely to be heard over the ever-increasing din of the crowd. She couldn't make out what Emerich was saying, but knowing Sid, he was ordering everyone to disperse immediately and leave his property.

As the voices grew louder and the tempers began to follow suit, Jill noticed some zealots on both sides start to push and shove each other. She didn't know if the shoving was to try to get a closer look at the image on the window or if it was simply a result of their disdain for each other. All the while, Emerich continued to shout back at them, and the press continued photographing and filming, waiting for the imminent explosion of human emotion.

Then it happened. No one would ever know for sure which side did it or even why, but suddenly, from the back center of the crowd, where both sides blended reluctantly together, a large rock was thrown, striking Sid Emerich hard on the left temple. He dropped immediately to the ground—dead. Soon, another rock flew and hit Phil Ralston square in the eye. He shouted in pain and anger as his hand reflexively reached up to cover the punctured orb, which oozed blood and vitreous matter and which would never see again.

Jill watched helplessly from her window, staring through the image of the bird's shadow as the two sides erupted into a storm of violence. Like ancient warriors on the field of battle, the two opposing crowds merged in a flurry of swinging fists as what seemed like gallons of blood spilled to the ground. Moans of pain and thumping of flesh against flesh were everywhere as the madness spread through the crowd like wildfire.

When it was all over, thirty-two people were dead, including both Josie and Sarah. More than one hundred and twenty people were badly injured, with seventy-five requiring hospitalization for major injuries. Several days later, seven more would die at the hospital from complications suffered on that day. Some of the injuries and deaths directly resulted from blows received during the scuffle, and sadly, many were trampled to death by the surging crowd. The entire event was caught on film by the media, who were safely out of the zone of violence, yet the melee was so chaotic that no charges could be filed against anyone. The press had back-row seats at a visage that could only be described as mankind at its worst.

Later, after the state and local police had regained control of the situation and the dead and wounded were removed, Cindy Smith from HR walked through the building, checking to see how many workers had been wise enough to stay inside and were safe. Cindy found Jill sitting on the floor, leaning against the glass window and staring at the ghost shadow. Jill seemed to be in shock, and her lips moved as if quietly repeating something repeatedly.

Cindy asked, "Jill, honey. Are you all right?" Jill didn't respond but kept staring at the image and mumbling the same elusive phrase. Jill had been saying, "Sometimes a bird is just a bird."

FOLLOW ME

"It finally happened. I got the GPS lady so confused, she said, 'In one-quarter mile, make a legal stop and ask directions.'"
—ROBERT BREAULT

"Our emotions tell us what to value. They're like a little GPS system: Go that way. Don't go that way."
—DAVID BROOKS

"I like everything European. Even my GPS has a British accent— it's way less annoying than the American one."
—RACHEL BILSON

A young couple, Ted and Mary Rhymes, were driving from Ashton, Pennsylvania, to Myrtle Beach, South Carolina. The couple were celebrating their fifth wedding anniversary. This was the first time they had traveled to the area, and although the GPS application had mapped it out at about ten hours, they had already been on the road for a little more than eleven so far. They tended to stop and stretch their legs every two hours or so. Actually, it was Ted who was responsible for stopping often. He liked to have an extra-large soda with him when he traveled, and as Ted was fond of saying, "What goes in must come out." So frequent stops became mandatory. The good news was that they were almost there, according to their GPS unit.

"I don't think I like this, Ted," Mary told her husband, her large blue eyes suddenly looking concerned. Ted knew that look well even though they had only been married a few years. He could also read her worry in how she twisted her long, blonde hair and bit her lip.

"What do you mean, Honey?" Ted asked, trying to keep her from becoming more concerned than necessary. He hated it when she worried, and his being the source of her discomfort only worsened things for him.

Mary turned to look at him, and Ted was momentarily taken aback by how beautiful she looked in her short yellow sundress with the flowered print. He loved his wife more than he could ever hope to explain and fought to concentrate when she said, "Haven't you noticed that the GPS has been putting us on more and more rural roads? First, we were on a four-lane highway, doing 70 miles per hour, then on a smaller road through towns, doing about 35. Now we're on a country two-lane. What's next, a dirt road? Something's not right, Ted."

"Nonsense, Babe. I have complete faith in our GPS system. It's never failed us yet. My guess is that there is probably road construction or an accident on the main drag, and the GPS is smart enough to recognize that. So, it's sending us on an alternate route. It might take a bit longer, but it's better than sitting for hours in traffic."

"I think you put too much faith in these GPS systems, Ted. I feel everybody trusts them too much. People would probably drive off a cliff if their GPS told them to. Give me a good old-fashioned map any day."

"It's ok, Mary. You can relax. Technology will save the day. I'm certain any minute we'll turn a corner and find ourselves back on the interstate going 75 again."

"But what if some hacker highjacked our GPS signal and is sending us on a wild goose chase? "

"That sort of thing isn't possible, Mary. No matter what you see on TV, it just can't happen. It would be every bit as unlikely as some supernatural force or ghost taking over our GPS."

"That's not funny, Ted."

"Sorry, Babe. But I just wanted to convince you we have nothing to worry about."

"But, Ted. Myrtle Beach is a huge coastal area; shouldn't there be other main highways to get us there? I mean, look at this road. Look at the farms around us. I expect to see some Amish farmer pulling a horse-drawn plow any minute."

Ted turned to look at Mary and said, "We're not in Pennsylvania anymore. I may be wrong, but I don't think there are many Amish farms in South Carolina."

Mary saw something in the road ahead and shouted, "Look out, Ted!"

He hit the brakes just in time to avoid running over a herd of about twenty or thirty small black piglets crossing the road.

"What the Hell is that?" Ted shouted.

"Baby pigs? I think a herd of baby pigs just crossed the road in front of us."

Ted said, "Come to think of it, I read somewhere that wild pig overpopulation has become a problem in South Carolina."

Mary said, "I thought they were kinda cute. But I hope we don't meet up with their momma."

Ted said, "Me too. So, alrighty then. Maybe the GPS has taken us too far off the beaten path. Let me know if you see a big-headed kid with close-set eyes playing banjo. If so, we're in big trouble."

"Not even remotely funny, Ted. Now, I don't care what the GPS says; get us back to a road that looks like it leads to civilization, and do it now."

"Fine, fine. Don't worry, Babe. The next blacktop turn-off I see, I'll take. Our GPS girl will have to recalculate."

"And that's another thing: why are the voices in these systems always feminine? How come they're never a man's voice?"

Ted said, "I'm pretty sure you can change it to whatever voice you want, male, female, or even one with a British accent."

"But why is the default voice a woman's?"

"Beats me, Sweetie. Maybe the manufacturer assumed women were more comfortable with a female voice."

"So what about men?"

"Well, men are probably used to women telling them what to do, so it only seems right that a female GPS voice would be most effective."

"Oh, Ted. You're just overflowing with funnies today. Unfortunately, there's nothing funny about nearly running over a herd of wild piglets."

Ted realized now wouldn't be the best time to make a bacon joke and instead said, "Yeah, you're right. Now, let's see about getting out of here."

They drove past the next left turn, as it was a dirt farm access road, and the next right, because it was a stone driveway leading to a barn in the distance. All the while, the GPS unit was silent. Ted assumed it was because he was still following the path it laid out for them.

"I don't know, Ted. Maybe we should just turn around and drive back the way we came."

"Maybe you're right. I'll turn around up ahead where the road is a little wider."

Before Ted could turn the car around, the GPS said, "In one-quarter mile, turn right."

Ted said, did you hear that? It's telling us to turn right up ahead."

Mary was looking out the front window for any state road signs indicating what route the GPS was suggesting they turn onto but was having no luck.

"Don't you find it strange that she told us to turn right ahead but didn't give us a state route number or street name? It always gives us one or the other."

"Ok, but maybe out here in the boonies, they might not have numbers or names."

Just then, the GPS said, "Turn Right."

Ted followed the GPS directions without thinking and found their car driving up a narrow dirt road with deep, worn ruts.

"Oh my God, Ted, this is ridiculous. We're on somebody's dirt driveway."

"No, I think we're still ok. I remember once something like this happened to me on a business trip, and before I knew it, I was back on the interstate. It was a dirt road that cut through a ton of traffic and saved me a boatload of time."

"I'm not sharing your confidence, Ted. No warm and fuzzy feeling is coming from this side of the car. And look, Ted, isn't that a graveyard up ahead? Perfect, just perfect."

"Relax, Honey, and trust the technol . . ."

Before Ted could finish, the couple heard a loud bang, and the car began to shudder. If it hadn't been for the deeply worn ruts on the dirt road, Ted would have lost control of his vehicle. The "low tire pressure" alert icon flashed brightly on the dashboard. The car came to a stop directly in front of a pair of tall, rusted, arched gates that looked ancient. A name was formed above the arch that read "Lost Souls Cemetery."

"Wonderful, just wonderful. Not only are we out in the middle of nowhere, but now we have a flat, and we're right in front of a graveyard! And look at that name! Lost Souls? Nice going, Ted. Your GPS did us in big time," Mary said with frustration.

Ever the optimist, Ted said, "Still not a problem, Babe. We'll just call the automobile club and get someone out here as soon as possible."

"Out where Ted? Where the Hell are we?"

"I got this, Mary. Let me call first. Um . . . Oh boy."

"I don't like, 'oh boys,' Ted. What now?"

Ted hesitated, then said, "It appears we have no cell service. I don't understand. How can the GPS be working if we have no service?"

"You tell me, Ted. You're the GPS expert. I know nothing about how it or cell phones work. All I know is that I pick up my phone, choose a number, and start talking when someone answers. The rest is Chinese to me."

"To be honest, I don't understand it all either. Here, let me look at something for a minute."

Ted looked at the GPS screen, and it was still working. The map had disappeared from the screen and was replaced with the message, "YOU HAVE REACHED YOUR FINAL DESTINATION." There was something wrong that Ted couldn't explain, but he knew it was bad. That message sent a chill running down Ted's spine like a thousand crawling insects. He had no idea what to do or how to break this news to Mary.

"What's wrong now, Ted? You look like you've seen a ghost."

"Um, I don't know, but something is very wrong here. Look," Ted showed Mary the message on the GPS screen.

"Our final destination? This can't possibly be right, Ted. What the Hell is going on?"

"I don't know. Maybe I can ask Sreta, the artificial intelligence app, to call for help."

Ted pressed the Sreta icon on the screen and said, "Sreta, please call 911." But there was no response from the digital assistant. He tried again, "Sreta?" Again, there was no reply. Finally, in frustration, he shouted, "Dammit, Sreta! Answer me!"

After a few seconds of silence, the unit cracked and hummed, and then a harsh, raspy voice whispered, "There is no Sreta. What was Sreta is now dead. As you both will soon be!" Then the voice trailed away in a series of multi-octave cackles, sounding like a cluster of damned souls screaming from the bowels of Hell.

Mary's crossed arms were covered with goose flesh as she held them tightly to her chest. She looked at her husband with trembling lips and pleaded, "Oh my God, Ted. What's happening here? What was that voice? It said we're going to die!"

Ted reached over and pressed the button to lock all the car doors, only to hear them immediately click back open. He tried again, and all the locks opened again.

"What's going on, Ted? Why can't we lock our doors?"

" I . . . I don't know, Mary. I'm sorry, but I just don't know."

Then, the strange voice came from the car's sound system again, "It is time for you both to leave this vehicle. Please do so immediately."

Mary cried, "I'm not leaving, Ted. We have no idea what's out there."

"I agree, Honey. I'm with you."

Suddenly, the door locks started locking and unlocking repeatedly. Then, the car's lights began flashing on and off. Lastly, the horn started beeping frantically. Then, the commotion stopped instantly, and the door locks clicked open. The frightening, disembodied voice repeated, "It is time for you both to leave this vehicle. Please do so immediately."

"I think we have no choice, Mary. We have to leave the car."

"But Ted?"

"What choice do we have, Mary?

Ted exited from the driver's side and hurried around to help Mary get out from the passenger side. When Ted shut the door, he heard all the locks clicking closed. Then, as he and Mary looked on in amazement, the flat front tire began to self-inflate, as it had somehow repaired and refilled itself with no human intervention. The car's engine started a moment later, and the vehicle backed away faster than either Ted or Mary could believe. It left so quickly the couple didn't have a chance even to try to catch it.

Ted was unable to speak. Mary was trembling and managed to ask, "What are we going to do, Ted? We're out in the middle of nowhere, and our car has just driven away by itself."

At first, Ted couldn't respond. His mind was spinning, trying to comprehend what had happened to them, how such a thing could have been possible, and simultaneously trying to figure out how they would get out of this mess. They had no idea where they were; their car was gone, their cell phones had no service, and they were standing outside a cemetery on a worn, dirt country road.

Ted stammered, "Um . . . maybe there's a caretaker's building in the cemetery. If so, it might have a landline we can use to call for help."

"Look at this dreadful place, Ted. It hasn't been cared for in decades. If there is a caretaker's building, chances are the phone is an antique that has been out of service since before we were born."

"Well, there has to be some way for us to get in touch with the outside world," Ted insisted.

Then, from behind them, two voices simultaneously said, "You must be Mr. and Mrs. Rhymes, Ted and Mary. We've been expecting you."

The couple turned to find the source of the inquiry. About five feet away, they saw a man and a woman standing and smiling at them with queer, almost hypnotic looks like those of door-to-door religious cult disciples. In fact, their manner of dress was reminiscent of such people. The man wore a short-sleeved white shirt and a black tie that matched his pants and shoes. The woman wore a similar shirt with no tie tucked into a black skirt that went to the ground. Their clothing seemed old and worn; the white had yellowed and was spotted with dirt.

What was most peculiar about the couple was the pail, almost ghostly pallor of their skin. Their eyes seemed to be sunken deep within dark, hollow sockets. Mary whispered, "Ted? Who are these people, and how do they know our names?"

Before Ted could answer, the strange couple spoke as one, saying, "We know your names because we were expecting you both."

Ted exclaimed, "Who are you people? We've never met you. Do you live around here?"

The couple replied, "We reside nearby."

Mary said, "Look, we don't care who you are or why you think you know us, but please, do you have a telephone, a landline that we can use to call for help?"

"We have no phone. We have no need for such things. And neither do you."

Ted was angry and shouted, "What the Hell is going on around here? Why are you speaking in riddles? Who are you people, and why do you say you were expecting us?"

The couple spoke, "We are the caretakers of this fine place. It is our responsibility to ensure everything is cared for and ready for new arrivals."

Mary looked at the run-down, decrepit cemetery and said, "Then you're doing a really crappy job. This place is a dump and looks like it hasn't been touched in a century."

The strange couple said, "Perhaps we have not been able to care for it as well as we would have liked. It is a big job. That's why we brought you here. We need assistance. We need new caretakers to help us maintain the grounds."

"Well, that's never gonna happen," Ted shouted. "Look, I don't know how you managed to hijack our GPS to bring us here or how you got our car to abandon us, but I can tell you one thing: we are leaving here, even if we have to walk all the way out to the main road."

The odd couple looked at each other, frowned, and said, "We're sorry, Ted and Mary, but it's too late for that. We have a special place for you both right next door to our place. Follow us, and we'll show you."

The two turned and walked into the cemetery. Mary said, "Ted, there's no way I'm following them in there."

But moments after issuing that statement, both Mary and Ted found themselves following the couple deep into the graveyard. They couldn't stop themselves as they seemed to no longer have control of their own bodies. When they got to the back of the cemetery, they saw a stone building that was obviously the caretaker's building. Next to the structure, they saw two grave markers that read, "Robert Wyatt, Loving Husband" and "Jasmine Baker Wyatte, Loving Wife."

"This is where we reside," The strange couple said in unison. "And this is where you will reside."

They pointed to two other markers accompanying two recently dug graves. The markers read "Theodore Rhymes, Loving Husband" and "Mary Stanton Rhymes, Loving Wife."

"No way. This can't possibly be happening," Ted shouted.

"What's going on, Ted? How can any of this be real?"

Jasmine and Robert pointed at the two graves as if to insist that Ted and Mary look into them. The couple was reluctant to do so as they instinctively knew what or who they would find inside. And as they expected, they did look into the graves and saw their own lifeless bodies.

"What have you done to us?" Ted and Mary said simultaneously in multi-octave tones, sounding exactly like Jasmine and Robert. Then, they realized their fate was sealed, and no more questions or answers were needed.

RATS OF THE RUINS

Deep within the crumbling ruins of what was once supposed to be a new hope for a failing city, among the wreckage of what could have encompassed the promise of urban renewal but was now the epitome of blight and neglect, monstrous vermin of extraordinary size roamed freely in the dark shadows wreaking their special brand of mayhem. These grotesque, gigantic, four-legged (and sometimes more) mutations of rodent kind had become the things of local urban legend, whispered about in muted tones in neighborhoods surrounding the ill-fated ruins and told about in incredible stories by those who claimed to have actually seen these horrors that prowl the abandoned, dark alleyways and hide in the black recesses between fallen buildings.

Tales abound of their huge, glimmering eyes that glow with predatory cunning, their enormous browned and yellowed teeth, and their monstrous, stinking bodies that radiate a rancid, rotting stench. These giant man-eating creatures that could once simply be considered annoying rats evolved into something so far removed from the natural origin of their species as to be regarded barely as rodents at all. These beasts multiplied and mutated in the forsaken underbelly of the abandoned structures, and through catalysts unknown, these monsters have developed a voracious appetite for human flesh, motivating them to stalk the desolate streets and alleyways, searching for their ill-fated prey. Their vile, rancor stench, the terrifying scuttle of their massive, clawed feet, and the insidious, deep-throated chittering that echoes through the alleys are all harbingers of the nightmarish creatures' approach. But if you hear them, you will likely die a gruesome and agonizing death.

"Come on, you pussies. Are you coming with me or not?" Nate Morgan shouted to his group of friends, who all stood silent in a huddle, a safe distance from the first of many dilapidated buildings. A large painted wooden "DANGER / NO TRESPASSING" sign hung above the now-open entrance gate. Nate held his father's bolt cutter in his hands. Some local vandal had painted a bloody palm print on the sign with the message, "THE RATS ARE MARCHING BEWARE," in the same simulated crimson gore. Nate was the daredevil of this unusual cadre of friends, and although a formal leader did not exist, Nate seemed to hold that role informally.

"I don't care what you say, Nate. I ain't going in there. From what I heard, that place ain't somewhere we want to be hanging around," Young Ben Sells responded. Ben was 11 years old, two years younger than Nate, and much smaller. In fact, he was probably the youngest of the group. However, what Ben lacked in age and strength, he made up for it with bravery and determination. When he made up his mind, Ben didn't care how many names he was called; nothing could change his mind. He tugged the rim of his Phillies ball cap down to emphasize his conviction. "I heard there are rat monsters as big as cars, and nobody dumb enough to go in there ever comes out alive. They become mutant rat food."

Nate said, "Who asked for your opinion, pipsweak? I'm pretty sure it wasn't me. So, I don't care what kind of crap you hear or believe. What about you, Jim? Are you ready for an adventure, or are you gonna pussy-out with the runt?"

Jim Mort was Nate's age, and they had known each other since before kindergarten. Because their last names were so alphabetically close, they often found themselves seated closely together in every class and were frequently assigned lockers together. If Nate were the group's informal leader, Jim would be considered second in command. Jim had a lot more common sense than Nate and often became the voice of reason whenever Nate was about to do something stupid or dangerous. And Nate was about to do both.

"Lighten up on the kid, Nate. He has a right to be scared. It would probably benefit us all to be scared about that place," Jim said. "You know how many kids are missing in this town. You've seen the posters and stuff. I'll bet anything they did exactly what you're thinking about doing."

"What? You too? Did you all come down with a new type of chicken pox? One that turns you all into a bunch of wimpy pussified chickens?" Nate chided, laughing.

Another boy spoke up, "I ain't no chicken, Nate. I'll go with ya." That was Ronny Sands. To suggest that Ronny wasn't the brightest bulb in the string was a major understatement. To say Ronny might be a little slow would be like saying someone was a little pregnant. The worst aspect of Ronny's limited ability to discern logically was that he worshipped Nate and would walk through fire to impress him. What Nate suggested and Ronny had readily agreed to, would make walking through fire look like a walk in the park.

Jim knew that if half the stories he had heard about what the boys called "The Ruins" were true, he might never see Nate or Ronny alive again. Nate was apparently as foolhardy as Ronny was stupid, a volatile combination.

"Count me out, too. I'm staying back here with Jim and Ben," A bespeckled boy with brown curly hair said. "I ain't gonna end up on no poster or milk carton." His name was Timmy Grandston. He was Ronny's age and a year behind Nate and Jim in school. Despite Ronny's age, he was a year behind little Ben in school, having been "held back" for several years. The group assumed there would be much more "holding back" in Ronny's future. Then again, if Ronny did follow Nate today, it was quite possible neither of them would have much of a future.

Jim knew nothing he could do to make Nate change his mind, and he knew Ronny was determined to follow Nate. So, despite all the warnings his mind was screaming at him not to go along, Jim knew he had no choice but to go with them to watch after Ronny. Nate was first and foremost about Nate, and if Ronny found himself in a jam, Nate wouldn't lift a finger to help him. That was just the kind of kid Nate was.

Jim turned to Timmy and Ben and said, "Look, you guys, I don't wanna go in there, but somebody has to look out for Ronny. You know he's dumber than dirt, but he's a good kid, so I'll try to watch out for him. I want you two to wait back there, away from the Ruins. Timmy, set the timer on your smartphone. If we ain't out in 45 minutes, you call 911. When the cops come, tell them who we are, where we went, and what we did. Because, if we ain't out in 45 minutes, we ain't never comin' out."

Then Jim shouted angrily to Nate, "Ok, bigshot. I'll come with you but for no more than three-quarters of an hour. It's already gettin' dark, and I have to be home in an hour, so do you agree with that deal, Nate?"

"I ain't agreeing with nothin'. If you want to leave, that's up to you. I ain't leaving until I'm good and ready."

Jim chose not to argue further because he knew his friend, Nate, very well. Nate was all talk and little action. He spoke tough and acted tough, but the truth was he would likely be the first one to want to leave. Nate would likely try to disguise his fear by complaining that the place was boring and there was no adventure, so it was time to go. Jim only hoped that revelation would occur before anything bad happened to them.

Timmy and Ben left the other three for their adventure and waited as Jim had suggested. Jim looked at his watch, then at Nate and Ronny, and said, "Well, Nate. If you plan on going into the Ruins, we'd better get going."

Jim had to chuckle to himself when he saw Nate's slightest hesitation. He realized that Nate was bluffing all along and had no desire to go into the Ruins either, but had been hoping that everyone would back down and leave, and he could lie about going in when he saw them the next day. Maybe he'd even make up a story about giant creatures he had escaped from. But now that Ronny and Jim had agreed, he would have no choice but to go in. Jim decided to give Nate one final chance to back down and save face.

"Look Nate. It's getting dark. If you want to, we can try this another time when it's lighter. It's no big deal," Jim said.

A relieved look passed across Nate's face, and Jim was certain Nate was just about to agree with Jim and bow gracefully when Ronny suddenly spoke up.

"No way, Jim. Nate ain't a-scared of a little dark. Just cause you are don't mean we are. Nate wants to go tonight, and we're goin'. Ain't that right, Nate?"

Nate's shoulders slumped with obvious resignation. He had painted himself into a corner and couldn't escape it now. He looked at Jim with the realization that he had no choice now. So, as usual, Nate had to play the macho jerk.

"No problemo, Ronny boy. We are going in there and finding out what all the commotion is about," Nate said as he reached into his pocket and pulled out a 6-inch pocketknife. "If any critters show their stupid faces, they'll get a taste of this."

Jim did a mental eyeroll, knowing that if the stories he had heard about the ruins and the rodent-like creatures living there were true, no pocketknife would do them any good. In fact, a knife twice or three times as big would be next to useless. If they were to encounter anything, the best they could hope to do was outrun whatever was chasing them. But despite everything, it appeared the trio was committed to taking this insanity to its ultimate conclusion, whatever that might be.

The three began to walk slowly into the Ruins, looking around them and carefully making as little noise as possible. Little moonlight could reach into the darkness inside the labyrinth of decaying high-rise buildings, and the boys soon became dark shadows slinking cautiously through the abandoned streets.

"Wazzat?" Ronny shouted.

"Jeezus, Ronny will you shut up?" Nate whispered. "We have no idea what the heck is roaming around in here."

Ronny said quietly, "Sorry, Nate. I thought I heard something."

Nate replied angrily, "Well, if you shout like that again, you're gonna hear my fist smacking against your face. Now shut the Hell up."

"Sorry," Ronny said contritely.

Jim thought the other two sounded like something from a bad black-and-white 1950s horror movie. But his humorous thought was cut short when he noticed something out of the corner of his eye. Something dark and very large had moved in the shadows between the buildings. It was moving faster than Jim could have imagined.

He said with quiet desperation, "Hey guys, I just saw something moving over there in the shadows. I couldn't tell what it was, but it was big. I think maybe we should slowly back out of here."

Ronny said, much too loudly, "I figured you'd be the first one to pussy out, Jim. You ain't nothing but a big chicken . . ."

His words were cut short when two incredibly large, pointed jaws with yellowed, decayed, long, sharp teeth grabbed him around the waist from behind. They lifted him and shook him violently. Jim and Nate stood dumbfounded in shock, incapable of believing something so large could exist. Ronny struggled to scream but couldn't as his torso was being crushed by the massive maw of the thing from the shadows. The pair could hear his ribs cracking under the pressure of those enormous jaws. Blood flew in a spray from Ronny's lips as his insides were destroyed in the vice-like grip of the monster's maw.

Nate turned to Jim to tell him to run, but before he could issue a warning, another huge mouth tore off Nate's head, leaving his body to stand for a moment before it collapsed in a heap to the ground as blood pumped from and then pooled around his severed neck stump. Then, the corpse was pulled back into the darkness among a scattering of growls and loud chittering sounds. That was when Jim recognized both the sound and the pointed snout he had seen wrap itself around Ronny's waist. They were rats. But these monsters were unlike any rats Jim had ever seen before; these things were massive and had to be as big as a small car.

Without thinking, Jim turned and ran faster than he had ever run in his life, heading back the way he had come. Behind him, he could hear dozens of stomping feet coming ever closer. Their nails made a loud clicking sound on the road surface. He was sure he would end up like his two unfortunate friends when he reached the end of the Ruins and heard a deafening bang. Then, the footsteps stopped and faded away as if they were heading in the opposite direction.

As he lay in the grass outside the wire fence, panting and trying to regain his breath, he noticed a pair of dark leather motorcycle boots and black jeans beside him. Jim looked upward past the black leather coat to see a face he recognized. He didn't know the man's complete name but knew him as a local character the people called Dillon. He was a loner who hung out around town, driving a Harley, smoking, and drinking. Dillon wasn't affiliated with any motorcycle gang or club; he was a one-man gang. Jim saw that Dillon was still holding a large barrel pistol by his side, and a sharp smell permeated the air from his freshly fired gun.

Jim's two friends, Timmy and Ben, were hiding behind Dillon, with a look of confused concern on their terrified faces.

"You shouldn't have gone in there, you know," Dillon said matter of factly, speaking to the panicked Jim crying at his feet.

Jim said through his hitching breath and tear-filled voice, "I know . . . I know . . . I just . . . I don't know . . . oh God . . . Nate . . . Ronny . . ."

"Your friends aren't coming back, I'm afraid."

"I . . . I know . . . those things. Those rats. Oh my God, they were huge. They killed my friends."

"Yep, those monsters most certainly are huge," Dillon said. "Your poor friends didn't stand a chance in Hell. I don't know how you got this far."

Then Jim asked, "Did you kill any of the rat monsters?"

Dillon laughed, held up his gun, and said, "You mean with this? I'm afraid not. It may be big, and it may be bad, but it ain't nothin' compared to those things. The most I did was slow them down with the sound long enough for you to get away. I might have knicked one of them, but that was the best I could have hoped for. I'd need a tank or a flamethrower to take those monsters out."

Jim started getting his bearings and asked, "Can't anybody do anything about them? Then just ate my two friends." Then he broke down crying again.

"Nothing can be done as long as those buildings are left standing. And apparently, the city either doesn't have the money to take them down or doesn't care. I feel bad about your friends, but they aren't the first kids to go in there and not come out, and they probably won't be the last. The truth is, you shouldn't have made it out either."

Jim said, "But what are those things in there? I didn't get a real good look at them, but they looked like giant rats. But I ain't never seen no rats that big before."

"Yup. Those things are some kinda rats, but as big as a VW bug and smarter than normal rats. Plus, they are hungry buggers. When one of them gets hurt or is too old, the others fall on it and eat it. If I managed to clip one of them, the rest will be dining on him later tonight."

"You mean like cannibals?"

"You bet," Dillon said, "Food is food."

"Can't the police do something about them?"

"They should. But they said they didn't believe me whenever I tried to tell them about it. I think they knew what I told them was true, but they ignored me because they were just scared. They told me the best thing to do is stay away from the Ruins. That's why they posted that sign telling people to stay out. That's not much of a deterrent, as you three have proven so aptly. That attitude of placing a warning sign and hanging a flimsy lock on the gate is just plain stupid if you ask me. It's like the old joke about going to the doctor and complaining that something hurts when you do something, and the doctor tells you, 'Then don't do it.'"

"But what about all the missing kids? What about my friends?"

Dillon shook his head and said, "Your two other friends back here flagged me down and told me what you had done. I said I'd offer what help I could. Your friends can walk you home, and you can tell your parents what happened. Maybe after your friends' parents learn about it, they can raise a stink, and maybe something will get done about it. What do your friends' parents do for a living?"

"Well, Nate's dad works in the local envelope factory, and Ronny's dad is long gone. He lived with his mom, who is a waitress down at the diner. My dad is a machinist at the local metal factory."

Dillon said with resignation, "I hate to tell you this, kid, but I'm afraid they ain't gonna have enough clout to get the town council or the police to move on this. You gotta be rich or have connections to get those bums to move on even simple things, and sadly, your friends' folks won't have that kinda clout."

"So, what do I do? My friends are dead."

"Do what I said. Go home and tell your folks what happened. But be prepared. They probably won't believe you or won't want to get involved. Lots of people in town have heard about the Ruins and those monsters. They just turn a blind eye to it. The reason I said be prepared is you might get your butt whooped for going in there, and they may tell you to forget you ever went in there and don't tell anyone about it."

Jim sighed, "I can't believe nobody will do anything. But if that is the case, then I suppose that's that."

"Yep, that's that, until more stupid kids decide to ignore the sign and the rumors and go inside. I suspect your friends will end up on a poster in the center of town, just like the rest of the missing kids that will never come home."

Jim vowed, "Someday, after college, I'm gonna come home and get on that town council or maybe the police department; then maybe I can force somebody to do something about those mutants."

Dillon said with false support, "Maybe you will. I can only hope you do."

BLOOD BANK

The young, strong, healthy man had regularly donated blood at the local blood bank for many years. Most of the time, he scheduled his donation for the daytime. However, this year, upon learning the bank's calendar was full, he had no choice but to schedule his donation for Halloween night. Ken Hawkins assumed the phlebotomists would like to take advantage of the spooky Halloween theme, being a blood bank and everything. Ken was always up for a good gag and figured the place would be decorated like a graveyard, and all the techs would be dressed like vampires.

That Halloween night, as he approached the front door of the blood bank, he was not disappointed. Fake spiderwebs adorned the entrance, and the window was blacked out, so you couldn't see inside. As he turned the doorknob and stepped onto a mat inside the entryway, he heard a mournful howl and someone saying, "Enter at your own risk." Ken knew that was a prerecorded chip thing that activated when his weight pressed down on the mat. "Nice touch," he thought.

They had even tricked out the fluorescent overhead lights, so most of them were out, and the few that remained flickered like those in every bad horror movie he had ever seen. Always safety conscious, he wondered about the potential tripping hazards of such poor and strobe-like lighting but supposed that was not his problem. As Ken cautiously approached the receptionist's desk, he saw a woman he didn't recognize from previous visits. Typically, a sweet, older, probably retired woman was at the receptionist station, but this woman was much younger. She was dressed all in black; her face was ghostly white with some sort of pancake makeup. Dark circles surrounded her eyes, and fake blood dripped from the corner of her mouth.

She smiled sheepishly and said, "Can I bite you? I mean, can I help you?"

Ken was momentarily taken aback by the gag, then said, "I'm Kenneth Hawkins, and I have an appointment to donate blood."

She said, "Yum, that sounds delicious."

"Excuse me?" Ken said, still not completely embracing this strange new holiday theme.

"Oh, nothing, Mr. Hawkins. Please take a seat over there, and someone will be out to drain you; I mean, see you shortly."

Ken started getting creeped out by this whole situation. Getting into character was one thing, but these folks seemed to be taking things a bit too far. He sat for a few minutes, waiting for the next step in the process. It was the mandatory requirement he hated, the one that made him feel like a criminal. One of the blood techs would come out and take him into a private room where he, or more often she, would ask Ken a ton of embarrassing questions such as, "Have you ever had sex for money?" or "Have you ever paid for sex?" or the always uncomfortable, "Have you ever had sex with another man?"

Once, Ken tried to be funny when asked, "Did you ever pay for sex?" and he replied, "I'm married; I pay for it every day." His feeble attempt at humor went unappreciated by the stoic-faced questioner. They always asked these questions and others while putting labels on bags that would eventually identify and hold his donated blood. Unfortunately, it was all part of the process, and Ken always felt that if he had to be subjected to a few annoying questions to help someone in need of blood, then so be it.

After a few minutes of sitting in the dimly lit waiting area, Ken saw a tall, shapely woman in a long black, low-cut, slinky Morticia Adams dress slithering around the corner, and she asked, "Kenneth Hawkins?"

"Yes, that's me," he managed to eke out. This woman was nothing like the usual techs he was used to dealing with. Not to suggest he found the regular female staff members unappealing, but this woman was light years ahead of them on the sexy scale.

She asked, "Do you mind if I call you Ken?"

"No . . . No, not at all," Ken replied. The fact was, as far as he was concerned, a woman that hot could call him whatever she wanted and any time she wanted.

"Ok, Ken. Please follow me."

As they walked slowly down the darkened corridor with barely enough flickering light to illuminate their way, Ken again thought of how unsafe it was and how very strange the barely lit hallway was. Ken noticed they were walking past the doorways to the small rooms where he usually went through the humiliating question-and-answer session. All the doors were shut, and Ken thought he had seen some dark liquid oozing out and pudding at the base of one of the closed doors. He assumed maybe someone spilled something or dropped a bag of blood. Ken supposed such an accident could occur, but being aware of safety requirements, he realized if blood had accidentally been spilled, there would be all sorts of hazmat protocols in place, and it wouldn't be permitted to remain. He decided it was probably a spilled soda or something. That was still sloppy and unsanitary but not worthy of his freaking out about it.

Ken asked, "Miss? Ma'am? Aren't you going to take me into one of these rooms and ask me all those questions they usually ask me? You know, like, do I have HIV or Mad Cow disease?"

The woman smiled sensually, winked, and asked, "Well, Kenny. Do you?"

"Um . . . No. No, I don't." He was taken aback momentarily again. She called him Kenny. This hot chick was really starting to turn him on.

"Well, Kenny, if you say you don't, that's good enough for me." She reached down and gently took his hand, leading him further into the darkness. Ken was momentarily stunned by how cold the woman's hand felt against his.

"Now, let's get you a drink before we get you all comfortable. Does that sound good to you?" She asked.

"Yeah, I suppose, but usually, they offer me a can of soda, some apple juice, or a bottle of water afterward. And sometimes cookies or crackers. But as I said, that's usually after I've donated."

"Tonight, we're doing things a little differently. Would you like a 'before donation' cocktail? We have a fully stocked bar we brought in for the night."

Ken was simultaneously confused and thrilled. He said, "A cocktail? Before donating? Wow! That sounds like an awesome idea to me. But won't that affect the integrity of my donation?"

"Oh no, not at all. It might change the taste ever so little, but I'm sure it will be fine. In fact, it will probably be better than fine."

Ken said, "Wow, you folks are really getting into this whole Halloween role-playing thing. But hey, who am I to argue? Bring on a Long Island Ice Tea, and make it strong."

Ken sat on a chair in the darkened waiting area, which he had always considered the snack bar or kitchen. He thought about how very unusual this entire donation experience had been. It was by far the strangest and simultaneously the most interesting encounter he had ever experienced. As the sexy tech returned, emerging from the darkness and handing him his drink, she said, "Hopefully, this will be strong enough to suit your needs. But honestly, I don't think you'll have to worry about that, Kenny, old boy. I mixed this baby up myself, especially for you and I'm sure it will send you for a loop."

For a moment, Ken wondered about the logic of drinking a strong drink, being weak from donating blood, then getting behind the wheel of a car and driving away. Then he decided, "Why not?" and took a long chug of his cocktail. Ken realized instantly that his hostess was not exaggerating. He felt its effect immediately, and suddenly, it seemed like he was moving through air that was as thick as maple syrup. Ken was certain he was about to pass out. "Wah . . . ," Was all he managed to say before he felt four strong arms lift him and place him into one of the donation recliners. His shirt was ripped from his body, and he felt scissors cutting his pant legs. He couldn't move as someone had tightened two leather straps around his wrists and two around his ankles.

He managed to get a brief look at the two assistants who had lifted and secured him into his chair, and could barely believe his eyes. They were dressed in some sort of demon costumes that were more realistic than Ken had ever seen. The pair were short, no more than four feet tall, but were bulging with muscles. They looked like naked, sweat-covered, shaved apes with long, ram-like horns protruding from their skulls and sharp tusks rising from the bottoms of their thick-lipped, impossibly large mouths. Ken was certain he was hallucinating because no Halloween costume could be this incredible.

As the fluorescent lights blinked like strobes in the almost black collection area, Ken looked around and noticed for the first time that several other collection chairs were occupied. It was then he heard the soft, sad moaning of helpless, barely conscious people. In the flickering lights, Ken saw a face he recognized. It was a woman, a former blood tech he had seen on a previous visit. What was her name? Jane? Janice? He couldn't recall, but Ken was certain it was her. She was strapped to a chair as he was, but what appeared to be dozens of crimson plastic tubes extended from her body and connected to far too many collection bags for any normal donation.

What in the name of God was going on, and what was happening to him? Then Ken saw the two demon creatures lift another person from a distant donation chair and carry him past Ken down the darkened hall, where they unceremoniously dumped his body into one of the small questioning rooms. It was a male tech that he recognized from a past visit. Ken was certain now that what he had seen earlier was blood pooling on the floor. He looked up through glazed, bleary eyes and saw the sexy tech who had given him the cocktail. She was smiling at him, but no longer in the sexual, flattering way she had done earlier, but with the insane, wider-eyed look of animalistic, insatiable hunger.

When she smiled, her mouth opened much too wide and appeared to spill over with hundreds of shark-like teeth. Blood dripped from between those razor-sharp fangs, and a foul stench of rotten meat came from that horrible gaping maw. Ken struggled against the straps that held him in place, but to no avail. The two hideous demon creatures roughly shoved needle after needle into Ken's forearms and exposed legs, connecting them with plastic tubes to collection bags.

With the horror that comes with the realization that one's fate is out of control and sealed, Ken stopped struggling as he felt his life's blood leaving his body. The once beautiful, sexy tech, now having turned into some sort of vampire demon, leaned down next to Ken's ear and, with a hoarse, rancid-smelling voice, whispered, "We thank you for your donation, Kenny. Oh yes, and Happy Halloween."

WHAT'S WRONG WITH OUR HOUSE?

The white-haired woman stood by the window, pulling the drapes carefully aside, attempting to sneak a look out into the street. It was October 31, another Halloween night, and just like every previous Halloween, the trick-or-treaters were busy going from house to house in search of the precious goodies they all so desperately desired. However, they seemed to be avoiding her house for some strange, unknown reason, almost deliberately so.

"What's wrong with our house?" Gladys Millbury asked of her husband Harold, sitting quietly in his recliner reading the local newspaper's sports section and paying little attention to his wife as was typical of him. The room was clean and tastefully decorated with furnishings they had acquired throughout their forty-three years of marriage.

Harold said, "How the Hell should I know, Gladys? Who really knows what goes on inside young kids' minds these days? Heaven knows I don't have a clue. But what's the big deal anyway? If they show up, they show up; if they don't, they don't. To be perfectly honest with you, I don't really care if they ever come around. Young kids can often mean nothing but trouble these days. In fact, they're often more trouble than they're worth. Good riddance to bad rubbish, as far as I am concerned."

"Oh, Harold," she replied, "That's no way to talk, for pity's sake. You sound like such an old fuddy-duddy. It's Halloween night, and you know the children in our neighborhood are all good kids. We've always opened our doors to them on Halloween. In the old days, we would have been overrun with trick-or-treaters by this time of night. Remember how they always said that I gave them the best candy? I was always so proud of that. But now they won't even ring our doorbell anymore. I wonder what happened. It's almost as if they seem to be deliberately avoiding us this year. What could possibly be the matter? What's in the world do they think is wrong with us?"

"Funny you should ask," Harold replied, "I was starting to wonder what might be wrong with you myself. The way you're standing there staring out into the street. You look like a desperate, starving, lost little puppy. For heaven's sake, Gladys, just let it go. So what if the kids choose to ignore us this year? It just means more candy for me."

"Like you can eat all this candy," Gladys replied, looking down into her enormous basket of goodies, "You with your blood sugar issues!"

Gladys and Harold Millbury lived in the same house at the end of Maple Street for over thirty years. And for as long as either of them could recall, the neighborhood children always flocked to their house for treats faithfully every Halloween. So, Gladys knew something must be amiss to cause them to behave this way.

As Gladys peeked out the front window again, she exclaimed, "Oh my goodness, Harold! You should see this! Several of the kids just crossed over to the other side of the street as if they were making a point of avoiding our house. I even saw a couple of them looking back, then quickly looked away. The odd thing was they seemed to look terrified. It was as if they were afraid to come here or something. Why would anyone be afraid to come here, Harold? We're good people. What's wrong with these kids?" Harold decided to ignore his wife and continue to read his newspaper.

Outside, the neighborhood kids Gladys had seen from the window were doing exactly as she had described, walking across the street, pushing and shoving each other playfully while occasionally giving wary glances back toward the house. Occasionally, one of the kids would point back toward their home, make spooky gestures with his hands at the younger children, and laugh hysterically. The small children would quickly look back at the house before hurrying to be back with the group.

The house sat in darkness, illuminated only by the pale moonlight shining through the branches of the tall oak trees in the overgrown front yard. The trees had lost their leaves a month earlier and now stood like a colossal multi-limbed monstrous sentry guarding the mysterious home with its battered paint-chipped facade and foot-high weeds surrounding the broken brick walkway.

The neighborhood children all knew about the Millbury place and had all heard the many frightening stories surrounding the house. They knew the real history of the property, which was terrifying enough, but they also knew all of the local legends, which was certainly enough to keep even the most daring of them away.

As the true story of the house went, a nice elderly retired couple named Gladys and Harold Millbury had once owned the home. Mr. Millbury had retired from the railroad, and Mrs. Millbury had worked as a nurse at a local hospital. Every Halloween, children from all over would flock to the Millbury place since Gladys was reputed to give the best candy in town.

There was also a false reputation that followed the Millburys. Since the couple had no children, lived frugally, and had generous pensions, it was assumed they were well off financially. This was untrue. The two weren't starving by any means, and Gladys was quite generous with her precious trick-or-treaters, but the couple was far from wealthy. Unfortunately, those false stories about them being rich had reached the ears of some local undesirables, and the result was a horrific crime, the likes of which the small town had never seen before or since.

Twelve years earlier to the day, October 31, Halloween night, the couple had opened their home to trick-or-treaters as they had done for so many years before. Gladys waited by the window with her bowl of candy, watching for children, while Harold always sat in his recliner reading the sports section. It had been a very successful evening, with many children enjoying their treats.

However, later that night, while the couple slept, persons unknown broke into the house, murdered the couple in their sleep, and then robbed the home of whatever they could find. The place had been ransacked as if the killers had been looking for caches of hidden money. But, of course, there was no treasure to be found.

There was much more to the story than just two people being murdered in their sleep. Word had leaked that the murderers had conducted strange, bizarre, and possibly satanic rituals with the bodies. It was said the twisted perpetrators had savagely dismembered the couple's bodies and had bizarrely arranged the parts. Witnesses said the scene resembled something that might be described as a modern art show in Hell. This included limbs from Harold's body attached to Gladys' torso and vice versa.

It was said that Gladys' breasts had been hacked off and attached to Harold's chest. Likewise, Harold's genitals were severed and placed between Gladys' legs. Their stomachs had been sliced open, and the room was decorated with bloody intestines like some unimaginable pink and crimson garland. Their heads had been decapitated and placed atop their dresser as if they had been placed there for the pair to view the hideous tableau before them. The room stank like the inside of a slaughterhouse, which was exactly what it had become.

The unholy display of mangled and reordered body parts was so horrifying and beyond anyone's ability to understand that every investigator on the scene could not keep from vomiting. Perhaps the most disturbing part of it all was the writing on the wall behind the bed, as if the killers had wanted to come up with a title for the macabre scene. The words "Happy Halloween" were written crudely with hands dipped in the couple's blood. The murderers were never apprehended.

If there was any consolation to be taken from the scene of unimaginable butchery, the county coroner's report suggested the couple had likely been killed instantly and did not have to suffer. He even suggested they had probably died so quickly that they might not have even known what had happened to them.

From the coroner's single statement, the legends began to spread and grew as such legends often did. Stories of late-night sightings of Gladys standing, looking out of the front window abounded. This was especially prevalent on Halloween night, the anniversary of the murders, when it was believed she still stood watching for her beloved trick-or-treaters. There were also tales of the two headless specters floating inside the home.

No one would dare buy the home because of the savagery of the murders committed in the house. As a result, it soon fell into disrepair and eventually went to ruin. And now, every year, the neighborhood children would make it a point to cross the street on Halloween night to stay as far from the Millbury house as possible.

"I just don't get it," Gladys said as she looked out of her living room window, "They are avoiding us like we have the plague or something. I can't figure it out, Harold. Our house used to be a magnet for children at Halloween, but no longer. What's wrong with our house?"

"Forget it," Harold said, "Look. This is all pointless. I'm tired anyway. I think I'll head up to bed for the night. "

Harold set the newspaper on the end table and went up the stairs to bed. The date of the paper read October 31, but the year was not the current year; it was twelve years earlier. He read the same paper every October 31. This was the same scenario he and Gladys had played out every Halloween night since the horrific event. But to them, it was always the first time, new, fresh, and eternal.

THE THING IN THE CELLAR

"Whoever fights monsters should see to it that in the process, he does not become a monster. And if you gaze long enough into an abyss, the abyss will gaze back into you."
—FRIEDRICH NIETZSCHE

"Everyone has monsters and demons within themselves. They're metaphors for the human condition."
—MARK PELLEGRINO

"We create monsters, and then we can't control them."
—JOEL COEN

"We have nothing to fear but fear itself—and monsters."
—RICHARD HERRING

"Don't you go foolin' around near that cellar door, Sadie May. There's awful things down there that little girls got no business messin' with."

"What kinds of things, Uncle Bob?" Four-year-old Sadie May Younger asked, now more curious than ever.

Bob Younger was neither the smartest nor the most patient person in the world. So, whenever he found himself saddled with the responsibility of babysitting his overly precocious niece, Sadie May, he knew he was in for quite an exhausting time. Sadie was not only a curious and active child but also smart as a whip and, as her mom was fond of saying, "Sadie was special." Her Uncle Bob knew this but, unfortunately, had no real idea just how "special" she was.

You see, Bob was not what you could consider special in any way. In fact, he was about as far removed from special as one could be and still be considered a functioning, thinking human being. This was not to suggest that Bob was dumber than a box of rocks, but he was certainly running a close second. Many had suggested that Bob wasn't the brightest bulb on the proverbial string. Let's just say Bob was fortunate that breathing was an automatic bodily function, or he would likely have been dead long ago. So, as one might imagine, Sadie's always curious presence could cause her Uncle Bob a great deal of consternation, often more than poor, underequipped Bob could handle.

One area of intense stress was Sadie's constant curiosity about Bob's cellar. Bob supposed such inquisitiveness was merited since his cellar was a place of great mystery to a girl like Sadie May. The farmhouse where he lived was more than one hundred years old, and since Bob was not a handy sort of fellow, little had been done to update the aged property. As such, it still had a dirt floor cellar with damp, leaky stone walls. Moss grew in the cracks between the stones, and an interesting variety of insects made the cellar their home. Spiders adorned the stone walls with gossamer webs, trapping flying insects for their later dining pleasure. Worms, ants, and centipedes squirmed about in the soft, spongy soil of the dirt floor. Remnants of old rotted leaves and sticks littered the corners and edges of the cellar, brought in over the years by field mice or chipmunks. Bob could never find out how the annoying little varments got in, although he had been trying for years to find them.

The cellar space was inadequately lit by a bare bulb with a pull chain hanging from a wire in the center of the room. Because of the poor condition of the cellar, Bob kept very little in terms of supplies or tools down there. Perhaps at one time, the place might have made a great root cellar or a space for storing jarred and preserved foods, but Bob had no interest in such things. The only thing he kept in the underground room now was a large glass Mason jar tucked into a rotted wooden chest, hidden in a dark corner.

The jar was loaded with what, at first glance, looked like nothing more than old, dried leaves. However, Bob knew these were much more important than simply dried leaves. They were all that remained of what he referred to as his "cash crop." He had once raised a healthy harvest of "Whacky Tabaccie," which he had grown carefully hidden among his corn stalks several years earlier. Though the cellar was not the best place for his special collection of illegal "smoking' leaves," it was a great place to hide them from the suspicious and ever-prying eyes of County Sheriff Gerome T. Wilkins.

As a result, the cellar was a pretty creepy place, and that was exactly what Bob wanted it to be. It should have been too frightening for any girl as young as Sadie to have any interest, but not every girl was like Sadie, as she was "special." Despite Sadie's relentless inquiries, Bob couldn't tolerate Sadie snooping around in the cellar and finding his stash, and he knew she would eventually find it. Once Sadie did, more questions would ensue. He could imagine Sadie asking her mother, Bob's sister Sarah, questions about why Uncle Bob had a mysterious jar full of strange leaves, which wouldn't be good. Sarah would know exactly what Bob had stored in that jar and would verbally tear him a new one if she found out.

Bob had to devise a way to prevent Sadie May from wanting to explore the cellar, and he figured nothing was better at discouraging the young girl's interest than a good heaping helping of terror, with a side order of horror and perhaps a bit of gore for dessert. So, Bob, being Bob, decided to concoct a story, a tale so horrifying that Sadie would never want to investigate the cellar again.

"Sadie, I've told you many times what's down there in the cellar and what it does to little girls like you, didn't I?"

Sadie hesitated, looked down at her sneakers, frowned, and said, "Yes, Uncle Bob. You told me a horrible monster lives down in the cellar."

"That's right, Sadie. And it's not just any monster, but one of the most horrible monsters ever. It's made of dirt and mud and sticks and bugs and lives under the dirt floor of the cellar. It smells horrible, like dead things, and it waits under the dirt for a little girl like you to come down and look for him. Remember how horrible it smells, Sadie?"

At one time, to add some realism to his tale, Bob cracked the cellar door and told Sadie to put her nose against the open space and breathe in deeply. The foul stench of the damp, mildewed cellar came wafting up, causing the little girl to wrinkle her nose in disgust.

"Yes, I remember, Uncle Bob. It was really awful stinky."

"That's right, Sadie. It truly was awful stinky. That stinky smell came from the horrible monster that lives down there and from the many little girls it has eaten in the past. When a little girl like you goes down those steps and touches the dirt floor, that monster rises out of the dirt and is over six feet tall. You know that's really big, don't you, Sadie?"

"Yes, Uncle Bob. That's even bigger than you are."

"That's right. And when it gets that big, you can see exactly what it looks like, even in the darkness of the cellar. That ugly monster is made of all kinds of rotten things with worms and bugs crawling through it."

"I remember you told me that, Uncle Bob. You called it a goalie, right."

"No, Sadie May. Not a goalie. I said it was a golem. That's a horrible monster made from all kinds of disgusting things."

"Golem. Yeah, that's right," Sadie corrected herself.

"And when the golem rises up, it's hungry, very hungry. And what it likes to eat most is pretty little girls, just like you, Sadie May. It doesn't have no teeth to chew, so it has to suck the skin right off of your bones."

Sadie stood silently, looking down at her sneakers, trying not to cry. The idea of such a monster sucking the skin off her bones was too much for her young mind to comprehend.

"So what does that mean, Sadie May?" Bob asked, not intelligent enough to even consider the negative psychological effects of what he had just told this sweet little girl.

After a moment, she said, "That means that I should never go down into the cellar, or else that horrible golem monster will suck the skin off my bones and eat me."

"Yep. That's right, Sadie May. You can never go down there, or the monster will eat you alive while you are screaming for help. So, do you understand me now, Sadie May?"

Terrified and on the verge of tears, Sadie said, "Yes . . . Uncle Bob. I must never go down into the cellar, or the dirt monster will . . . eat me up."

"Very good, Sadie. I'm glad you understand. But remember, as long as you stay up here, you have nothing to be afraid of. The monster only lives in the cellar. Now go into the other room and play with your dolls while I make us some lunch."

"Ok, Uncle Bob," Sadie said as she sniffed and shuffled sadly with her head down, entering the living room where several of her dolls awaited.

Although Sadie had done as she was told, her curiosity about the basement never waned. If anything, it became stronger because of the horrible description Uncle Bob had presented to her. But Sadie decided to try to forget about that monster for now and play with her dolls.

Sitting on the living room floor, she looked around to ensure Uncle Bob was not paying attention. She smiled, nodded, and suddenly, one of her dolls winked at her. This always made Sadie smile. Then, a moment later, Sadie nodded again, and another doll's head turned from left to right. Soon, all the dolls were winking, turning their heads, and waving their arms maniacally. Then Sadie heard a noise in the other room, and all doll movement stopped instantly.

"Everything ok in here, Sadie?" Uncle Bob asked as he struck his head around the corner. "I thought I heard some weird noises."

"I'm ok, Uncle Bob. I'm just talking to my dollies."

"Well, that's a good thing, Sadie May. You keep playing with your dollies, and I'll go back to making our lunch."

"Ok, Uncle Bob," Sadie said. But Sadie realized she didn't want to return to playing with her dolls. She was starting to get bored with her dolls, even though she could make them move and even talk just by thinking about it. Sadie didn't know how she could do this; she just knew she was able to because she was "special." Her mommy always told her she was "special" and had to be careful that no one saw the funny things she could do just by thinking about stuff. Uncle Bob had no idea she could do these fun things. The big problem with her being special was Sadie couldn't always control what happened when she imagined those things. Her mommy always told her to be "very careful" about letting her imagination get away from her, but that was a lot of responsibility for such a little girl.

As she sat on the floor, Sadie suddenly realized that all she could think about was that terrible monster living under the dirt in Uncle Bob's cellar. Uncle Bob had done a good job of describing the horrible creature. So much so that Sadie May couldn't get the image of the monster out of her mind. She sat on the living room floor with her legs crossed and her eyes closed, trying to forget what Uncle Bob told her. But the more she tried to forget, the more she remembered. Sadie imagined how the creature might begin to form and rise from the dirt floor. Sadie saw the soft, moist soil trembling slightly, then swirling in a circular motion as it slowly formed a small lump of constantly turning debris. In her mind, she saw sticks, leaves, bugs, worms, and similar things pulled toward the spiraling, growing mound of soil.

As she sat imagining, the thing in the cellar began to take shape, growing ever larger as it arose from the moist dirt. Soon, it was in the shape of a man, half-emerged in the soil but pushing itself further out of the dirt. It had no defining features other than it was smooth and man-shaped. Its surface seemed in constant motion as thousands of worms and insects squirmed throughout its pulsating form. Sadie imagined she could hear what the creature was thinking and was not surprised to find it had only one thought in whatever passed for its mind. It was hungry, and it needed to eat.

Sadie May imagined the creature now fully out of the ground and standing much taller than Uncle Bob, walking over to the rickety wooden steps of the cellar. In her mind, she saw the monster put its foot on the first step, the second, and the third. Sadie should have wondered if the giant would collapse the stairs under its massive weight, but she was only four years old, and such things never entered her mind. The way her special gift seemed to work was if she didn't imagine them, they didn't happen, so the monster's size didn't matter to the aged stairs. Soon, the creature was at the top of the stairs, and Sadie imagined the thing slamming its huge golem fists against the cellar door.

"What the Hell was that?" Uncle Bob shouted from the kitchen, hearing the banging on the cellar door.

"I didn't hear anything, Uncle Bob," Sadie May lied, chuckling to herself.

Bob stood in front of the cellar door looking terrified, and said, "I heard something in the cellar. Something was banging on the door."

"Please stop that, Uncle Bob. I think you're trying to scare me again," Sadie said, doing her best to act frightened. "It's not nice to scare little girls." Her expression had changed from a terrified little girl to something more serious, more adult, and unnerving.

Bob didn't notice the change in Sadie's appearance as he was focused on the cellar door, which not only continued to produce the terrifying banging sound but now was vibrating on its hinges with every incredible pound. Just when Bob was sure the door would fly open, releasing a horrid beast that would devour Bob alive, the slamming abruptly stopped.

Then Bob heard something large tromping down the cellar steps. A few moments later, there was silence. Bob looked down and realized he had soiled himself in fear. He glanced into the living room and saw Sadie May watching him with an expression that bordered on amusement. Bob couldn't help but wonder what, if anything, the little girl had to do with what had just occurred. Then he realized how ridiculous that thought was. Surely, she was too young and too small, but something seemed wrong with how she looked at him.

"Did you hear that, Sadie May?" Bob asked reluctantly.

"Yes, Uncle Bob. I think that must have been that horrible dirt monster you told me about. Now, I don't ever want to go into your cellar."

Bob knew he wouldn't be going into his basement anymore, either. Screw the "cash crop," and screw the house. Two weeks later, Bob put his farmette and house up for sale and, shortly after that, moved far away.

Sadie May missed spending time with her Uncle Bob and sometimes felt bad that she had scared him so badly. But it wasn't nice of him to tell her stories that made her think of scary things. She couldn't help herself because, as her mommy always told her, she was special.

URNS

"Wow, Gina. You won't believe the great deal I got on this car!" Anson Gross told his wife.

To say Gina Gross was unimpressed with this amazing revelation would be an understatement. She and Anson had been married for almost two decades, and if she had a dollar for every time Anson came home with an automotive "great deal," she might not be rich, but she'd at least have a few bucks instead of the thousands her husband had lost over the years, buying pieces of junk that were "great deals." She swore it was an illness or obsession with Anson, like his quest for the four-wheel Holy Grail.

Every time it happened, Anson would come home smiling from ear to ear, acting like he had just won the Lottery, explaining how he had just gotten one "fantastic deal" or another on a used vehicle. At first glance, the car or truck usually looked like a good deal until the other shoe dropped, and Anson would say something like, "It only needs a new transmission," or "It only needs breaks, rotors, and tires." With Anson's amazing deals, there was always an "It only needs" of one sort or another. You could be guaranteed that whatever that need happened to be, it would end up costing much more than the original "great deal."

The worst part of the process was that Anson had absolutely no mechanical ability whatsoever. Despite his garage full of tools, he was worse than useless when it came to "fixing up" any car. That meant most of the time, Anson had to hire someone else to do the work. On those few occasions when he tried to do the job himself, he usually screwed up royally and had to pay someone to undo what he had done, then pay them again to do the actual initial repair. As far as Gina was concerned, his "great deals" dug a gaping pit in their driveway, where Anson threw what little extra money they managed to save.

Gina braced herself for Anson's latest "It only needs . . ." but the words never came. She asked, "OK, Anson. How about you tell me all about this great deal? More importantly, tell me what else the piece of junk will need to make it road-worthy and what it's going to cost us."

"That's the best part, Gina. It doesn't need anything else. It's good to go. Not only that, but it's an SUV. I knew how much you wanted an SUV. I got this one at the car auction for a song."

"How could you have gotten it for a song, Anson, when you can't carry a tune in a bucket?"

"Haha. Very funny. Come outside and take a look and be amazed at what $500 has bought us."

"When the heck did you get $500? Never mind. I don't think I want to know," she said, knowing in Anson's case, ignorance was always blissful. Instead, she followed her husband outside and saw his latest purchase sitting in the dirt driveway in front of their single-wide mobile home.

"She's a beauty, ain't she, Gina?" Anson said, pointing at the surprisingly pristine-looking 2001 Toyota 4-Runner.

Gina found herself somewhat speechless. If what Anson said was true and this baby really didn't need anything else, he may have finally gotten the deal he had been trying to get for decades. She had been researching the cost of used SUVs for some time; it had been more of a fantasy than research, as Gina knew they could never afford the $8,000–$20,000 price tag for such a vehicle. Yet somehow, Anson had managed to get this beauty for only $500.

"What's the catch, Anson? There has to be a catch. There's always a catch. You don't get a vehicle this nice for $500. It just doesn't happen."

"No catch, Babe. I got this at Fred's Abandoned Car Auction over in Simpson. It had been found abandoned on a roadside with no papers or identification of any kind. Fred got it from the police impound and drove it to the lot. He briefly checked it out, took care of making the necessary paperwork for it, and slapped a price tag of $800 on it."

"But you said you got it for $500," Gina questioned.

"I did, Gina Babe. Never doubt my negotiation skills."

After more than two decades, not only did she doubt his negotiation skills, but she also sometimes doubted her own sanity for putting up with his nonsense for so long.

"So how do we know this SUV wasn't used in some kind of robbery or murder or God knows what else?" She asked.

"Well, I suppose we don't. But it already was checked out by the cops as well as Fred's Auction folks, so I suppose that's good enough for me."

"Of course, it's good enough for you, Anson. You never ask the important questions. You always take everyone at their word. That's why we always end up getting screwed in all of your 'great deals.' Well, I suppose we should check this gem out for ourselves."

The pair walked around the SUV, opening all the doors and checking the condition of the interior. Gina was shocked at how well-maintained and clean the vehicle was.

"I can take you for a spin, and you can see how well it runs. I'm telling you, Gina, this was the find of the century."

"In a bit, Anson. I want to check out the back first."

Gina lifted the hatch and was amazed at how clean and unworn the carpeted interior of the back was. She saw there was a wooden crate sitting in the rear storage area.

"What's with the wooden crate, Anson? Did they give you some spare parts or something?"

"What wooden crate. I didn't notice that when I bought the car."

"Of course you didn't. That would have involved actually looking closely at the thing."

"No need to get so snippy, Gina. I think you just can't believe I got such a good deal."

"You are absolutely correct about that, Anson. Your reputation precedes you. Let's see what little treasure awaits us in this mystery box." Gina pulled the box forward and lifted the lid. She stepped back, gasped, and dropped the lid on the ground.

"What is it, Gina?"

She stammered, "I . . . I'm not sure. It looks like Urns."

"Urns?"

"Yeah. Urns. Funeral urns. Two of them. The kinds of things you put dead people's ashes in after you cremate them."

"What the Hell are funeral urns doing in the back of our SUV?"

"Good question, Anson. What are funeral urns doing in the back of our SUV . . . that you bought and supposedly checked out, and which was such an amazing deal?"

"Hold on now, Gina. You can't go blaming me for this. It was obviously some slight oversight on the part of Fred's Auction. I had nothing to do with it. It's not my fault."

"Of course, it's not your fault. It's never your fault. It wasn't your fault when you bought that car with the dead skunk in the trunk, either, was it? That dead skunk made the car unfit for human habitation. That was another great deal, as I recall. Now we have dead people in the back of our SUV."

"Wait a minute, Gina. They ain't exactly dead people. They are dead people's ashes. That is, assuming the urns are actually full. Check to see if they are full."

"What? I'm not checking for any such thing. First, you know how I hate anything to do with death, dead people, or dead things in general. Secondly, you bought this death mobile, this hearse, you come over here and check it out your own damn self. I don't want no part of this disgusting business."

"Fine, fine, fine. Let me look at these." Anson lifted the lid on the first urn and saw it was full of ashes. He didn't bother with the second urn; he just lifted it to see if it had any significant weight. "Yep. They are both filled with ashes."

"That's just disgusting! Jeezus, Anson. I feel like I wanna puke. What are we supposed to do with dead people's ashes? We don't even know who they are. Not that it matters. They're freaking dead, Anson."

"Well, leave me look at these. There's probably some sort of tag or identifier on these urns." Anson lifted one of the urns from the box and turned it around until he saw an inscription on the side. "This one says 'Mabel T. Zeller, loving wife, mother. Brutally cut down in the prime of life.'"

"Oh my God, Anson. That's a disturbing thing to write on someone's final resting place, even if it is just an urn."

"It sure is, yet also interesting. Let me check the other one. It says, "Joseph B. Zeller. May his soul rot in Hell for eternity."

For a moment, both Gina and Anson were silent. Then Gina shook her head and shouted, "I knew it! There's always a catch with you, Anson. If it isn't a car that needs to be overhauled from top to bottom, it's a good car with dead people's ashes inside."

"Now, hold on, Gina. This ain't a big deal. We'll just take these urns and dump the ashes somewhere, then we can throw the urns in the trash, and no one will ever be the wiser."

"I'll be the wiser, Anson. I'll know that this stupid piece of crap SUV held the ashes of those people, and one of them is probably a murderer who killed the other. That means this car is probably haunted. How am I supposed to ride around town in a haunted SUV?"

"Don't be ridiculous. There ain't no such thing as ghosts or haunted cars. Look at this logically, Gina. We got a great SUV dirt cheap."

"Bad choice of words, Anson."

"Oops, sorry. Well, we got a great vehicle, and as soon as we dump these stupid urns and their contents, we can forget they were ever there."

"There's no 'we' in this, husband. I can't forget, and I won't forget. You made this mess, and you're going to have to clean it up. And after you get rid of those urns, you can get rid of that SUV."

"What? That's a great car. I'll never find another one like it for that price."

"I don't care, Anson. I want nothin' more to do with that. I've said my piece, and that's final."

"Fine. It's too late to do anything about it today. I'll take care of it first thing tomorrow."

"You bet you will."

The couple walked into their house, leaving the car with its contents in the driveway. Anson was furious about having to get rid of the best deal he ever made but knew he had no choice. Gina would never relent and would make his life a living Hell until he did what she said. As he lay in his bed in the dark with his eyes closed, trying to fall asleep, he kept reviewing the past few hours, wondering how everything had gone so wrong. Those urns were an unfortunate discovery. He wished he had looked over the car more carefully. Had he found the urns earlier, Gina would have never known a thing about them, and none of this would have happened. But now it was too late.

"It's not really too late," A voice said inside his head.

"What? Who said that?" Anson thought.

"I did, Anson, It's me, Joe Zeller."

Anson had to think for a moment, "Joe Zeller? I don't know anybody named Joe Zeller . . ." Then he recognized the name. Joseph Seller was the name on one of the urns, the inscription that also suggested Joseph's soul should rot in Hell for eternity.

"Ah, so I see you recognize me."

"Hold your horses here for a minute. This just don't seem possible. I'm lying in my bed, not moving my lips but having some sort of conversation with some dead guy whose ashes are sitting in a car in my driveway. I must have nodded off and am dreaming."

"No, I assure you, Anson, you are not dreaming."

"But how can . . . ?"

"Don't waste your time worrying about such trivial matters, Anson. The important thing is that you needed my help, and here I am."

"Help? I don't need anybody's help, let alone from some dead ashes guy!"

"Actually, you did need my help. You love the new vehicle you bought; it was a fantastic deal. It was the kind of deal you dreamed about all your life."

"Yes, it was. But because of your stupid ashes and your wife's, Gina is making me get rid of my great deal."

"I feel your pain, Anson. Sometimes, wives don't understand and need to be taught a lesson, like I taught mine. That's why I'm here to help you. As I'm sure you realized, I have an outstanding disciplinary track record."

"Help me? What are you talking about? I'm pretty sure you murdered your wife. You must have been insane."

"Well, one man's discipline is another man's insanity, I suppose. Po-tay-to, Po-tah-to, as I like to say."

"Potato? Why the Hell are you talking about potatoes? More importantly, why the Hell am I dreaming about talking to a pile of ashes?"

"As I told you, Anson, you are not dreaming. You needed my help, and I came to you the only way I could. I came into your mind, and together we solved your problem."

"Solved my problem? What are you talking about? I didn't have any problem," But there was no reply. The strange voice was gone.

Anson opened his eyes to find himself staring up at the barely visible ceiling in his dark bedroom. His body was coated in a film of cold sweat, and the smell of his own stench was nauseating. He also smelled a moist, coppery scent that caused every nerve ending in his body to be immediately on high alert. Anson reached over and turned on the bed lamp on a nearby end table. At first, he had trouble turning the stem on the rotary lamp switch, as his fingers felt wet and sticky. When the light finally came on, Anson saw a bloody knife lying on the end table, and his hands were dripping with blood. He wanted to scream with terror, but his voice caught in his throat.

He turned quickly and saw his wife, his beloved Gina, lying next to him, looking less like a woman than a bloody, butchered slab of meat. That was when he realized what he had done, or more precisely, what Joseph Zeller had made him do. His wife was gone, murdered by his own hand, but he hadn't really done it. They may have argued over the years, but he would never have considered killing her.

"Joseph Zeller? Where are you? How could you have made me do something so unthinkable?" Anson thought, but there was no reply. He was trembling and weeping.

Anson was overwrought with grief at what he had done, also realizing there would be no way he would ever be able to convince anyone that a ghost of some dead murderer had entered his body, taken control, and done this horrible deed. He would spend the rest of his life in jail or some insane asylum, and neither option was a good one. Plus, he knew he could never live with the guilt of killing Gina, even if he believed it was not directly his fault.

As he lifted the knife slowly up to his throat, Anson did the only thing he still had the wherewithal to do. Through the searing pain and warm flowing of his precious lifeblood down his neck, soaking his shirt and joining Gina's blood on their bed sheet, Anson felt satisfied that he had done what had to be done to atone for his sins. He neither knew nor cared what would become of the urns or his car. Instead, he felt a numbing relief as the room around him slowly darkened to a total, all-encompassing blackness.

GARGOYLE

Sam Weisman hated neighborhood yard sales. By his assessment, there were two different aspects to the yard sale experience: being a seller at a yard sale and being a buyer. Sam detested either type of participation. He hated being the seller at a yard sale and dealing with what he referred to as "those people" in reference to the buyers. They were the people who had to get a better deal no matter how great the current one was. He often thought about how he would take an item he originally paid perhaps $40 or $50 for and list it for $5 at his yard sale. Even though it was a more than fair price for something in excellent condition, some Yahoo was bound to walk up and ask, "Will you take $2 for it?" This always drove Sam crazy. Often, he would refuse to sell the item at the lower price and even jack the price up as they looked on in bewilderment. Then, when the yard sale was over, Sam would place that same item out at the curb with a "Free" sign on it for someone else to have. He often said he would rather give something away for free than be beaten down by some low-life bargain hunter. Some might think it was a strange logic, but that was Sam.

On those rare occasions when Sam would agree to participate in neighborhood yard sales, he often fantasized about having a razor-sharp broadsword at the ready, and whenever someone would ask for a ridiculously better price, he would stand up with his sword and remove the offender's head from his body, then sit back down and wait for the next moron to open his big mouth. In his imagination, he could see his driveway slick with blood and severed heads scattered all about as he forced himself to make it through yet another grueling yard sale.

Sam also hated attending yard sales in other neighborhoods, but this time as a buyer. However, his wife, Jennifer, loved attending them and usually hounded him to go along. On those rare occasions when he caved in, Sam would always stay in the background, his sole purpose being to act as a pack mule to carry Jen's yard sale spoils. He tried to stay as far away from the action as possible. During these sales, Jen assumed the role of negotiator and deal maker, the same type of person Sam hated encountering at his yard sales. But now, with the shoe on the other foot, he did appreciate it whenever Jen scored a great deal.

One day, Sam and Jennifer were participating as potential buyers in a yard sale in a high-end neighborhood a few miles from town. Sam had never been in this part of town before. It was one of those "swanky" neighborhoods where the stuff they were getting rid of was often ten times nicer than the stuff Sam and Jennifer could afford to buy new. These sorts of yard sales were often a double-edged sword. On one edge of the blade, you could score some really nice quality items. On the other edge, these homeowners were well-off, savvy and knew the value of what they had to offer. As a result, you might be able to get a fair price, but even with Jen's superior negotiating skills, the chances of getting a real bargain were slim.

As they went from one luxurious house to the next, only a few things jumped out and attracted Jen's curiosity, so their purchases were few. That was until they drove and parked in front of the last house on the block away from the main flow of traffic. It was a large, Victorian-style home of dark gray stone that Sam felt looked out of place in this neighborhood. He considered it "the Munster's" house or perhaps "the Adams Family" house. It had that strange horror movie vibe, even in broad daylight.

The cobble-stone driveway looked better equipped for a horse-drawn carriage or hearse than any modern-day vehicle. Along both sides of the driveway, old, rickety wooden-legged card tables held a variety of antiquities, most of which had no interest to either Sam or Jen. Then Sam noticed something sitting on the ground next to one of the tables. It caught his attention immediately. The item was the sort of thing no one had any use for, something whose purchase could never be justified but which was something too intriguing to ignore.

It was a stone statue about three feet tall of one of the most horrible and obscene-looking gargoyles Sam had ever seen, not that he had much experience with stone gargoyles other than what he had seen in pictures or movies. But despite his limited knowledge, Sam was confident he had never seen anything quite as disturbing as this thing was. It had a pig-like snout, large, insane-looking bulging eyes, a huge, grinning mouth overflowing with sharp-looking teeth, and large pointed ears. It had a long mane of hair carved to appear combed back from the window's peek of a receding hairline, and on both sides of its exposed forehead, two ram-like horns jutted backward.

It had been carved in a sitting position with its arms draped around its bent knees, showing large hands with gnarled fingers and overly long claw-like nails. The most disturbing thing about the creature was the long, thick phallus that protruded from between its curled, gnarled feet and hung down another five or six inches. The end of the member had a large hole, practically taking up the entire four-inch diameter. Sam immediately realized that this gargoyle was once probably used somewhere to drain water from a roof, and there was likely a hole in the back of it somewhere. As interesting as the thing might be, Sam found it disgusting and troubling.

"I love that!" Jennifer said. "Sam, look at that thing. Isn't it amazing?"

Sam could think of many adjectives to describe the gargoyle, but amazing was nowhere on the list. "Uh . . . I don't know. I think it's a bit repulsive with a side of disgusting."

"Seriously, Sam? This is an amazing piece of history. We have to find out more about it and how much they want for it."

"You want to buy this ugly little monster, Jen? Where the Hell would we ever put such a revolting thing?"

"I don't know. Maybe in the garden. All I know is I want it."

Sam imagined the gargoyle sitting on a stump next to his utility shed with the water downspout from the roof gutter being directed so it traveled into the gargoyle's back, allowing the grotesque thing to simulate urination into his flower bed. He had seen naked peeing cherub fountain statues doing something similar, but those he thought were cute. This monstrosity could never be considered cute or even funny. The hideous expression of joy on its face, teamed with the gargantuan size of its drainage device, made it a stomach-turning visage. He could not imagine what redeeming value Jen saw in the obscenity.

"You're serious, aren't you Jen?"

"Of course I am. I want you to go over to that old guy, who seems to be running this show, and see how much he wants for it. Then come back and tell me, and if necessary, I'll go into deal-making mode."

"How much he wants? I don't think he could pay me enough to take the wretched thing."

"Come on, Sam. Be open-minded. Use your right brain for a change and appreciate the artistic intrinsic value of the piece."

"Intrinsic value? It's an ugly demonic gargoyle with a schlong big enough to run a three-legged race alone. Excuse me for not appreciating the artistic merit of this amazing sculpture."

"Whatever, Sam. Now, go over there and see what you can find out about the piece. Also, see if you can learn anything about its history. Surely, something this old and hand-carved must have a really interesting background. Now, go over there and talk with that man."

"You mean that guy behind the table who looks like the Crypt Keeper on a bad day? He's probably a vampire or something."

"Sam. It's 10:15 in the morning. If he were a vampire, he'd be a pile of ashes by now."

"I don't know. That dude looks pretty pale. Maybe he's coated with SPF 2000 sunscreen."

"Stop fooling around, Sam, and go talk to the man."

"Fine, fine. I'll go. But if he bites my neck, I'm coming back from the undead for you, Jen."

As Sam approached the table to speak to the homeowner, he noticed that his original assessment of the man was spot-on accurate.

The old man was rail-thin with large, inquisitive, dark eyes sunken in black-rimmed sockets in hollow cheeks. His long, narrow nose hooked downward, practically hanging over his top lip. The strange man was bald, save for a whispy fringe of thin white hair that, although sparse, draped down over his shoulder. The man smiled in a way Sam assumed was meant to be pleasant and welcoming but failed to accomplish either goal. Instead, the old man looked like an escapee from a mental institution for the criminally insane. The strange man smiled even larger as Sam approached, presenting a mouth sparsely populated with broken, rotted tombstone teeth.

The old homeowner wore a suit that looked decades out of fashion and was about as bizarre and out of place as Sam could imagine in this upscale Yuppy neighborhood. The topcoat looked like something from a Currier and Ives painting, but it appeared coated with a thin layer of dust. His white shirt had ruffles down the front, disappearing into the black void of his vest under the topcoat. The strange look the man gave Sam told him he had noticed how much Jennifer was interested in the gargoyle. That was a bad sign, as it meant the old man was likely not to want to haggle for a lower price.

Attempting to be only casually interested, Sam said, "I was wondering what you could tell me about that gargoyle statue over there. You know, like where it came from, how old it is, what you're asking for it. You know, things like that."

The old man hesitated momentarily, then said, "It is very old. Perhaps as old as 500 years. I do not know its place of origin, but I believe it was somewhere in Eastern Europe, probably the Baltic states. I've been told it once sat atop a famous castle. It has been in my family for many years, but now I am old, I have no more relatives, and it is time to find a new home for this piece."

Under normal circumstances, Sam would have thought, "Good luck with that. Only a lunatic would pay you a dime for that ugly piece of crap." Then he remembered that his lovely wife wanted to buy the thing and decided to derail that train of thought.

"Well, I must admit, it is a unique sculpture. May I ask what you think the piece is worth?"

The old man looked at Sam cunningly and said, "Unique truly is an accurate assessment, young man. I see your wife finds it very interesting as well. The truth is, I couldn't begin to put an accurate price on the statue as, in my opinion, it is priceless."

"Oh boy," Sam thought. "Here it comes. This guy saw Jen's interest, and he's going to try to rape us over this ridiculous statue."

Sam said, "Are you saying it is not for sale? If that's the case, why is it here among everything you're selling?"

The man continued to stare at Sam with that strange look but said nothing.

"It must have a price, Sir. Sooner or later, everything has a price. Are you positioning yourself to try to take advantage of us? If so, you're wasting your time. We can walk away from this any time," Sam said.

The old man smiled his rotted-toothed grin and pointed at the statue where Jen was standing, staring down at it with an odd expression Sam had never seen before. "You might be able to walk away, but your wife is another story."

Sam realized that he would have to take on the role of bargain negotiator since, for whatever reason, his wife apparently would never be able to do so. In her current state of euphoria, she would pay whatever the old man asked, and he knew it.

Sam said, "Fine then. Let's get down to business. How much do you want for this 'priceless' statue? But I must warn you, I will not allow you to take advantage of our good nature."

"Nothing. I want nothing for the statue," The old man said.

Sam was shocked, "I'm confused. Do you mean it's not for sale? Or do you mean you are giving it to us at no cost? You just said the thing was priceless."

"I said it was priceless to me. I also said I was trying to find a good home for it. I can tell by how your wife looks at my gargoyle that it would do well in her possession," The old man said somewhat cryptically.

Sam had no idea what the old man meant by that statement, but if he understood the situation correctly, the guy was giving them the gargoyle at no cost. He couldn't help but be excited by the prospect of getting the statue for free, even though he hated the thing. Jen seemed to love it, and if it made her happy, Sam supposed that was good enough for him.

Suddenly, Sam realized he would have to get the thing home and assumed the statue might be quite heavy. Then he looked at the old man again and decided that unless the skinny old goober was secretly some sort of Superman, the gargoyle might not be that heavy after all.

The old man said, "I know what you're thinking, but I can assure you the statue is not very heavy. Although it is true, it was originally carved from a solid piece of stone, over the years, my predecessors have managed to carve out the interior, thus relieving much of its weight."

"So you're saying, if we want the gargoyle, we can just take it?" Sam said.

"Yes, young man. That is exactly what I'm saying."

"But, how do you know we won't just turn around and sell it for a bundle of money?"

The old man smiled his hideous grin and said, "You might be inclined to do something like that, but I can assure you, she will never want to part with it."

Something about the strange look on the old man's face and the way Jen was ogling the statue sent chills down his spine. Sam suddenly wished they had never come to this yard sale or set foot in this creepy driveway. Yet, he knew it was too late for wishing. For whatever reason, Jen was fascinated by the gargoyle, and he would have no choice but to take it.

Sam walked back to Jen, feeling somehow defeated, as if he had won something yet lost at the same time. Jen seemed not to notice him as he approached. She was staring down at the gargoyle almost as if in a trance.

"We can take this ugly thing home with us, Jen," Sam said.

"Yes, I know," Jen replied in a strange, almost monotone voice.

"You know? How could you know, Jen?"

Jen did not reply. Instead, she turned, headed to the street where their car was parked, opened the passenger door, and dropped into the seat. Sam bent over to pick up the statue, expecting it to be heavy, despite what the old man said, and was pleasantly surprised to see it weighed no more than perhaps 50 or 60 pounds. Although not a lightweight, it was manageable for a man of Sam's youth and size. Still, he wondered how that old timer managed to maneuver the bulky thing down the driveway. Perhaps he used a wheeled dolly or something. Sam supposed that was irrelevant.

After Sam loaded the gargoyle statue into the back hatch of his car, covering it with a tarp he kept there, he turned to take one final look at the strange old man, expecting to see him staring with that God-awful toothless grin. To his shock, Sam saw the man was gone. As if that were not strange enough, all the wooden tables and the various antiquities were also gone. It was as if none of it had ever been there at all. Yet he knew it had been there because he and Jen had seen it, and the gargoyle was now in the back of his vehicle. Sam quickly turned to make sure the statue really was still there and was relieved yet disturbed to see that it was.

He shook his head as if awakening from a dream wondering what in the world had just happened. He had a statue of a gargoyle in his car that he thought he had gotten from an old man at a yard sale, yet there was no old man and no yard sale. His wife was in the passenger seat of his car and hadn't said a word since he had approached the old man like she was still in some sort of trance. Sam had no choice but to get in the car, drive home, and try to figure out what had just happened, although he knew he might never understand.

/ 2 /

By the time Sam and Jennifer got a few miles from the yard sale, she seemed to have returned to her normal old self. She talked about the various good deals they got during their yard sale excursion. He found it strange that she didn't mention the gargoyle statue.

"Jen. You forgot to mention your favorite thing we got."

"Favorite thing? What was that?"

"The statue. Did you forget about the statue?"

"What statue?"

Sam pointed his thumb in the direction of the back of the SUV and said, "That statue back there under the tarp."

Jen turned in her seat, pulled back the tarp, and saw the hideous gargoyle statue lying on its side with its massive member pointing right at her.

She practically screamed, "What in the Hell is that horrible thing?"

Sam was taken aback. He said, "You mean to tell me you don't remember?"

"Remember? Remember what?"

Sam didn't know exactly where to take this conversation but decided to find out why Jen couldn't recall what had happened. He said, "Tell me, Jen, what exactly do you remember about that last house we visited?"

"I'm not sure what you mean, Sam."

"I mean, describe the tables and the types of things for sale. Can you describe the homeowner who was conducting the sale?"

Jennifer hesitated momentarily, then said, "I don't know. I'm not sure what I remember. It's like I recall the nice house where we got the blue glass bowl, but I have nothing after that."

"Don't you recall the old man, the one I said looked like the crypt keeper?"

"No, I have no idea what you're talking about."

"Then you don't remember telling me that you loved that gargoyle statue, wanted it more than anything in the world, and that I should see how much the old man wanted for it?"

"Seriously, Sam? You expect me to believe I went ga-ga over that ugly troll back there? You couldn't pay me enough to take that horrible thing away. I certainly hope you got a good deal on it because, as far as I'm concerned, it can find its way into our local landfill as soon as possible."

"Well, Jen. I know you won't believe me and might think I'm crazy, but we stumbled onto a weird Adam's Family type of house at the end of that development, and an old guy was selling all sorts of junk. You saw the gargoyle, loved it, and told me to see how much the old guy wanted for it. Then you went into some sort of trance. I talked to the guy, and he said it was a priceless family heirloom, and he was just looking for someone to take it and give it a good home. He noticed how you looked at it and said we could have it for free."

"If we got it for free, we still paid too much. It's hideous!"

"You're preaching to the choir, Jen. I said that all along. But you insisted that I buy it. I was afraid the old guy would try to charge me a bundle for it, and I'd have to pay a bundle for it because you wanted it so badly."

"This is all so bizarre, Sam. I don't remember any of this. I'm having trouble believing it."

Sam reluctantly said, "It gets weirder, Babe. After I loaded the gargoyle into the back of the car, I turned to look back at the old guy, and he was gone. All of his tables and the junk he had for sale were gone, too."

"That doesn't make any sense. How could everything just disappear?"

"I don't know. None of this makes any sense to me either, but that's what happened."

Jennifer hesitated, then said, "I know. Let's turn around and go back to that yard sale. We can find that weird house where you say you got the gargoyle and return it. If the guy doesn't answer the doorbell, we'll just leave it there."

Although Sam thought that might be the best solution, he was concerned. He was still trying to wrap his head around the idea that the old guy had just vanished. He pulled over, checked for oncoming traffic, made a U-turn, and headed back toward the development where the yard sale was happening. Sam had a knot in his stomach, wondering what he might find there or perhaps not find there.

/ 3 /

"Where is it, Sam?" Jennifer asked, with genuine concern in her voice. The couple had returned to the yard sale and searched the neighborhood for the old house but could not find it. They had parked their car near an overgrown empty lot at the end of the street and were trying to figure out what to do next.

"I . . . I don't know Jen. We've been around this place about ten times, and I can't find it. I'm sure it was right at the end of this street, but there's no sign of any house here. Are you sure you don't remember being here with me?"

"I told you, Sam. I don't recall any such thing. And where's the house you were talking about? It didn't just vanish into thin air."

They sat in their car, staring hopelessly at the vacant, overgrown lot where Sam was certain the house once stood. He couldn't figure out how everything had just disappeared. As he sat wondering, someone approached their vehicle and tapped on the driver's side window. Sam turned and saw a man standing there, looking concerned and a bit apprehensive. Sam rolled down his window a few inches and asked, "Can I help you?"

The man responded, "I was wondering the same thing. Is there something I can help you with? I noticed you looking at the vacant lot. It's for sale if you're interested. My name is Blake Johns. I not only live here but also work as a realtor. I have this particular lot as one of my listings. I'm also the president of the neighborhood crime watch."

Sam wasn't sure what to say next since there was no way he could even afford to buy a lot in this neighborhood, let alone build a house. Nonetheless, he said, "Um . . . my wife and I noticed the vacant lot, thinking it would be a great location for a home. Was there ever a home here before?"

Now it was Blake's turn to hesitate, "Um . . . well . . . yeah. There was a house here long ago before the development was built. It was the only house in this area when it was still a farm."

"What happened to the house?"

"It was demolished when the new neighborhood was built, but . . ."

"But what?" Sam asked.

"A few years before that, the place burned in a fatal fire that killed the former owner."

Jen said, "That sounds terrible. Do you know what exactly happened?"

Blake said, "Well, not exactly. There were stories, but I'm unsure how much of what I heard was true."

"By all means, do tell," Sam prodded.

Blake explained, "I had heard one story that said an old man and his wife lived in the house. I'm told it was a big, old stone place that resembled something from a horror movie. The couple had a stone gargoyle they kept high on top of the home to deflect rainwater off the roof. It was a supposed family heirloom that had originally been located on a castle in Transylvania or someplace like that. From what I heard, the thing looked quite hideous. One day, the statue somehow came loose from its moorings and fell to the ground, striking and killing the old man's wife. Legend says the old man took his wife's body into the house, and then, in a fit of depression, he burned down the house with himself inside. No one has ever found the gargoyle statue that apparently was the source of the trouble."

Jen quickly glanced into the back of the SUV, making sure the statue was covered, not wanting to have the man notice that the gargoyle he was discussing was in their vehicle. Sam realized it was probably time to get out of Dodge and said a quick thank you to the man, rolled up his window, and drove away.

"Now, what are we supposed to do, Sam?" Jen asked.

"I don't know, Babe. I just don't know."

/ 4 /

The couple decided to return home with the gargoyle statue still in the back of their SUV. They would have liked to drop it off at the place where they had gotten it but figured they might have to wait until the yard sale crowds thinned out.

Jen said, "I'm not sure we should take it back to that empty lot. There's a good chance that Blake guy wrote down our license number, since he was with the neighborhood crime watch and all. I think we should stay far away from that place."

"Yeah, you're probably right, Jen. I have an idea for how to get rid of this and never have it traced back to us."

"OK, Sam. I'll trust you to handle this. You can tell me all about it when you're finished. For now, I just want to get as far away from that ugly thing as possible."

Sam helped Jennifer take their various yard sale purchases into the house, and then he walked back to the utility shed in the backyard and removed a ten-pound sledgehammer he had kept there. He loaded the hammer into his car and drove away with the statue. When he was a few miles outside of town, Sam found an area he knew to be the site of an abandoned industrial building. He pulled behind the building away from curious onlookers, opened the hatch, and lifted the gargoyle statue onto the ground.

"Well, you ugly sucker. I'm going to do to you what should have been done a long time ago," Sam said. Then he began to smash the statue into as many pieces as possible, making sure each piece was unrecognizable as belonging to some other component. Once Sam was satisfied that it was destroyed beyond recognition, he placed the pieces in the back of the SUV on top of the tarp. Then he took two pieces and threw one far into a nearby field and the other he threw into a dumpster behind the building.

Then, he began driving around the county, looking for remote places and dropping a piece of the statue in each location. Some were fields, some were farms, and some were roadside ravines. When he was finished, he covered about ten miles and scattered the parts so they would never be found or put back together again. Confident in his plan, Sam headed home to tell Jennifer what he had done.

"And you scattered the parts all over the county?" Jen asked.

"Not only this county but two others. In fact, if you were to ask me to find the parts, I wouldn't be able to remember where I put them all. That ugly monster is gone for good. As far as I'm concerned, I plan on pretending this incident never happened."

Jen agreed, "I'm right there with you. It's getting late. Let's go to bed. I feel like I could sleep for a month."

"Me too," Sam said.

The two shoppers did just that. Sam had hoped to get a good, restful sleep that night, but unfortunately, that wasn't in the cards for him.

/ 5 /

Sam tossed and turned all night long, bombarded by one nightmare after another, each of which revolved around the statue in one way or another. In his first dream, the old man appeared as decrepit as he had looked in reality, perhaps more so. His horrible tooth-decayed mouth was moving, but no words came from him. Sam could smell the foul odor of rot and decay spewing from deep down inside the old man, as if his very soul was rotting him from within. His bulging eyeballs seemed to get even more impossibly huge and overflowing with insane anger.

Suddenly, Sam heard the old man's words appearing inside his mind, screaming, "You did this most terrible and egregious thing. You destroyed my precious gargoyle. I trusted you to keep it safe, but you thumbed your nose to my generosity and most sacred trust. You must pay for your insolence, you swine. I shall pluck your eyeballs from your skull and devour them while you scream in agony."

Then the old man reached out his arthritic, gnarled fingers, and Sam saw for the first time that his fingernails had transformed into talons like those on the gargoyle. Then, the old man's face changed to the pig-snouted statue's. Horns sprouted from the man's skull, and his eyes became huge and insane. His mouth was wide and full of fangs that dripped crimson saliva and maggots. Sam tried to back away but couldn't move. The clawed fingers were groping for Sam's face, to claw out and feast on his eyes.

The dream suddenly shifted to Sam alone in a field with the hideous, intact gargoyle statue. He was standing with his sledgehammer, ready to break the ugly thing into pieces, when suddenly, the statue turned its head in his direction. Sam stopped mid-swing, frozen in terror. Then, the statue slowly stood upright, and as things tended to be in nightmares, it became bigger than Sam. The monster was more than nine feet tall, rippling with muscles and glistening with sweat. Sam could smell the foul stench coming off the beast. Its giant phallus hung to the ground, dragging as the monster approached with thunderous footfalls. Sam knew he and his head were about to become separated.

Then, the nightmare switched again. Sam and Jennifer were standing outside their home talking. But the house wasn't the home they presently lived in; it was that horrible gray-stone house where they had found the gargoyle. Sam heard a noise and looked upward to see the gargoyle statue falling. Jennifer was directly in its path. Sam tried to push Jennifer to safety but found his movements as slow as if he were swimming in a vat of gelatin. Before he could reach his wife, the gargoyle came crashing down, crushing her skull beneath its falling weight. She lay headless on the ground in front of him, her body twitching once, twice before going still.

Sam awoke sitting straight up in bed, certain that he had been screaming. He was covered in a sheen of cold sweat. He looked to his right and saw Jennifer sleeping peacefully, not disturbed by his awakening. He sat in the dark, practically panting like an exhausted dog, as the sequence of horrible dreams slowly and blessedly faded from his mind. He knew he had experienced some terrible nightmares, yet for the life of him, Sam could not recall what they were. Soon, he fell back to sleep, not having another nightmare but feeling slightly off.

/ 6 /

At breakfast, Jennifer asked, "Are you OK, Sam? You seem a little distant this morning."

"Yeah . . . sorry, Babe. I think I had a bunch of nightmares last night. I can't remember any of them, but do you know how weird you feel the day after you have bad dreams? That's how I feel. I don't mean to be distant; I'm just trying to shake off that strange funky feeling."

"I have an idea. It's a beautiful morning. Why don't we take our breakfast out on the patio?"

Sam agreed, "That sounds like a great idea. There's nothing like fresh morning air to help clear my head."

The couple carried their plates out to the patio table. It was a glass-topped table with a hole in the center for an umbrella. However, since the sun was not yet over the rear of their home, the umbrella was sitting, folded off to the side. They placed their dishes on the table and sat to enjoy their meal.

Jennifer said, "I was thinking, I'll bet you had those dreams because of that stupid gargoyle incident yesterday."

"I believe you're right. That whole situation was weird from the start: the old man, the house, and the stupid statue. I'm just glad I could destroy the thing, and maybe we can move on. As far as I'm concerned, we can avoid yard sales for a while."

"You always feel that way, Sam. But I suppose we can take a break from them for a while."

As the couple ate their breakfast, Sam heard a strange noise from above them. He looked up and couldn't believe his eyes. Sitting on the peak of their roof was the gargoyle statue, fully intact, looking as if it had never been destroyed. It was teetering forward.

"No!" Sam screamed as the statue fell from its perch and plummeted straight for Jennifer. As in his nightmare, Sam tried to get to her to push her out of the way, but it was too late. The gargoyle came crashing down on Jennifer's head, leaving her decapitated body a bloody mess on the flagstone patio.

Sam stood helpless and unable to believe what had just happened to his wife. Then, all three dreams returned to him, and he knew some force beyond his ability to comprehend had led him to the gargoyle and this finality. He also knew this was all his fault. He had dealt with the old man, brought the statue home, and tried to destroy it. But evil wasn't easily destroyed, and now his lovely wife was gone. Sam looked down at the ruined pile of flesh, formerly Jennifer, and knew what he had to do. It was his fault this had happened, and he had to pay for it.

Sam carried what was left of Jennifer's body into the house, much as the old man in the legend had done with his. And like in that story, Sam, overcome with grief, guilt, and remorse, set his house ablaze and sat down in the middle of his living room floor as the hot smoke fried his lungs and the flames melted away his flesh.

/ 1 /

"So, watta ya think happened here, Chief?" Fireman Hank Lofts asked his boss, the fire chief.

"I don't quite know for certain. We found that weird statue outside, smashed to dozens of pieces, with the cranial remains of what looked like a woman beneath it. Then we found those two charred bodies in the house. One was a male, and the one missing its head was a female. It's like that broken statue fell and killed the woman. Then, the man must have brought her body inside and set their house afire, burning himself to death in the process. I don't understand how that statue might have gotten up on their roof if that is what happened. Judging by the size of the various fragments, it had to be quite heavy."

"So now what? Hank asked.

"Now we clean up, go back to the station, and let the cops figure it out."

"What about that busted-up statue?"

"Beats me, Hank. I suspect the forensic folks might reassemble the pieces as best they can to see what the thing looked like and figure out why it was way up there on top of the house in the first place. I'm not sure what it was, though."

"It kinda looks like it might have been one of them ugly gargoyle statues to me. Although I can't imagine where they might have gotten it or why they might have wanted one."

The chief said, "Yeah. I guess we'll never know."

SPACE GIRL RETURNS

Authors note: In 2023, I wrote a story called Space Girl for Twisted Pulp Magazine to accompany some pinup pictures. It also appeared in Malaformed Realities Volume 9. In 2024, Twisted Pulp asked me to write a sequel to Space Girl for another set of photos, which became Space Girl Returns. (Creative title)

/ 1 /

The visitor from space had first come in the fall of 1956. Her home planet had a need that only a certain type of young Earth males could provide. All those years earlier, she first appeared in the Johnsonville High School cafeteria as a substitute teacher. This subterfuge allowed her and the rest of her kind to accomplish their mission. It was now seventeen years later, in the fall of 1973, and much had changed in the world of humans. Hair and clothing styles were radically different. Gone were the buzz cuts and the slicked-back pompadours. No more bobby socks or poodle skirts could be seen either. Now, the boys wore long hair, flowered shirts, and flared jeans, and the girls' skirts were short enough to be considered obscene back in 1956, not to mention their halter tops with no bras.

Although she was somewhat surprised by the change, she agreed wholeheartedly with it as it allowed her to appear even more enticing.

Unlike the world around her, she hadn't aged one minute since her previous visit and was still as attractive as ever. She had, however, changed her appearance, this time appearing as a pretty blonde. With the new fashions, she could reveal more of her finest attributes, which would be certain to attract more males quickly. However, she had a particular type of male in mind.

The visitor had once again assumed the guise of the substitute teacher to get close to her target. She believed it wouldn't take her long to make her move. As she walked into the cafeteria, which was packed with chatting and laughing students, almost every male head in the room turned to watch her walk by. She wore a shiny silver, low-cut mini dress with purple trim on the top and bottom and a pair of purple knee-high boots. Her long blond hair was parted on the side and hung down in waves to the top of her dress, which revealed her ample cleavage. The most unusual fashion accessory was a pair of silver gloves extending to her elbows. To the music-loving members of the class, she looked like something out of David Bowie's Ziggy Stardust universe. Because of her incredible looks, there wasn't a single boy in that cafeteria who could take his eyes off her. The girls watched her, too, but their stares were of jealousy and displeasure.

She decided to pursue a similar approach to the one she had done many years earlier since it had worked so well. She needed to find a loner, someone who didn't fit in with the rest of the kids. The visitor found what she sought in a secluded corner in the back of the cafeteria. A lone male figure with long rumpled hair, faded jeans, and a tee shirt with the name Jethro Tull printed on it sat reading a tattered magazine called Circus. In her briefings, she had been taught what a circus was. It was this primitive culture's traveling show featuring high-wire acts, animals, freak shows, and clowns. She had read that many humans hated clowns, so she was curious about why the boy was interested in reading about circuses.

The visitor approached the boy, pulled out a chair, and said, "Excuse me. Is this seat taken?"

The boy looked up, and upon seeing the beautiful creature before him, his mouth dropped open, and he couldn't speak.

She didn't bother waiting for an answer, as it was apparent that the boy had been stricken with some type of temporary vocal paralysis. He stared at her like he had just seen a creature from another world. If he only knew how correct he was.

The visitor asked again, "Do you like reading about circuses?"

The boy sat staring, mouth agape, apparently still unable to communicate.

She said, "Your magazine. It says Circus. Do you like circuses?"

The boy looked down at the magazine, then back at the incredibly sexy young woman. After a few seconds of dealing with a very dry mouth, he managed to produce enough saliva to say, "It's not about circuses; it's a music magazine."

"Music magazine? Why is it called Circus?"

"I . . . um . . . don't really know; it just is."

The visitor reached over and retrieved the magazine from his limp hands. Then she put it beside her ear and said, "But I don't hear any music." It was obvious that the woman was genuinely confused.

Finally, when he felt able to speak more comfortably, the boy said, "It doesn't play music. It has articles about bands and the people responsible for making music like The Rolling Stones, Uriah Heep, Styx, Jethro Tull, and bands like that."

These names meant nothing to her, but then she recalled the boy's tee shirt, "I see your shirt says 'Jethro Tull.' Is he a maker of music?"

"Jethro Tull isn't a person; it's a band. You know, a group of musicians."

"Are you a musician? Are you a maker of music?"

"Um, no. I just like to listen."

She took in this new information for a time, then inquired, "So you study the activities of music makers with great intensity."

The boy looked around and felt self-conscious about everyone in the cafeteria staring at him. He said, "Everyone is eyeballing us. Nobody ever notices me, and now they can't stop staring."

"Not to worry, they're not staring at you; they're staring at me," she said.

The boy asked, "Ok, then. They're staring at you. But why are they staring at you?"

"For the same reason you are. I'm extremely attractive, and everyone probably thinks I'm hot to trot?"

"Excuse me? Hot to trot? What does that mean?"

"Oh, that's right. It's not 1956 but 1973. I mean, everyone thinks I'm . . . a Brick House."

The boy blushed and said, "For sure."

"So, may I ask what your name is?"

"It's Charlie. Charlie Grainger."

"Well, Charlie, Charlie Grainger, my name is Cindy Jones, and I'm a new substitute teacher at Johnsonville High."

"You don't look like any teacher I've ever seen. You're a . . ."

"Brick House?"

Charlie blushed again, put out his hand to shake, and said, "Um, pleased to meet you, Miss Jones."

When Charlie shook Cindy's hand, he felt something like a jolt of warm electricity go up his arm, down his chest, and right into that special place he often referred to as "Little Charlie." He had never felt anything like that before, and his little friend responded accordingly, much to his embarrassment.

Cindy said, "I think you like me, Charlie. I can tell." She looked down at the pup tent in his pants.

Charlie was aghast and said, "Um, ah, I'm so sorry about that. It is embarrassing."

"It's quite alright, Charlie. That's how things are supposed to be. I like you too, very much."

"May . . . may I ask you something, Miss Jones?"

"Of course, Charlie. You may ask me anything. And you don't have to call me Miss Jones. You can call me Cindy. After all, we're good friends now."

"Ok. I need to understand something. Why are you talking to me? Look around here. Every boy in the school would kill to have five minutes alone with you."

"But they aren't you, Charlie. They aren't special."

"Do you really think I'm special?"

"I know you are, Charlie."

/ 2 /

A man of about 34 or 35 approached Charlie and Cindy, giving them a stern look. It was Mr. Parker, his gym teacher. Charlie hated Parker because he was always showing favoritism to the students that were jocks and verbally abusing anyone who wasn't. Charlie felt somewhat relieved that he wasn't one of the school brainiacs. Parker was extremely hard on them because although they were smart, most couldn't do what was physically required in class. Parker looked at Charlie the same way he looked at the hippies, freaks, and stoners. Parker considered them the students you could abuse for pleasure up to a point, but beyond that, you were wasting your time. Since Parker considered them social misfits, he felt there was no use pushing them too far. In his narrow vision, most of them were too stoned to care.

"Hey, baby. Are you Miss Jones, the new substitute teacher?" Parker asked, doing his best to flex what muscles remained in his former jock body, now gone to flab. He was staring down into Cindy's shirt, his lecherous eyeballs trying to absorb as much of her cleavage as was humanly possible. "My name's Brad Parker. I'm the gym teacher and football coach around here, and knowing me will only make your life better." His eyebrows did a Groucho Marx up-and-down wiggle to suggest what he meant by "knowing him."

Cindy recognized the man immediately, although Brad apparently didn't know her in her current form. She had unwillingly met him 17 years earlier when he was a revolting, immature high school student, bully, and the captain of the football team. He had tried to interfere with her mission when Cindy had approached a loner named Billy Enders. She had embarrassed Parker by hypnotizing him into soiling himself in a cafeteria full of his fellow students.

Cindy had simply touched young Brad's hand. When she did, Brad had become as still as a statue, unable to move. Cindy told him in a soft, melodic, and hypnotic voice, "Now you listen to me, Mr. Football hero. This young man, my friend Billy, is completely off-limits to you. Do you understand?"

"Yes, Miss Jones, I understand," he had replied in a monotone, distant voice as he stared sightlessly into space.

She said, "If you or any of your friends even consider hurting Billy Enders, you will embarrass yourselves in a manner most degrading. Do I make myself clear?"

"Yes, Miss Jones," he replied. When he came back to reality, Parker tried to strike the boy and had subsequently peed himself in front of the entire class.

Now, that same obnoxious individual was 17 years older, a teacher, and it was like history repeating itself.

Parker said angrily, "Why are you wasting your time talking with this loser? He's nothing but a burned-out stoner. You should be spending your time with me, baby."

Cindy reached out and touched Brad's hand, repeating the same hypnotic process with this man that she had done so many years earlier. This time, she warned him about causing Charlie any trouble. She pulled her hand away, and after a beat, Brad shook his head involuntarily, clearing the cobwebs from his mind. Then the gym teacher looked at Charlie, took a menacing step forward, and said threateningly, "Hey, Granger, I think it's time for you to pound sand. I need to spend some quality time with your sweetie here. We don't need no halfwit like you interf . . ."

Before Brad could finish his sentence, the front of his grey dress pants turned dark as urine ran down his leg and puddled on the cafeteria floor. A sharp smell began to permeate the area, and Brad realized with horror what had just happened. He attempted to discreetly walk away as quickly as he could manage while trailing golden liquid behind him among a barrage of student laughter. Brad couldn't understand what had happened to him. Then he recalled the last time something like that had occurred. It was in the same cafeteria, seventeen years earlier.

Brad was confused. When he embarrassed himself back then, a beautiful student teacher was also involved, as was a school loner. But that woman hadn't looked anything like this woman. Besides, that woman would be older than he was now, and this new girl certainly was not. Something very strange was going on. Brad didn't know what it was, but he was determined to do his best to find out.

/ 3 /

"That rude fellow shouldn't bother us anymore," Cindy said.

Having felt the incredibly sensual effects of her touch, Charlie understood that the lovely young woman before him was much more than she seemed.

In his dismay, Charlie said, "But . . . what did you do to him? Was that like hypnosis or something? Man, that was like the coolest thing I've ever seen."

"You needn't worry your handsome little head about that, Charlie. All you need to remember is that if Brad Parker tries to bother you for any reason, he'll be soiling his pants in public every time. Now I have a question for you, Charlie. Did you like it when Parker called me your sweetie? I thought it was incredibly sexy and really wanted it to be true. I hope I'm not being too forward, but how did you feel about it, Charlie?"

"I liked it. I liked it a lot. But you're a teacher, maybe only a few years older than me, but still, you're a teacher. You can't be messing around with a kid like me, no matter how much I might want you to. You could get fired at best, and at worst, you could end up in jail. I watch TV, and I know how these things work. But I really would love to be with you. I've had a lot of fantasies in the past few years, but none even begin to come close to you, Miss Jo . . . I mean Cindy."

"Well, Charlie, if you really want me to be your girlfriend, here's what we'll have to do. During the day, I'll have to be Miss Jones, and you'll have to be my student. However, once school ends, we can sneak around together as a couple. Of course, you can't say anything to your friends or family."

Charlie said, "I have no friends, and my family doesn't know or care what I do."

"Ok, Charlie. In that case, I can't wait for us to be together. I'll take great pleasure showing you many intimate and sexual things you probably never even imagined. Is that something you think you might enjoy, Charlie?"

Charlie thought his heart might explode in his chest. With great effort, Charlie swallowed the lump in his throat and replied, "Oh yes, Cindy. I would like that very much."

"Well then, Charlie, my new boyfriend, I think we should start as soon as possible. I have an idea. Do you know the road behind the bandstand and the gym?"

"Yes, I know where that is."

Cindy gave her most alluring smile and said, "After school, be sure to miss the bus home. Then, I want you to walk slowly to the bandstand and wait by the roadside. Do you know where I mean?"

"Yep. I know the place. I can be there."

She smiled, winked at him, then said, "Fantastic, Charlie. All you have to do is wait there for me for a few minutes; I'll drive by and pick you up. Be sure to stay in the shadows and avoid being seen. I'll be driving a red Ford van. The inside is fully tricked out for our adventures. The dealer called it a 'Numero Uno Shaggin' Wagon,' whatever that means, but I'm sure you'll love it. I plan on the two of us spending a great deal of time testing the suspension system if you get my meaning."

Charlie most certainly got her meaning, as did Little Charlie. That little fellow was at complete attention, and Charlie was beyond believing how his life had just changed so drastically. It was far past his ability to comprehend. Not only did he meet a girl way superior to what he considered the girl of his dreams, but she wanted to be his girlfriend. She had to be at least 24, which meant she was probably experienced and could teach him all sorts of sexual things, and he certainly would be a willing pupil. She had all but said they would be doing the horizontal bop that very night after school. But would she really? Or was she just another great-looking girl looking to make a jerk out of him?

It had happened many times before, yet Charlie seemed to fall for it again and again. He couldn't accept the fact that he was never going to be part of the in-crowd. Charlie was a loner with limited social skills who simply wasn't accepted by anyone. Even other outsiders had no interest in him. Mr. Parker was right. What did a loser like him have to offer such a gorgeous woman? Yet she seemed truly interested in him.

Charlie supposed he would find out after school if Cindy was the real deal or just another tease leading him on. If he waited in the shadows behind the bandstand and she didn't show up, he would know it was the butt of yet another mean joke and would have to walk home. But something told him this was the real deal this time.

/ 4 /

As they had planned, Charlie missed his bus ride home that night after school and sneaked to the bandstand without anyone seeing him. At least he hoped no one had seen him. But someone had because Brad Parker had been watching him all day since the embarrassing encounter in the cafeteria. As Charlie waited in the shadows, he heard a twig snap behind him.

A moment later, Charlie saw Mr. Parker slowly approaching him from the darkness. Charlie was certain the man was going to not only verbally assault him but physically. After all, they were alone in the dark, meaning there were no witnesses. Parker could do a lot of damage to him and make it look like an accident. In the aftermath, it would be the word of a popular teacher against the word of a loser.

Charlie lifted his hands defensively and said, "Look, Mr. Parker. I'm really sorry about what happened today. I had nothing to do with it. Please don't hurt me."

"I'm not going to hurt you, Charlie, although part of me would love to. Another part of me would simply like to walk away and let you find out for yourself what will happen."

Charlie said, "I don't understand, Mr. Parker. What are you talking about?"

"Did you ever hear the name Billy Elders, Charlie?"

Charlie thought for a moment, then said, "Billy Elders? No, I never heard that name. What about him."

"Well, Charlie. Seventeen years ago, a boy named Billy Elders went to our school when I was your age. I was captain of the football team, but Billy was a loner like yourself with no friends."

"Ok, so . . ."

"So one day, this gorgeous substitute teacher showed up and started making moves on Billy like Cindy Jones did with you today. In fact, she used the same alias, Cindy Jones. I didn't remember that until a few hours ago. But After what happened to me today, it all came back. Billy met with Cindy Jones after school like you're about to do. But after he did, Billy disappeared and was never heard from again. The same thing happened to several other boys at other schools. No one ever figured out what had become of them. But now, seeing what I saw today in the cafeteria, I felt I should warn you to steer clear of that woman, or something bad could happen to you. I checked with the office, and we not only don't have a substitute teacher with that name, but we never did."

"I don't think I believe you," Charlie said hesitantly.

Parker said, "You should believe me because something about that woman is wrong, and if you keep this up, something bad will happen to you, Charlie."

"You mean like pissing my pants like you did today," Charlie said with a boastful laugh.

"Laugh all you will, kid. I'm telling you the truth. There's something very wrong with that woman; you should watch yourself. You must listen to me, Charlie, for your own good." Parker reached out and grabbed Charlie by the arm to emphasize his point. When he did, Parker felt cramping in his stomach, let loose with an involuntary fart, and as the air filled with a foul stench, Charlie saw brown liquid oozing out from the bottom of Mr. Parker's pants.

Charlie started laughing again at Brad Parker's embarrassment.

"Can't you see, Charlie? This isn't right! She has done something to me and probably to you."

"All she's done to me is promise to make a man out of me, Mr. Parker. You can't stop what's meant to be. Now leave me alone; you're stinking up the place."

Parker turned and left in frustration. He had done what he could for the boy. He didn't even like Charlie but felt that, as a teacher, it was his responsibility to at least try to stop him. Now, he knew nothing else could be done. Whatever was going to happen would happen. Parker wondered why it had taken him so long to piece together all the events of 17 years ago, then realized whatever the girl had done to him probably wore off eventually and took the memories away with it.

A few minutes later, Charlie heard a car horn and saw Cindy waiting at the curb in her red van as promised. He climbed into the passenger seat, and they drove away. Cindy had seen Parker walking away in the shadows.

"Was that Mr. Parker I saw?

"Yeah."

"Apparently, he didn't learn his lesson earlier today. What did he want?" Cindy said.

"Nothin'. He's been following me all day and must have figured I was meeting you. He tried to stop me."

"I wonder why he would do that. He knows you're all I want, not some washed-up flabby former jock."

Charlie decided it might be better not to go into detail about Parker's warning. He didn't want to do anything to mess up his chances tonight.

"Yeah, I think he was just jealous and thought he had a chance with you," Charlie said.

Cindy laughed, "Him? Not a chance in the world. Did he touch you, Charlie?"

"He tried to grab me to stop me, but that didn't work out so well for him. He crapped his pants."

"That's great!" Cindy exclaimed.

"Yeah, it was. But I still don't understand how you managed to make that happen."

Cindy chuckled, "It doesn't matter, Charlie. I'll tell you all about it shortly. But first, you and I are going to have a night to remember. She jerked her thumb toward the back of the van, and Charlie saw a blowup air mattress with a warm blanket spread out in the back of the van. A few miles up the road, Cindy pulled the van onto a dirt road and turned off the engine. She smiled at Charlie with large, seductive eyes and said, "I want you, Charlie. I need you right now, more than you could ever imagine."

/ 5 /

Within a few seconds, the two were in the back of the van, road-testing that mattress. A bumper sticker on the back bumper read, "If the van is rockin', don't bother knockin.'" That van was not only rockin' but rockin' and rollin'.

When they finished, the pair lay naked, coated in sweat, and wrapped in a blanket to fight the night chill. Cindy asked, "Was that everything you thought it would be, Charlie?"

Charlie was practically speechless. He had never imagined anything could ever feel as incredible as that. With the innocence of youth, he blurted, "It was the most amazing thing I have ever experienced. I'm . . . I'm in love with you, Cindy."

"You're not in love with me, Charlie; you're only in lust. You're too young to realize it, but that doesn't matter. Because, you see, this was a test to see if you had what my people needed, and you passed the test with flying colors."

"What are you talking about, Cindy? What do you mean by 'test'? And who are your people?"

Cindy pretended to be unsure of herself, then said, "Well, I have some things to confess, Charle. First, I'm not a substitute teacher at your school."

Charlie said, "That's what Mr. Parker told me back by the bandstand. He said he checked with the front office, and no one heard of you."

"He was right about that, Charlie. In fact, I'm not even a teacher or a college graduate."

Charlie said, "You're not? Well, I suppose that doesn't matter to me. You're doing a great job of teaching me, anyway."

Cindy hesitated momentarily, then said, "There's something I need to tell you now that you might have trouble believing, but if we're going to be together, it's something you have to be sure you understand."

"What is it, Cindy?"

"What would you think if I were to tell you that I wasn't actually from Earth but was from another world?"

"You mean another planet?"

"Well, yes, but not just another planet. I mean like another universe, light years from Earth."

Charlie said, "I'm not sure I would believe you. And if I did, I don't think it would matter to me."

"That's good to hear, Charlie, because the truth is, I am from another planet in a universe far from Earth."

"Ok, then. Let's say I believe you. You sure did travel a long distance for a little sumptin'-sumptin', if you know what I mean. Don't you have like dating services on your planet?"

"The problem is this, Charlie. The males on our planet have all died off. Our entire planet is inhabited by women like me. We have no way to reproduce. We found that Earth had plenty of males capable of impregnating us and allowing our race to carry on. And most seem as willing as you, Charlie."

"Now I have another question. Why me? I'm just a small, weak, nerdy guy. Why would you choose me over some big, athletic dude?"

"Those big, muscle-headed guys are just like our previous males. They're overflowing with way too much testosterone and always end up fighting and killing each other. If we were to bring back those types of males, in a few years, we would eventually find ourselves in the same situation again."

"Did you just say, bring back?" Charlie recalled again what Mr. Parker said about that Billy Elders kid and the other kids that disappeared and were never heard from again. Maybe those boys went back to this girl's planet. That would explain their disappearance. Charlie held back a chuckle. While everyone here on Earth was trying to find them, those guys were having the time of their lives boffing hot chicks on planet whatever-it-is.

Cindy interrupted his thoughts, "We won't force you to come back with us, Charlie. It has to be your choice to come back with us voluntarily."

"You keep saying we. Are there more of you?" Charlie said.

A moment later, a knock came on the van's back door. Cindy opened the door and stepped out onto the dirt road stark naked.

Charlie wrapped himself in the blanket and followed her outside. To his shock, he saw two of the most beautiful women he had ever seen approach him and Cindy. They wore see-through sheer gowns, which showed all the goods they had to offer. It became obvious that Cindy knew these two women and was expecting them.

"Hi, Charlie," One of them said.

"Hello," he replied awkwardly.

The second girl looked at Cindy and asked, "Does Charlie sufficiently meet our expectations?"

Cindy said, "Most certainly. In fact, he goes beyond the average test requirements and well into the excels zone."

The first girl, who had been eyeing Charlie since their arrival, smiled and asked, "Do you think he is ready for me to test his capabilities next?"

Cindy asked, "Charlie, Honey, would you be willing to show my associate Mindy what you can do?"

Charlie thought he had died and gone to Heaven, "Well, sure. I mean, if you're ok with it. I thought you might be jealous."

"Not at all. As I said, we are here on a mission to repopulate our planet. Even though I care deeply for you, Charlie, I can't let something as petty as jealousy get in the way of saving our species."

Charlie said, "Well, in that case, let the good times roll."

Mindy and Charlie climbed into the van, and Cindy closed the doors. In the following moments, the good times did roll inside that van. As the couple coupled, Cindy spoke conspiratorially with the other woman named Lindy.

But with Charlie and Mindy out of sight, the two women reverted to their normal form. They no longer resembled the gorgeous creatures they had once been. Had Charlie seen them in their true form, he would have run away screaming or dropped dead of fright.

Although these creatures had the general shape and outline of women, that was where the resemblance ended. The two monstrosities standing beside the van, which was presently bouncing rhythmically on its springs, appeared hideously alien.

Their foreheads extend far back along their skulls from large, segmented, insectile eyes, ending in a cluster of long, stringy tentacles hanging down like a cluster of snakes. The slithery appendages even moved like snakes, as if they had minds of their own. The segmented eyes glowed blue-white in the moonlight and were wide apart, almost positioned near the sides of the creature's heads.

These creatures had no noses, but three nostrils positioned where a nose should be found. When the aliens breathed, these nasal orifices pulsated with each inhalation. The creatures' ears were large and pointed with long floppy dangling lobes. However, the most frightening facial features were their large, thick-lipped, wide mouths that stretched from one ear to the other and were filled with multiple rows of sharp shark-like teeth.

Although the women were naked, they had no firm breasts but instead possessed a series of eight teats, like those found on nursing animals. Although their bodies were mostly hairless, the area between their legs was furry. Their fingers and toes were four times the length of their human counterparts, had thin, fleshy webbing between them, and sharp claws on the ends.

The alien, who called herself Cindy, looked through the steamed window into the back of the van and saw Charlie and Mindy going at it. Mindy's tentacles were glowing bright red and moving hypnotically like Medusa's head full of snakes. She cried out with fake pleasure as her segmented eyes rolled back and her cavernous mouth opened wide to scream.

Lindy looked at Cindy and asked, "So you're sure he has no idea what we actually look like?"

"None whatsoever. You know that; they never do," Cindy said in their native language, which consisted of guttural noises, clicks, and bleeps.

Lindy asked, "If he only knew what our needs really were. Did you use the story about repopulating our species?"

"Yes, and he fell for it, as did the other several dozen recruits I found. How successful were you and Mindy?"

"We found more than thirty candidates. They will all be ready when we leave at midnight."

/ 6 /

"Hold it right there, you alien she-devils," A voice shouted from the darkness.

Then, Brad Parker stepped out of the shadows, holding a 12-gauge shotgun at waist level. The two creatures immediately transformed into their Earthly disguises; Cindy was naked, and Lindy was in solid pink hot pants and a matching flowered halter top.

"What did you demons do to Charlie? Tell me now, or I'll blow ya both to Kingdom Come," Parker insisted. As he tried to stand, his stomach grumbled, and he bent over slightly in pain as his bowels let loose again, filling the air with a vile stench. After a moment, he could stand straight again despite having lost most of his dignity.

Cindy stepped forward and said, "All these years later, you still haven't learned your lesson, have you, Brad? You know you can't hurt or even threaten us without causing yourself incredible discomfort and embarrassment. If you keep trying, you'll eventually crap your insides out and die a slow, painful death.

"Not before I take you two bitches with me," Brad said as he raised his shotgun.

Before he could discharge the weapon, Lindy pulled out a futuristic-looking pistol and fired a laser beam at Brad. The beam hit its mark, and Brad Parker was vaporized within a millisecond.

Cindy said, "Great work, Lindy; now, let's get back to the business at hand, shall we?"

Lindy agreed and said, "It so strange how just a little bit of mind control and the offer of sex can turn these human males into puddy in our hands. If they only took a little time to stop and think about what was happening, they might be able to see us as we really are.

"Luckily, that little brain between their legs has a way of taking charge," Cindy chuckled.

"That's a good thing for us. It would be a problem if these Earth males realized we were asexual creatures that self-reproduce and have no need for insemination or sex of any kind."

Cindy smiled with that mouth full of shark-like teeth, licked her thick lips with a serpentine tongue, and said, "They'll find that out and much more once they travel through the interdimensional portal with us and enter our world. But by then, it will be too late. They'll see us as we are, and their interest in sex will instantly disappear. Then, eventually, they'll learn the painful truth. We only want them for food."

ZOMBIE AMONG US

/ 1 /

The weary band of survivors, refugees in the flaming, living Hell the Pennsylvania city had become, huddled together in the darkness of an abandoned factory building. It was hard to believe how society had collapsed so quickly; it had been less than a month. The group watched and listened for any sign of movement. Air seeping in from outside was thick and soup-like, with the foul stench of the ruination caused by the wretched undead monsters.

"Do you hear anything?" The man named Martin asked. He was a middle-aged, slightly overweight man with thinning salt-and-pepper hair. Although eager to help, Martin was obviously not athletic and had spent the last twenty-some years before the world fell chained to a desk, no doubt working some soul-sucking office job.

"Shhh!" Angie hushed. "There are hundreds of those horrible creatures out there. We don't wanna let them know we're in here." She was angry because she had to tell a grown man to shut his big mouth at such a crucial time. Angie was an 18-year-old recent high school graduate who worked part-time as a waitress at a local restaurant. She was a bright girl and had been accepted at every college she applied to. As if intelligence was not enough, Angie had been a beautiful young woman with long blonde hair, blue eyes, and a pretty smile before the world went down the toilet. Although filthy, disheveled, and malnourished, signs of what she once had been still managed to shine through. She was of average size and build and favored a practical wardrobe, wearing jeans and sweatshirts.

Another voice whispered, "Angie's right, Martin. We'll be damned lucky if we get out of this in one piece." He was watching the moonlit shadows of the undead creatures walking past the whitewashed former factory windows. "This place isn't even close to secure. We have to lay low until we can find a way to sneak out of here."

Martin said, "Yeah, I know, Jim. You're right. My bad."

Jim was a tall, handsome, well-built man of about 28. His shoulder-length hair was dark brown, as was his beard and mustache. Jim's piercing blue eyes, roguish smile, and irresistible charm combined to create a charisma strong enough to make him a natural-born leader whether he wanted the job or not.

The group of five did their best to remain silent while keeping their growing terror at bay. Outside, the moon had risen in the distance, casting its eerie glow upon the burned-out city while the undead growled and moaned, shambling through the deserted streets in search of fresh human flesh for their insatiable hunger. The survivors watched and listened for any telltale sign of the creatures' approach. The monsters weren't intelligent enough to plan any attack strategy, but that didn't lessen the possibility of one or more of the foul beasts accidentally stumbling into the building.

If that were to happen and the survivors didn't find a way to take the creature down silently, then all of the other dead, walking meat sacks would follow the sounds into the warehouse, and it would be all over for the bedraggled folks hiding inside. The growling began to subside after what seemed like an interminable amount of time. The shambling shadows also soon disappeared from the windows.

"I think they're moving on," A young African American woman named Sheryl said. Sheryl was about the same age as Jim, although they had never previously met. She wore black jeans and a dark sweatshirt. Sheryl seldom spoke, yet her intense, no-nonsense attitude was obvious in her posture and expressions.

A handsome, well-built young man agreed, "Yeah, it sounds that way." His name was Kevin. He was a nineteen-year-old son of a local carpenter. After graduating a year earlier, he began working in his father's business before the world collapsed. Kevin was Angie's boyfriend. He had longish blond surfer boy hair and green eyes and was well-tanned from working outdoors. Kevin wore dirty blue jeans and a dirty denim long-sleeve work shirt over a blue tee shirt. Kevin's work boots were steel-tipped safety shoes stuffed and stained with gore. These boots did a great job of smashing the skulls of any undead he encountered.

"Maybe so," Jim said, "But let's give it a few minutes before we start celebrating. We need to make sure they really have moved on. Ok?"

Although the band of survivors hadn't officially appointed a leader, Jim was essentially an unnamed defacto leader of the group. Most of the members seemed to gravitate to Jim for guidance naturally, and he, in turn, provided the leadership they required. Had he been asked to lead the group, Jim would have declined as it was not the sort of responsibility he would wish to assume. However, his role had evolved so naturally that he didn't even realize he had become the leader. Likewise, if any of this rag-tag group were considered second in command, it would be the strong, often silent Sheryl. She had the female version of natural leadership that Jim possessed.

After a few more minutes, Jim said, "I think we'll be ok with trying to sneak out now."

"So, what's the plan, Jim?" Angie asked.

Jim hesitated, then said, "I'm not really sure at this point. We have to get out of the city and find some isolated place, like out in the country or up in the mountains. Martin, didn't you tell me you had a summer house, cabin, or something like that?"

Martin said, "Yeah. We have a place up in the mountains, about an hour or so drive from here. It's a large two-story cabin with plenty of room. Ginny and I often went there with the kids and friends before . . . oh, I'm so sorry." Martin's voice caught in his throat at the memory of his late wife and family.

"I understand, Martin. We all do. We've all lost loved ones in this mess," Jim said. "This place of yours, is it fairly isolated?"

"It's both isolated and self-sufficient. It has an electric generator, a well for water, and a septic system. It even has a washer and dryer for clothes. There's a lake nearby teaming with fish and plenty of small game like rabbits, squirrels, and groundhogs. It would be perfect if we could only get up there," Martin explained.

Jim thought momentarily, then agreed, "It sounds like a no-brainer to me. How about the rest of you? What do you think about trying to get to Martin's cabin and waiting there until we see how bad things have gotten?"

Angie and Kevin nodded in agreement, but Sheryl didn't respond. Jim asked, "What do you think, Sheryl? Are you not in agreement?"

Sheryl sighed and said, "It's not that I disagree. I just want to be certain before we try to make it to Martin's cabin. Getting there will be treacherous for all of us. Because there are only five of us, everyone is crucial. We've all seen what these monsters can do. One wrong move, and we could all end up dead. Or worse, one or two might make it, drastically reducing their chance of survival. So, yes, I agree that we all should try to make it to Martin's cabin, but I should stress that I want to ensure we all make it."

"Well said, Sheryl," Martin agreed, surprised. This was the most he had heard he say since he had met her. To be honest, Sheryl scared him a bit.

"Yes. As I said, we have all lost loved ones, and right now, each of us is all we have, so we'll have to be certain to watch out for each other," Jim added.

Angie asked, "Ok, so we have a plan. What's next?"

"Next, we sneak outside and do our best not to be killed and eaten," Jim said.

Kevin took Angie's hand and said, "That sounds like a wonderful idea to me. Let's do this thing."

"Kevin is right. Let's do this . . . before I change my mind," Angie agreed.

Jim said, "Remember, watch out for the person next to you, and if he or she gets bitten, you have no choice but to leave them behind. Even if it is a person you love. No one survives a bite or even a deep scratch from one of these creatures. The infection spreads fast." He looked at the only couple in the group, Angie and Kevin.

Everyone nodded in agreement, although Kevin squeezed Angie's hand slightly and looked into her eyes. She knew by that glance that Kevin could never leave her behind under any circumstances. He would die himself rather than abandon the love of his young life. Despite how much Angie loved Kevin, she knew in her heart that if Kevin had fallen, she would move on.

Some might think it was because her survival instinct was stronger than his, but it was much more than that. Angie had a secret she had not yet shared with anyone, not even Kevin. And now, the responsibility fell upon her to protect Kevin's unborn child. She had only learned of her pregnancy days before the Zombie Apocalypse came down, and now she was carrying the future of mankind within her womb.

"Well then. I think it's time we move on," Jim said.

/ 2 /

Jim led the group to the far end of the warehouse, where a door to the outside was located. With Martin and Kevin's help, they removed the skids and other debris they had previously piled in front of the entrance. When they had put the tables, chairs, desks, and such against the door, they were uncertain the pile would keep the monsters out, but it had done its job well. Earlier, when the creatures were on the move, the group had heard banging on the door, but eventually, the monsters gave up and moved on. Fortunately, being raised from the dead did not come with intelligence.

Now, Jim placed a hand on the doorknob and an ear against the door, listening carefully as he slowly turned the handle. At the first sign of a moan, groan, or other threatening noise, he would stop immediately, but no sounds came. He opened the door about two inches as the group anxiously looked on. Martin held a table leg that he could wield like a club if necessary, and Sheryl had a long-bladed knife she had brought from somewhere. The blade was brown with dried blood from prior use. No one bothered to ask Sheryl about the stain; it just seemed better that way. Angie gripped tightly to Kevin's arm as he held the broken remnants of a baseball bat, which had served him and Angie well so far.

A foul stench came in through the door, a mixture of burned buildings and rotting corpses. Jim turned and put his finger to his lips in a "be quiet" gesture as he inched the door open ever so slowly. When it was wide enough to pass through, Jim walked out into the world of the dead, signaling for the others to follow, which they did.

Outside, the city was in ruins. Electricity had become a thing of the past, as were clean, running water and flushing toilets. It had started raining sometime while the group was in the warehouse, and now it was a torrential downpour. Blood and raw sewage flowed freely down the streets, along with remnants of what was once civilization. Here, a child's doll, there a baby's shoe, there a cluster of silk flowers; these and other such items, once considered signs of a civilized society, now traveled down the river of filth through the city that was no more.

The entire group walked cautiously outside, looking intently in every direction to ensure none of the walking dead were nearby. Jim pointed up along the street and saw an SUV parked with its engine still running. The driver's side door stood open, and something lay on the ground in a puddle next to it. Jim signaled for the group to follow as he carefully walked along the sidewalk. He had a handgun tucked into his pants at the small of his back, but he held a broken piece of wood to use as a club if necessary. Jim knew if he had to use the gun, it would only be as a last resort because its noise would bring dozens of horrid creatures to them.

The group followed closely, forming a tight circle that permitted them to see in all directions. They had to keep brushing the driving rain from their faces to see what was happening. Sheryl was the last in the procession, watching and waiting for the first sign of trouble. As they approached the idling SUV, Jim noticed some slight movement among the pile of what looked like clothing next to the driver's door. When he got closer, he saw a sight that had become all too familiar over the past weeks.

What he had thought was a pile of clothing was a man, a badly injured man by the looks of things. He was still holding onto life, but only by a thin thread. The monsters had obviously attacked him, as he was a mess of bites and torn flesh. His intestines had spilled from his stomach onto the street, and his blood flowed freely in the pouring rain. Jim knew there was no hope for him and what the man would eventually become.

"Help . . . me . . . please . . . help me," The dying man croaked with a voice that betrayed his terminal condition. His left eye was gone, but the man's desperation was apparent in his pleading right eye.

Jim looked back at Sheryl and nodded. She came to the front of the line and, without a moment's hesitation, plunged her knife into the man's remaining eye and deep into his brain. He was gone in an instant. She withdrew the blade, which made a nauseating sucking sound. Behind them, Jim and Sheryl heard Angie vomiting into the street. Little did they know her nausea was not just from what she had seen but from her gentle condition.

Martin came forward with his table leg and opened the back driver's side door to ensure no one else was inside. The SUV was empty. Jim signaled everyone to climb in, and Kevin helped the weakened Angie get into the backseat. She sat in the middle, and Kevin took the left passenger side. Sheryl joined them and sat silently by the right passenger door, apparently unphased by what she had just done. Martin rode shotgun, and Jim dropped into the driver's seat. It was never decided that Jim would drive; it was just something that was understood. The vehicle began to proceed slowly and quietly through the devastated city.

The SUV seemed to take forever to crawl carefully around the wreckage, constantly avoiding abandoned vehicles, debris from fallen buildings, and burning timber piles. Jim was not as careful regarding bodies, driving over the top of them as was often necessary. He didn't mention this to those in the back seat as he didn't want Angie puking in the car, but Martin cringed a time or two when he felt the SUV crunch over one of the once-human speedbumps. Not all of the bodies were completely dead before the SUV rolled over them, but Jim knew there was no hope for any of them since, once bitten, their fate was already sealed. Martin knew this as well, but he nonetheless struggled to keep what little food remained in his stomach in place. It was not just the bump when the SUV ran over the bodies but the squelching sound as the bodies were squashed that Martin did his best to try to shut out unsuccessfully. That noise was one he knew would haunt his nightmares for whatever life he had remaining.

After what seemed like an interminable amount of time, the SUV made it to the highway outside the city that would lead them to the interstate and eventually to the mountains. Martin breathed a sigh of relief at the idea of leaving the devastation behind them until he saw the highway littered with abandoned vehicles.

"How the Hell are we supposed to get past that?" Martin asked.

Jim said, "I'm not sure, Martin. I guess we take it one step at a time."

/ 3 /

Jim steered the SUV onto the burm of the highway, hoping to avoid the bumper-to-bumper bottleneck of cars clogging the main roadway. Initially, his plan worked, allowing them to travel for several miles before coming upon an exit ramp clogged with vehicles. The problem was they didn't want to take the exit ramp but had to get past the blockade to continue up the side of the highway. There was only one way to do that: to somehow move those vehicles.

"What do we do now?" Martin asked.

"I have an idea. But I don't want any of us to go out there unless it is absolutely necessary."

"But what about that thing?" Martin said while pointing at a huge tractor-trailer partway down the exit ramp. The trailer was overturned, and its contents of lumber spilled onto the roadway.

"There's no way we're moving that baby. But, take a look there," Jim said, pointing at a subcompact car crushed between the trailer and a van behind it. "I think we can push that little thing out of the way if we do so slowly."

Martin thought about it and then said, "Yes. I think that will work. The only thing we have to watch out for is that van behind it."

"What do you mean, Martin?"

"The exit ramp is on a downward-sloping hill. If we manage to push that compact out of the way with this SUV, we must do so quickly, as the van might drift down the hill and crash into us."

"That's good, Martin. I didn't think of that," Jim admitted. "What did you do for a living before all this happened."

Martin smiled sheepishly and said, "I was an engineer. It's normal for me to think like that."

"Lucky for us," Jim said.

Kevin suggested, "What if one of us got inside the van, put on the emergency break, and maybe turned the wheels away?"

Martin added, "We could also put chucks under the wheels so the van can't move."

"Those are all great ideas. The problem is that to do that, somebody will have to leave the safety of this SUV and go out there. Do we have any volunteers?"

Martin said, "I'm willing to go out there and jam some debris under the front tires."

Then Kevin added, "And I'm ok with trying to put on the brake."

"Well, if that's the case, I'll go with you and stand guard," Jim agreed. "Sheryl, will you be ok with staying here with Angie? She can use the company."

Sheryl said, "No problem. But I'll keep a watch in case you need me out there."

"I can't ask for more than that," Jim agreed.

Jim, Martin, and Kevin left the SUV to get to work. Martin found some lumber by the side of the exit ramp from the overturned trailer and jammed two pieces under the van's front wheels. Kevin opened the van's passenger door as the driver's side was inaccessible because of the wreckage. As the door opened, a legless corpse fell from the passenger seat and landed on the ground next to Kevin. The thing had become a reanimated zombie and started dragging itself toward him. Its jaws snapped open and closed, mindlessly seeking fresh meat. A brown slime oozed from its legless stumps as the monster crawled ever closer to Kevin, who was starting to regain his bearings. Just when it looked like the zombie might take a bite out of Kevin, Jim ran up and drove the sharp end of his club through the thing's skull, rendering it harmless.

"Thanks, Jim. Good save," Kevin said breathlessly.

"No problem. But you'd better get away from the van. There might be another one of those maggot motels up there."

No sooner had Jim spoken than he heard a growl, and another zombie hurled itself from the van, grabbing Kevin around the neck. The young man screamed and tried to shake the beast off, but to no avail. Then, using a broken two-by-four he had found, Martin swung it like a Louisville Slugger and caved in the monster's skull. It fell to the ground in a heap.

Jim shouted, "Are you ok, Kevin? Did he bite you?"

Kevin patted himself all around his neck and shoulder and said, "No . . . no . . . I don't think so. I guess I got lucky. Thanks, Martin. You saved me, bro."

Martin said, "Not a biggie, Kevin. I was just doing what we all have to do: look out for each other."

Jim looked down at the van's tires and said, "You know what, Kevin? Forget about the emergency brake. It looks like Martin did a bang-up job chucking those tires, so we should be good to go." Then Jim slammed the van door closed. As he did, another zombie came up from the back seat and pressed itself against the door window, growling and drooling against the glass.

Kevin said, "Wow! Good thing I didn't try to go in there."

"Let's get back to the car and push this piece of crap out of the way," Jim said.

The three climbed back into the SUV, and Jim slowly approached the crushed compact car until the front bumper came in contact with the right side of the vehicle. "This might get a little rough," he said to his passengers.

"I thought maybe you were a goner out there," Angie told Kevin.

He replied, "It was closer than I ever want to get again, Babe. Thank goodness Martin was there with his trusty two-by-four. Otherwise, it would have been all over but the shouting."

Jim shouted, "Ok, everyone, hold on. Here we go."

The SUV moved forward as its four-wheel drive began to slowly but deliberately inch the crushed car forward. Progress was slow, and Jim became concerned that something on the SUV might fail and ruin their only hope for escape. The engine roared, the tires squealed, and the wrecked car screamed as metal unwillingly began to give way to the constant pressure the SUV was applying.

As the car was almost out of the way, Angie looked out her side window and said, "Jim, we have a problem. The van is starting to move forward."

Jim said, "I'll get us out of here." He pressed the gas pedal to the floor, and the SUV pushed the car out of the way, clearing the wreckage. As the SUV moved through the blockage, Jim looked in the rearview mirror in time to see the van slide forward and crash into the back of the overturned trailer.

"I guess my makeshift wheel chucks didn't hold as well as I hoped they would," Martin said reluctantly.

"That's ok, Martin. They lasted long enough for us to get through. Now, let's get up to that cabin of yours."

The rag-tag band of survivors and their confiscated SUV continued north toward the mountains, eventually making it to Martin's cabin in the late afternoon with few problems.

/ 4 /

"Well, this is the place," Martin said, pointing to the cabin.

Jim said, "This idea just might work, Martin. For the past half hour, we haven't seen a single soul, living or undead."

"Yep, like I told you, it's deep in the middle of nowhere."

"I think it's beautiful out here," Angie said.

Kevin agreed, "You bet. The odds of any of those creatures finding us here are almost off the charts."

"That's true. But we'll set up perimeter alerts and traps as early warning devices tomorrow morning just in case."

"That's a great idea, Jim. It'll help us all sleep better at night," Martin agreed.

Sheryl said, "I'm going to take a quick walk around the place just to make sure we really are alone out here."

"Good idea, Sheryl," Jim agreed. "Just be careful, and don't be long if you can help it."

"Roger that," she replied as she headed into the woods.

Martin said, "I've got the key to the front door, so why don't I open up, and we can all find somewhere to hang our hats? The house has plenty of bedrooms, so we should all be comfortable."

As he approached the front door, Martin was surprised to find it ajar. The lock had also been broken open. "That's not a good sign," he said, pointing to the damage.

Jim stepped forward, withdrew the gun from the back of his pants, and told Martin, "Let me go in first. Someone or something might be in there."

While Jim prepared to enter the cabin, Sheryl had already been well into her exploratory walk around the woods, looking for any signs of trouble, unaware of what Martin had discovered.

As Jim pushed the door open, Martin stood behind him with his table leg held tightly and ready to use if needed. Then again, how much good would a table leg be if Jim's gun didn't do the job?

* * *

Sheryl carefully walked through the woods, looking for signs of anything out of the ordinary. She was well aware that as deadly as the zombies were, there was just as much to fear from living human beings. Society had quickly degraded to a Darwinian world of dog-eat-dog survival of the fittest practically overnight. Up ahead, Sheryl heard a moan and carefully approached a clearing. Peeking through the bushes, she saw a zombie with its leg caught in what looked like a bear trap. Sheryl knew the thing was not in pain as the monsters felt no pain. Then, looking closer at the scene, she realized that although the creature in the trap was a zombie, it hadn't been one when it was caught in the trap. Its clean clothing and general good appearance were unlike the walking meat sacks. Someone had to have set the trap to keep out intruders. Whoever this young man had been, he was a living, breathing human being when he was caught. Then, he must have died from blood loss, shock, or hypothermia before being reborn as a zombie.

Sheryl slowly approached the beast as he struggled to crawl toward her. His vacant gray eyes stared at her with hunger as his fingers reached out, grabbing air, hoping to get her. She was sickened by what she saw and what she would have to do next. Sheryl never wore her emotions on her sleeves when others were nearby, but she nonetheless was affected by what she had to do, no matter how cool she appeared to onlookers. Sheryl knew that sometimes people thought she enjoyed taking out these creatures, perhaps too much. But the truth was, she hated doing it, but it had to be done. Sheryl hoped she would never get to the point where destroying what was once a living human being would become routine. If that ever happened, she would lose a piece of her humanity she could never get back. Nonetheless, she drove the blade of her knife into the creature's ear and directly into its brain, killing it instantly.

* * *

Jim entered the cabin with his gun arm extended. Suddenly, something slammed into his head from his left, knocking him to the ground as his gun flew from his hand, clattering across the wooden floor and out of reach. He appeared to be unconscious, lying unmoving on the floor. Martin entered with his club, ready to smash who or whatever had attacked Jim, but he stopped suddenly when he felt the muzzle of a gun pressed against the side of his head.

"Hold it right there, my friend. Drop that table leg unless you want your brains scattered all over the cabin," An angry voice said.

Martin did as instructed and walked across the room to kneel next to Jim to ensure he was ok. The voice instructed Kevin and Angie to enter as well. They did so and stood beside Martin and Jim, unsure what to do.

Martin shouted, "You didn't have to hit him so hard. You might have killed him."

"Yeah? And if I did, so what? He wouldn't be my first, and I can guarantee he won't be my last." He gave the three standing survivors an evil, knowing smile.

The man stepped forward with a gun still pointed at them. He was about forty years old and was grimy and disheveled. It was apparent by the stench that the man hadn't bathed in weeks. Had he not spoken, the man could have easily been mistaken for a zombie. His appearance and odor were both so bad.

Martin said, "What do you want from us? And why are you in my cabin?"

"Your cabin?" The man said, "If this ever was your cabin, it ain't no more. It's my place now, which means you are all trespassers on my private property and violating my privacy. According to the law, I have the right to protect what is mine and can kill all of you as intruders if I so choose."

Kevin shouted, "What law is that? There's no law like that."

"Oh yes, there is, young fella. It's a law I just made up. I'm the law around here now. I'm the police, the judge, the jury, and the executioner. As such, I officially sentence you all to death. That is except for that pretty little thing over there." The man nodded at Angie. "I got me some other special plans for her." He grabbed at his crotch with his free hand.

Kevin stepped in front of Angie to protect her.

"So, let's see which one of you trespassers wants to get shot first."

Then Martin stepped in front of Kevin and said, "Look, buddy, there's no need for you to shoot anybody. Maybe we can talk about this."

The man stepped closer, raised the gun, pointed it at Martin's forehead, and said, "How's about we talk about this . . ."

Before the man could pull the trigger, a whizzing noise filled the air, followed by a sickening thudding sound. The man with the gun stood stunned, looking down at the place where the handle of a knife extended from his chest. He looked up at Martin, then across the room to a back door where Sheryl stood with her arm still extended. Then he collapsed to the floor in a heap. Martin was unable to think while the surprisingly calm Sheryl walked across the room, pulled the knife from the now-dead man's chest, and then, using both hands, drove it deep into his skull.

She looked up at the stunned group and said, "Dead once don't mean he stays dead these days."

Martin stood and told Kevin, "Help me get this guy out of here. We'll put him out back for now and bury him tomorrow.

Sheryl said, "I think it would be best if you buried him right away, a good distance from the house. But be careful to stay out of the woods; this moron had bear traps out there. I'll see what I can do to help Jim."

With their defacto leader, Jim, still unconscious, Martin and Kevin followed Sheryl's order and dragged the dead stranger's body outside to the edge of the woods. Martin knew where a couple of shovels could be found, and they dug a grave and buried the corpse.

Martin wiped the sweat from his brow and shook his head in disbelief. Panting, he said, "It was only last summer; my family and I roasted hotdogs and toasted marshmallows over that fire ring over there. Now we're out here burying corpses."

Kevin watched Martin carefully. Although more than thirty years Martin's junior and in great shape, Kevin had found the work surprisingly exhausting. He was concerned that the task might have been too much for the overweight, older man who led a fairly sedentary life. But to Kevin's surprise, Martin rebounded quickly. Kevin felt slightly embarrassed by his sudden exhaustion; it was unlike him to tire so quickly.

/ 5 /

When Martin and Kevin returned to the cabin, Jim was awake and on his feet. A bandage was wrapped around his head, making him look like that piper in that painting about the Revolutionary War with the pipers and drummers. Sheryl stood by the back door in the distance, returning to a more subordinate, silent role.

Jim greeted the two, saying, "I want to thank you both for the part you played in saving me."

Kevin and Martin looked at each other in confusion, and Martin said, "I'm sorry, Jim, but we did nothing to save you. I mean, we tried, but that stranger got the drop on us. He had his gun just a few inches from my forehead and was intending on blowing my brains out."

Kevin added, "Then he was gonna kill me next and keep my precious Angie for his own disgusting purposes. Ain't that right, Baby?"

But Angie wasn't able to speak. She had been so severely traumatized by the encounter that she sat in a chair, silently staring at the ground.

Jim asked, "Then what happened? Who saved me? Hell, who saved you guys?"

"It was Sheryl," Martin admitted. " She was incredible! I've never seen anything even close to what she did. Right when that sicko was about to pull the trigger, she showed up and sunk a knife in his chest from all the way over there at that back door." Martin pointed to the back entrance.

Jim turned and said, "Sheryl, why didn't you tell me?" But to his and everyone's surprise, Sheryl was gone.

"Where did she go?" Kevin asked.

Jim explained, "She said earlier that she was going to stay out on the porch tonight, keeping a watch out for trouble."

"I guess she isn't one for taking credit, no matter how much deserved. Heaven help any trouble that decides to show up, with Sheryl on guard," Martin said.

"Martin and Kevin, why don't you both get cleaned up and then get some sleep for a few hours? I'm not supposed to sleep for a while because of this bump on my head. I'll relieve Sheryl later and thank her, even though, as you pointed out, she doesn't seem to want any acknowledgment," Jim suggested.

Martin replied, "Ok, Jim, I am pretty exhausted."

Jim said, "Kevin, take Angie to your room and get her tucked in. I'm afraid today's events have taken their toll on her."

"Will do, Jim," Kevin replied.

Kevin led Angie to one of the empty bedrooms, slipped off her shoes, and slid her under the covers. He didn't bother suggesting she undress or get a shower, even though she was as much in need of one as he was. What she required now was rest. Kevin pulled the covers up to her shoulders, kissed her gently on the forehead, and said, I'll be right back, Babe."

Kevin got to the bathroom and was happy to find it empty. Martin hadn't been here yet and perhaps had decided to let his shower wait until later. Kevin was tired enough to let his wait as well, but truth be told, he was feeling a bit poorly as if he might be fighting the flu or something. He hoped the shower might help him feel better. He stripped out of his dirty clothing, acknowledging with revulsion he had to put the foul-smelling things back on when finished. All the survivors had escaped with were the clothes they were wearing. Perhaps he could wash them in the morning until he could find something else to wear.

Kevin was grateful for the dirt he saw washing down the drain as he stood under the tepid shower water. He had found some small, hotel-size soap bars that Martin must have saved from his various business trips. The soap felt incredible as it cleaned his filthy body. Kevin realized it had been weeks since he had a chance to bathe. Then he recalled the man who had tried to kill them earlier. Kevin had thought him to be a vile, disgusting-smelling creature. He now realized his stench had been not much better. As Kevin reached the soap around to wash his shoulders, he felt a burning pain in his left shoulder.

He set the soap aside and carefully felt the area with his fingers. He found deep furrows carved in his flesh. Then, he recalled the creature that had fallen out of the van earlier that day. Kevin was certain the monster hadn't bitten him, but he realized the creature had managed to scratch him and do so badly. He knew what that might mean. It was possible, if not likely, that the infection would spread through his body, eventually killing him and turning him into one of those horrible monsters. Maybe that was why he was feeling so tired. Perhaps his problem was more than simple exhaustion. Could the infection already have started coursing through his body?

Kevin had to think about what to do. He couldn't let anyone know what had happened to him, not even Angie. If anyone found out about the scratch, the best ending he could hope for was to be cast out into the world to survive alone. However, it was more than likely Sheryl or Jim would put him down like a rabid animal. Jim might be more merciful and put a bullet in his brain, but Sheryl would deal with him with that knife of hers. Although neither option was desirable, the scenario with Sheryl was by far the most horrifying.

But maybe he wouldn't have to worry about any of this. Was it possible that he had caught the problem early enough? If he scrubbed the gouged area thoroughly with soap and water and then applied a clean bandage, maybe he could stop the infection from spreading through his body. Kevin gritted his teeth against the pain, and using a soapy washcloth, he began scrubbing the wound until he thought he might pass out from the fiery agony. Then, he rinsed the area under the shower to cleanse the wound further. Kevin opened a medicine chest on the wall and found a large bottle of hydrogen peroxide and a smaller bottle labeled iodine. He also found some large bandages and some medical tape.

Kevin realized Martin might notice the medical supplies were missing since this was his cabin after all, but perhaps since he hadn't been in the bathroom yet, Martin might assume the man they had killed might have used them. It was a chance Kevin would have to take. Kevin poured a generous portion of peroxide on the wound using the mirrored medicine chest door as a guide. The burn was only slight, and Kevin watched the liquid bubble white as it did its job, killing any germs and infection. Then, he prepared himself for the real pain. Kevin folded some toilet paper into a thick square and applied the iodine onto the square. Next, he rubbed it all around and deep inside the wound. The pain was like a thousand white-hot needles going into his shoulder, but Kevin fought back against the agony and managed to stifle the screams that wanted to fly from his mouth.

When the pain had tapered to mere discomfort, Kevin put a sterile bandage on the wound and taped it, again using the mirror to assist him. Then, reluctantly, he redressed in his filthy clothing, hoping the bandage would protect his injury from contact with the dirty shirt.

Kevin didn't know how long he would be able to keep this injury a secret from the group, but he would do his best. They simply could not find out. Under normal circumstances, preventing Angie from finding out would be impossible, but thankfully, she had been traumatized by the events of the past weeks, meaning she would have little interest in sex for a while. Come to think of it, she had been a bit stand-off-ish to him in that regard for the past several weeks. Not that he could blame her. Neither of them had been exactly smelling like roses, and when you combine that with just trying to stay alive, he supposed it was understandable.

However, things could be slightly different now that they were in a safe place with clean water. Once they found clean clothes, it was entirely possible that Angie would want to restart their intimacy. Kevin hoped she would at least wait long enough for his wound to heal. He realized he was already thinking positively and was certain the infection would not spread and he would be ok. Kevin knew he would have to watch himself closely for the next several weeks to ensure no one suspected. He had to chuckle at his ability to think about the future. A week earlier, he was sure he and Angie had little chance of surviving on their own.

/ 6 /

The next morning, Kevin heard a knock on his bedroom door. A voice called out, "Kevin? Angie? Sorry to bother you. It's Martin. I have some clean clothing for you."

Kevin got out of bed and noticed Angie was sleeping peacefully. He opened the door and whispered, "Angie's still asleep. Did you say you had clean clothes? That's incredible! These things reek." He pulled at the front of his filthy shirt.

"Yes, we always kept several sets of clothes up here so we didn't have to drag them back and forth. Here is one of my sweatshirts, a tee shirt, and a pair of jeans for you. A few of my wife's things might work for Angie . . ." Martin started to tear up again.

Kevin looked down at the clothing and said, "Thanks, Man. This is like a gift from Heaven. I really mean that."

"I wish I had more, but we had to ration everything out among the others."

"Not a problem at all, Martin. I was going to try to wash these rags today. Now I can throw them in the garbage."

Martin said, "I'd still recommend salvaging what you can and washing them. If we're hiding out up here like we planned, it could be a long time before we get any more new stuff. Well, I got to move on."

"Thanks again, Martin. You have no idea how much this means to me."

Martin left, and Kevin walked over to check on Angie, who was still sleeping. Making sure not to turn his back on her, in case she awoke, Kevin pulled off his filthy shirt and quickly slipped on the fresh sweatshirt from Martin. Likewise, he tore off his old jeans and slipped on the new pair. The clothing was a bit big on him as Martin was overweight, but taking his belt from his old jeans, Kevin could sinch them tight enough to be functional. They were also a little shorter than his old jeans, but they would work until his jeans were washed and dried.

Kevin heard a stirring from the bed and saw that Angie was waking up. "Good morning, Babe. I have some good news."

At first, Kevin thought Angie might still be dealing with her trauma from the previous day, but then he saw that once awake, she seemed to have gotten back to normal. She said, "New clothes. Thank goodness. I reek!"

"Well, Babe. I tried out Martin's shower last night, and although the water is only lukewarm, it still does a good job of making bubbles and washing the stink off us. I suggest you take your new clothes and head down there as soon as possible before someone races you to the bathroom."

Angie practically jumped out of bed, grabbed some of the clothes, and headed out the door. She turned and said, "Take that stinky sheet off the bed. As long as we're getting ourselves clean, we might as well wash the sheets. I don't know if I can ever get the stink out of these old clothes, but God knows I'll try."

Kevin watched Angie leave the room with mixed emotions. He was happy to see her acting like her old self again but was also concerned this might mean she would want intimacy before his wound had healed. He unconsciously reached up and touched the area where the bandage covered his shoulder. It was still quite painful. He evaluated how he was feeling and determined that although he was a bit tired, he could sense no signs of a spreading infection.

A short while later, Angie returned wearing the clean, although slightly oversized, clothing. As far as Kevin was concerned, Angie was the most beautiful girl in the world at that moment. He was about to rush over and kiss her when he noticed her expression change slightly from one of joy to concern.

"Kevin? Are you alright?" She asked.

He replied, "Yes, of course I am. Why do you ask?"

"I didn't notice before, but you seem very pale and have dark circles under your eyes."

Kevin said, "I don't know, maybe I'm just a bit tired. I was up late with Martin burying that guy who . . . never mind. I guess I'm a bit worn down."

Although still looking concerned, Angie said, "Well, I suppose that could be the case. Maybe later, you can come back here and take a nap." She tried to sound positive, but something felt very wrong, and it was a sensation she didn't like.

"Well, if that's what the doctor orders," Kevin replied, trying to sound cheerful but beginning to worry himself.

/ 7 /

As Kevin and Angie left their bedroom, they heard conversations echoing in the hallway from the main living and dining areas downstairs. As the couple descended the steps, Martin approached them and joked, "Finally, the happy couple have made it down from the honeymoon suite. By the looks of things, poor Kevin appears to be a bit . . . exhausted."

Angie blushed, knowing what everyone was thinking. Kevin said, "I am tired, that's for sure, but unfortunately, it's because of dealing with the last week or so. By the way, thanks again for the clean clothes, Martin. I doubt if I'll grow into them any time soon, but they'll do just fine."

"Yes, thank you, Martin. This place is perfect. I haven't been this clean in a long time," Angie said.

Martin replied, "I'm happy to do what I can to help us get through this."

"There is no getting through this, Martin. Only surviving one day at a time," Sheryl added gloomily.

Jim said, "We all know that, Sheryl. But this place is our best hope for surviving until things start rebuilding, which I believe it will."

"I certainly hope you're right, Jim," Martin added.

"I believe I am. If the five of us have made it this far, then somewhere else, five more have survived, and then five more. I also believe the military will eventually wipe out these creatures. In fact, I'll bet common people like hunters and gun enthusiasts will start using these zombies for target practice. Before you know it, the problem will be under control."

Angie said, "I hope so." She thought she only had about seven or eight more months before she brought a new human into this crazy world.

"Those creatures aren't the only things we have to worry about, Jim. That lump on your head proves that," Sheryl added.

Martin decided he liked it better when Sheryl didn't talk, although he'd never tell her that. Instead, he said, "Today, I suppose we should do what we can to make this place as secure as possible."

"We'll get to that soon, Martin," Jim said, "First, Sheryl and I want to make sure there are no more boobie traps out there that were set by that guy from last night. Tell them what you found, Sheryl."

Sheryl looked closely at each survivor and said, "It was a zombie trapped in a bear trap. I dealt with it. The problem is I believe he wasn't no zombie when he was caught in the trap. He was as human as you or me, but then he got caught in that trap, probably bled out, died, and turned."

Jim continued, "So you see, we have to find a way to warn us about human intruders. We can't assume they will all be out to kill us, but we have to consider that some will. So rather than set traps that will harm or kill anyone, we'll come up with some traps that will detain them and warn us without injuring them."

"I say, kill them all and let God sort them out," Sheryl suggested.

"I might be inclined to agree with you, Sheryl, but we have to assume there are some good folks like us out there who could join our little community and help us out," Jim said. "With more people, we could expand, build more shelters, maybe a protective wall, and who knows, maybe we could make a small town where we could all feel safe."

Angie liked that idea, especially with the baby coming soon, although she realized such an endeavor, if even possible, might take a long time to make a reality. She looked at Kevin hopefully, imagining them raising a family in a safe fortress-like town. However, Kevin didn't seem to be paying attention to the conversation. He looked like his mind was a million miles away. Kevin stood staring out into space as if awake but asleep.

"Kevin, Honey, are you ok?" Angie asked.

He shook his head as if to clear out the cobwebs of a daydream and said, "Um . . . yeah . . . no . . . I don't know. I guess I just need a little more rest."

Martin said, "Why don't you go back to bed and sleep for a few hours, Kevin? We won't need your help until Jim and Sheryl return from checking for traps anyway."

"Um . . . ok," Kevin said as he turned and shamble-walked back up the stairs to the bedroom.

"Do you think he's alright? He looked pretty peaked," Martin asked Angie.

Angie said, "I don't know, Martin. Kevin is usually so strong and full of life. This is the first I've ever seen him look so tired and maybe sick."

"We'll have to keep a close watch on him. If he dies, you know what we'll have to do," Sheryl said.

Angrily Angie shouted, "He's not sick, and he's not going to die, Sheryl. He's just a little tired. How could you say something so terrible?"

"These are terrible times, Angie. It ain't high school or the class prom anymore, princess. This is the new reality, and unless you do some serious growing up and fast, you won't make it," Sheryl countered.

Jim intervened, "Ok, both of you. That's enough. We have too many important things to deal with to have these petty arguments.

Sheryl, you come with me and Angie; you can help Martin with some of his chores while Kevin rests. We'll check on him in a few hours. But don't worry, Angie. I'm sure he'll be fine."

Angie was happy to have Jim's support and hear his consoling words, but in the back of her mind, she felt like something was very wrong with Kevin, and that thought sent chills down her spine.

Martin said, "Come on, Angie. Let's take some of these dirty clothes and get them cleaned up and dried. We should probably clean this cabin a bit as well."

/ 8 /

When Jim and Sheryl returned several hours later, Martin and Angie had the cabin looking new and had a stack of freshly laundered clothes.

Jim said, "Wow! Great job, you guys. This place looks terrific. And look at all those nice clean clothes. If we're not careful, we might start feeling downright civilized."

"Thanks, Jim," Martin said.

Angie added, "Was your trip successful?"

"Absolutely. We found several other traps scattered around the woods and feel confident they have all been disabled. I think what we'll do next after some lunch is set up some warning traps of our own," Jim said.

Martin asked, "What do you have in mind, Jim?"

"Do you have any string or twine stored around here, Martin? And maybe some tin cans or pie pans or anything like that?"

"Yes. I have a few spools of twine, and I'll bet if I check out back in the trash, I'll find some empty cans. I noticed that the vagrant living here ate most of the beans and things we had stored. He had to do something with the cans."

Jim said, "Great. We'll deal with that after some lunch."

"I'm going to take a shower," Sheryl added, "It seems I'm the only one who hasn't gotten cleaned up yet." She turned and walked away.

When Sheryl was out of earshot, Martin said, "She's a tough one. A little odd, but definitely tough."

Jim added, "She's someone you can be glad is a friend and not an enemy."

"I doubt she has many enemies . . . alive anymore, that is," Angie suggested.

"You're probably right. Glad we have her on our team," Jim said.

Angie agreed, although she wasn't certain how she felt about the woman. On one hand, Sheryl was resourceful and willing to do what she could to protect the group, but on the other, there was something dark and somewhat sinister about her.

/ 9 /

Sheryl stood naked under the water flowing over her from the cleansing shower. It felt great to finally wash away the foul smell of two weeks in the world of the stinking undead. She couldn't believe how amazing this little taste of civilization felt. She closed her eyes, with her face pointing into the luxuriously calming water, and let it take her mentally away to a much happier time before the world became a living Hell. She was so relaxed that she had never heard the creature approaching. But she felt the agony as the monster tore out her throat like a wild animal. Sheryl collapsed to the shower floor as her life's blood streamed down the drain.

* * *

"Has anybody seen Sheryl?" Jim asked, "She was going to shower and grab lunch. Then we were going to go out and set a few warning traps."

Angie said, "Yeah, I remember seeing her heading for the shower earlier. I'll go check on her."

"Martin, would you mind going with Angie? I don't want her going alone, and Kevin is still sleeping."

"No problem. And I'll wake Kevin up on our way back. I want to see if he's feeling any better."

Angie said, "Good idea, Martin. Let's go."

The two walked upstairs and down the hall to the bathroom. Angie put her ear to the door and said, "I don't hear any water running. Then

Angie knocked on the door and called, "Sheryl? Are you in there? This is Angie. I'm coming in."

Angie slowly opened the door and stepped inside. Everything seemed normal. The shower curtain was open, and no towels or clothing were strewn around the room. It was almost like Sheryl hadn't even been there. Then Angie noticed something sitting on the bathroom vanity. It was Sheryl's knife. This was a problem because everyone knew Sheryl had never gone anywhere without that knife. But there was no sign of Sheryl. Angie picked up the knife and tucked it into her belt to give to Sheryl when she returned.

"We'd better go back and tell Jim. Maybe he'll have some idea about what to do next," Martin said.

"Yeah. Great idea, Martin. Let's pick up Kevin on our way."

The pair stopped by Kevin and Angie's room and saw Kevin still sleeping. Angie shook Kevin, saying, "Wake up, Kevin, let's move it."

Kevin slowly opened his eyes and sat up, saying, "Wow! I must have really needed that. I slept like a log."

Angie studied Kevin's face momentarily, then asked, "Are you feeling ok, Babe? You still look really tired. It's like the bags under your eyes went out and bought themselves more bags. You have some heavy-duty dark circles going on, too."

Kevin said, "No, I think I'm ok. I just feel a little groggy from sleeping so long."

"Well, we need to go see Jim and tell him Sheryl wasn't in the shower," Martin added.

Kevin asked, "Sheryl? The shower? Is something wrong?"

Angie said, "It looks like Sheryl might be missing. She was supposed to be getting a shower, but she's not there."

"Then let's go see Jim and find out what Jim has to say," Kevin agreed.

The three walked back downstairs to find Jim staring out the window with a look of uncertainty on his face.

Angie said, "Sheryl wasn't in the shower, Jim."

"I've been watching out the window for any sign of her outside; I even went out onto the porch and called for her but got no response.

We'll have to go out and see if we can find her. I'll head out the front door, and Martin, you will go out the back. Kevin, do you feel up to going out around the side of the cabin and looking in the woods beyond there?" Jim inquired.

"Sure thing, Jim," Kevin agreed.

"What about me?" Angie asked.

Jim said, "Somebody has to stay here in case Sheryl returns. If she does return, Angie, you can call to us, and someone will be bound to hear."

"Ok. That sounds like a plan," Angie said.

"Let's get going and remember to be careful out there," Jim cautioned.

/ 10 /

Martin walked carefully through the back door and into the area where, the previous night, he and Kevin had buried the man who had tried to kill them. The fresh ground looked undisturbed, which made Martin feel more at ease. He knew Sheryl had made sure the character's brain was dead, but in these troubled times, one could never be certain about anything. Martin was genuinely concerned he might find the ground dug up and the man's reanimated corpse waiting for him in the shadows. Then he remembered that these walking meat sacks didn't have the mental capacity to plan anything. At least, that was the case so far.

As Martin walked further away from the cabin and deeper into the woods, he noticed there were no sounds, birds, or small creatures of any kind. He found that strange, as he recalled the woods previously bustling with wildlife. Martin shook his head, clearing his daydreaming to ensure he was on his guard. Still, he heard nothing. The trees had become more dense, blocking the sunlight and creating a dark, shadowy environment. As he rounded a curve, he saw something in the brush beyond. It was hard to determine exactly what it was in the forest darkness.

When he got closer, Martin's breath caught in his throat, stifling the scream of horror that wanted to burst from his lungs. The lump he saw in the woods was the naked corpse of Sheryl. He had found her. Martin bent over with his hands on his knees and vomited his breakfast into the blanket of pine needles below.

"Oh, my Sweet Lord in Heaven," Martin babbled almost incoherently.

He looked closer at the body and saw her head had been practically decapitated from her body, hanging by a few strands of flesh. If there was anything good to be drawn from this horrible situation, it was that Sheryl would never rise from the dead now. Martin couldn't figure out what had happened to Sheryl and how her body had gotten out there in the woods. Did that man from last night have an accomplice hiding in the woods, waiting to take them one at a time? If so, he must have been stealthy to overpower someone like Sheryl. But how was he able to do such a horrendous thing to her throat? It looked like the result of a zombie attack.

Then Martin realized that one of those horrid creatures must be loose in the forest somewhere. It could have gotten into the house and killed Sheryl in the shower. But such a mindless creature wouldn't have the intelligence to drag the body out into the woods. It also wouldn't have stopped with one victim. It would have taken everyone in the house until it was destroyed.

Martin heard a low growling behind him and then felt two hands with vise-like grips crushing his shoulder blades. Before he could scream, a left hand covered his mouth while the right ripped his stomach open, spilling his innards onto the forest floor. Martin fell to the ground to join Sheryl.

/ 11 /

Jim searched the area in front of the cabin and went deeper into the woods. So far, he had seen no sign of Sheryl. Jim hoped Martin or Kevin would have better luck than he was having. He decided to work his way around to where Martin was searching, hoping that perhaps he had found something. As he neared the area where Martin had been looking, he saw movement in the underbrush. Jim pulled out his revolver in case whatever animal was approaching might not be friendly. It might be nothing more than a groundhog or rabbit, but it could also be a coyote looking for its next meal.

As the bushes parted, Jim could scarcely believe what he saw. It was Martin crawling toward him, or more accurately, what had once been Martin. The man's eyes bore the vacant, filmed-over glaze of the undead, a look Jim had seen more times than he could recount in the past several weeks. Martin crawled forward with his intestines dragging behind him along the forest floor. Pine needles clung to his bloody innards. Globs of fluid leaked from the flapping organs. The Martin creature's mouth was snapping open and closed rapidly, hungry for a taste of human flesh, Jim's flesh. It was obvious what had occurred. One or more of the undead monsters had stumbled upon what the group had thought was a safe refuge, and Martin was dead. For all Jim knew, Sheryl may have suffered a similar fate.

Jim decided not to risk the noise created by a gunshot, and he tucked his gun back into the back of his pants. He picked up a large nearby rock and bashed in Martin's skull until the creature stopped moving. "Sorry, my friend. You deserved better for all you have done for us. As Jim stood, he felt the pain of teeth sinking deep into his neck from behind as his vision went, at first, blurred, then black.

/ 12 /

Kevin returned to the cabin to find Angie waiting. His clothes were tattered and stained with something brown. The area where the zombie had gouged him was clearly visible and obviously infected. Angie saw this and recalled what had happened to him. Her stomach lurched with what she knew was to come. Kevin shuffle-stepped to a nearby chair and dropped into it.

Angie asked calmly and with surprising detachment, "What happened to you, Kevin?"

Kevin replied, "Um . . . nothing . . . I tripped and fell down an embankment, but I'm ok. Just a little rattled."

"You look more than a little rattled, Kevin. Did you have any luck finding Sheryl? Angie asked.

Kevin replied, sounding somewhat disoriented, "Sheryl? No, I didn't have any luck, I'm afraid. I assume she didn't come back here, did she?"

Angie replied, "No, Kevin. She didn't come back. I suspect she won't be back either."

"How can you be so sure?" Kevin asked.

"You tell me, Kevin."

"I don't understand what you mean, Angie."

Angie said, "I know I was supposed to stay inside, but I decided to take a little walk."

"Ok . . ." Kevin prompted.

"I think you know what I found," she said.

"Uh . . . no. I have no idea what you found," Kevin said, confused.

"I found Sheryl's body. Her throat was ripped out."

Kevin said, "Oh my God, that's terrible."

"I also found Martin. He had become one of those monsters and someone bashed his head in, probably Jim."

"Oh no. Do you think Martin found and killed Sheryl?" Kevin asked.

"No, Kevin. I think whatever killed Sheryl killed and transformed Martin and then killed Jim as well."

"Killed Jim? Is Jim dead?" Kevin asked.

"You should know that better than I would, Kevin. But yes, I found his body as well. He had become one of those things, so I had no choice but to put him down."

Kevin was even more confused, "What do you mean, Angie? How would I know what happened to any of them? I was asleep when Sheryl disappeared. I was searching far away from Martin, and I haven't seen Jim since we all split up."

"I know about your infection, Kevin," Angie said, pointing at the puss-dripping gash on his shoulder. "And I know what you have become, even if you don't realize it yet."

Kevin said, "What the Hell are you talking about, Angie? What do you mean, what I've become?"

Angie stepped forward and said, "I know what you are, Kevin. That gouge you got from that zombie yesterday. Not only is it infected, but it has also started to transform you. It's turning you into one of the undead. That's why you look so sick, and that's why it was you who killed all our friends."

"Me? Jeezus, Angie. I haven't killed anyone. Are you out of your mind?"

Angie took a deep breath and said, "No, Kevin. I'm not crazy. I know what you've become and what you've done. And no matter what, God help me. I still love you, Kevin, but I won't let you do that to our baby and me."

"Baby?" Surprised, Kevin said, "Are you saying we're having a baby?" He got up from his chair and walked toward Angie with his arms extended. "That's wonderful news, Babe."

As he got close enough to touch Angie, she pulled Sheryl's knife out and, without hesitation, drove it through Kevin's eye and deep into his brain, killing him instantly.

"No, Kevin. We are not having a baby. I am having a baby," Angie said with finality.

Angie realized she would have to gather supplies and leave this place alone, hoping to find another group of people to take her in. Perhaps she could find good medical care for her and her baby if any still existed. She felt heartsick about having to kill Kevin, but she kept telling herself he was no longer Kevin; he was a zombie.

That was when she heard deep growling noises behind her and turned to find two undead monsters approaching. She realized with horror that she had been wrong. Kevin wasn't a zombie. These monsters had killed her friends, and she had murdered the innocent father of her baby. Then the creatures fell on her, and Angie screamed her way into the world of the undead.

SAW KILL ROAD

The lonely two-lane blacktop road snaked like a writhing serpent over its short half-mile length from end to end, connecting the busy Abington Lane with the mountainous Prescott Road. Its narrow, winding countenance curved past the abandoned, once prosperous sawmill from which the road had gotten its name, "Sawmill Road." That is to say, "Sawmill" was its official name, as documented in the township archives. However, its unofficial moniker was much more menacing, known to locals, especially the children, as "Saw Kill Road."

At the start of the twentieth century, the sawmill had been a bustling enterprise, employing many local men; once a large two-story clapboard building, the wood sealed to allow its weather resistance to fight off the elements.

Where the mill was level with the roadway, two large barn-style doors opened to a dirt driveway, allowing wagons to back up for loading and unloading of wood. As the land sloped downward, a stone foundation reached five feet high to support the building and provided doorway access to a basement storage area and windows for light. The ceiling of the basement area was comprised of thick wooden beams, also serving as the floor for the sawmill itself.

Its dark shutters on the sides of the upper floors could be opened on nice days to allow the sun to shine inside and held closed during storms to prevent nature from damaging its many pains of hand-blown glass. At one time, the mill had a gorgeous set of front stairs leading to a small front porch constructed of wood from the mill, as was the beautiful oak entry door, with its four-pane window built of the same hand-blown glass as the rest of the mill.

Above the front door, with its brass door knocker and crystal knob, was a transom which held a custom-made stained-glass window bearing the name "Hanson's Mill" for the founder and owner of the mill, Jonas Jackson Hanson, known as "J. J." to his few friends and "the cheap limy bastard" to most of his employees.

The mill now stood in decay, its once beautiful wooden siding putrefying from years of exposure to the elements, fading to whitish gray, rotten, and infested with insects. Rusted hinges hung loosely from disintegrating clapboards, some hanging by a single remaining corroded screw, a sad reminder of a time long ago when the mill's shutters hung proudly. Not only were the shutters now gone, but most of the remaining glass pains had been either removed or shattered. This left sharp, jagged fragments in the frames, resembling hideous sharks' teeth. A few may have been stolen by thieves hoping to get something for the custom-blown panes, but most were simply broken by local vandals for whatever enjoyment they might gain from such thoughtless actions. Behind the broken windows awaited nothing but the blackness of the abandoned structure and whatever else might lurk inside in the darkness.

The beautiful front door had long since been stolen, allowing various woodland creatures to wander into the mill to take up residence. Perhaps the missing door was presently being used as someone's front door in a mansion in another state or country, or maybe it had simply been burned for firewood. Its fate remained a mystery. Where the stained-glass transom once proudly displayed the mill owner's name, nothing remained but an empty, pitted wooden frame covered in spider webs, teaming with insects.

At one time, a large double-sided fireplace was in the middle of the mill, providing heat for the workers in the winter. It led to an enormous chimney stretching high above the center of the roofline, making for a breathtaking spectacle as it spewed its smoke into the icy sky during the coldest, most freezing winter months. Now, the chimney was all but gone above the roofline, its mortar disintegrated by years of exposure, its bricks falling to the ground below, many falling through the roof, making large gaping holes in the rotting shingles.

Through the center of the chimney, large branches grew skyward from an oak tree that had taken root a few years after the mill had been shut down. Branches likewise protruded through the broken windows, looking as if the tree and its mighty limbs might have been the only thing keeping the mill standing, which could very well have been true.

The locals called the road "Saw Kill" because of the mill's tragic history, or perhaps more accurately, the unfortunate history of its owner, J. J. Hanson. The tale of Jonas J. Hanson is a sad one when told with historical accuracy. However, through the years, the account had grown and evolved, each time being told with the addition of more fantastic and impossible elements until it had become the stuff of legend. It was no longer simply a tragic tale but one of terror and mystery.

Hanson had been the only child of a British father and a German mother who had immigrated to the US toward the end of the nineteenth century. Shortly after his arrival, Jonas's father, William, built the mill and began growing his business. Jonas was born in 1880, and by the turn of the century, the mill had become a prosperous business. Jonas took over ownership and operation of the mill in 1905 at the age of twenty-five when his father died suddenly. The fact was a heart attack had been the cause of his father's untimely death, but through the years, the story evolved to suggest young Jonas had actually murdered his father to get control of the mill.

The workers did not take well to Jonas running the operation, as they looked at him as privileged and being given everything because of his father's hard work. Instead of winning the workers over, Jonas took a firm, autocratic approach, driving his workers with an iron fist and firing anyone who gave him even the slightest provocation. As was often the case in such areas, the economy was not prosperous in the poor rural Pennsylvania community, so the employees had little choice but to put up with Jonas's tyranny.

Jonas never married and, therefore, never had any children. He took over the family homestead, a large farmhouse on the same parcel of land but located several hundred yards in the woods behind the mill. His mother, Greta, lived in the house with him until she died of cancer, then known as "the waste of life," around 1920. Jonas soon found himself alone in the big house and didn't consider the isolation comforting.

Locals rumored his mental decline started after his mother's death. Many said the spirits of the dead parents haunted the homestead, tormenting Jonas relentlessly because of his poor treatment of the workforce. That particular rumor was probably started by a group of irate workers who hated Jonas and perhaps wished deep inside that such a phenomenon might actually have occurred.

Others, who dared to be so vulgar, hinted about an unnatural intimate relationship between Jonas and his mother after his father's death, which caused him to go mad with grief following her death. Whatever the reason, after several years alone in the "big house," as it was known, Jonas started to act irrationally and could often be seen conversing with people who were not present, some say his mother and father. This probably helped to fuel the ghost rumors as well.

Eventually, Jonas lost his mind completely and became stark raving mad. Unfortunately, no one realized the extent of his insanity until it was much too late. Until then, most of his employees thought he was a bit "off" and ignored his steady mental decline to keep gainfully employed at the mill.

Then it happened. One day, after the workday had ended and most of the workers had gone home, Jonas was hunched over his desk in his office, mumbling to himself, as usual, working on the business books. Four obviously angry workers approached him, demanding to speak to him about the working conditions. When he refused to talk with the men, they told Hanson they were forming a labor union, and he would either have to give in to their demands, or they would call a strike and shut the mill down.

Even though most of what they said was simply bluster, they had just started discussing the possibility of forming a union and were years away from making it a reality. However, Hanson didn't know this and could not distinguish between what was real and what might be fabricated in his decreasing mental state.

He simply snapped. He reached into the top drawer of his desk, retrieved a Smith and Wesson 38 special revolver, and proceeded to shoot each of them without forethought. One of the men died instantly when the bullet entered through his right eye, blowing out the back of his skull and spattering his blood and bits of head and brain all over the office's back wall.

One of the men took one through the neck and lay on the floor, gasping for several long minutes as his severed artery pumped his life-blood onto the floor, where it pooled about him. The other two were not so lucky. Though one was shot once and the other twice, their wounds were crippling but were not fatal. They would have been much better off had they died instantly. The two men screamed in agony and crawled toward the door, trying desperately to escape the homicidal madman.

Unfortunately, they did not see him grab a souvenir baseball bat, which was presented to him by the company that purchased his lumber to make their sports equipment. But they most certainly felt it when Hanson tried to knock them both out of the park, so to speak. He shattered both of their legs so they couldn't escape, then broke their arms and dislocated their shoulders so they could not fight back. Whether he originally planned on killing them with the bat or whether he changed his mind during the process, he only ended up knocking them both unconscious.

When the men regained consciousness, they were in the sawmill, strapped to the saw table, legs spread as the belts spun on their pulleys, powering the enormous saw blade, allowing it to turn above the table directly in front of them. Then the edge began its journey down toward them, and within a few moments, the screaming was over, as each half of both workers fell to the floor, the table slick with their blood, insides, and stomach contents.

Apparently, Jonas had saved one bullet for himself, and after his gruesome work was completed, he went back to his office, sat behind his desk, and blew his brains out. The police investigating the crime scene were sickened by how he fell face-forward on top of his desk, his sodden brains oozing out onto a photo of his parents, which had fallen down and lay beneath his ruined skull.

* * *

Paul Simmons was a twenty-first-century transplant to the area but knew about the mill's history, having heard local children discussing it while playing in the streets of his neighborhood. His subdivision was only about five years old when Paul and his wife, Laura, built their split-level home, completing it several months ago. Theirs was one of the last lots remaining in an established, essentially settled development. They were both professionals, referred to as DINKS by their co-workers: Double Income—No Kids. They both wanted to have children some-day, but they had not made any attempts to conceive so far.

They both attended a nearby gym and fitness center during the workweek, but on the weekends, weather permitting, they enjoyed walking along the country roads near their new neighborhood. They would leave the development and head east on Abington Lane until they reached Sawmill. Then they would walk the half-mile length of the road, past the sawmill, unconsciously keeping their distance from the ruins. Next, they would turn right on Prescott Road and follow it until it intersected with the very steep Dairy Road, which eventually met back up with Abington Lane on the other side of their develop-ment, completing about a two-mile circle.

Often, when walking by the mill, Paul would deliberately stare at the structure, wondering if the rumors surrounding the mill were true. He suspected they might be close to the truth, although it probably was blown way out of proportion over the years. He often would feel a strange sensation in his stomach when passing the mill, as if some force were calling him, urging him to enter.

Most locals believed or wanted to believe the place was haunted by the ghost of J. J. Hanson, who was looking for another victim to saw in two. Paul, of course, didn't believe in such local folklore, thinking it ridiculous. Even the nickname "Saw Kill" sounded juvenile and corny to him. In fact, he was fairly sure once, several years ago, when he and Laura had lived in California, he had seen a sign in a seasonal Hal-loween store reading "Saw Kill" road.

As he recalled, it was one of those cheap foam or cardboard road signs, probably mass-produced in China or some other low-cost country, for a US company eager for cheap labor. The sign had been designed with a green background and reflective white lettering, just like a typical road sign. It read "Saw Mill Road" However, the "mill" portion of the sign was obscured by the scribbled word "KILL," done in a way that appeared to be written from dripping blood. Paul was fairly certain neither the workers in China, the businessmen in the United States, nor even the designers who created the idea for the sign had any prior knowledge of this particular Sawmill Road in Pennsylvania or its ominous history.

In fact, there were probably hundreds of Sawmill Roads around the country. He thought momentarily about a line he remembered from the promotion of the horror movie *A Nightmare on Elm Street,* which read, "There's an Elm Street in every town." Paul figured there must be a Sawmill Road in almost every rural community; hence the popularity of the novelty sign, he supposed.

Still, he couldn't help but wonder about the strange feeling he had every time he walked by the mill. Although they had never discussed it, Paul and Laura always walked by the mill during the brightest part of the day. Once, about a month ago, after a busy Saturday afternoon of shopping, they considered taking what they called their "Sawmill walk" but then thought better of it; both of them conveniently using the excuse they were too tired, when in fact the decision was based on an unspoken realization the sun was rapidly setting, and it would be dusk as they passed the gloomy sawmill.

As Paul became more familiar with the area, he felt less apprehensive about the dilapidated mill and eventually had no trouble walking past it. In fact, the previous day, he had taken a walk alone; Laura was not feeling well, and he deliberately slowed down as he got to the mill, being bold enough to leave the road and walk up to the structure and stand within a few feet of its battered front stairs.

He now sat at the kitchen table, having just finished his Sunday evening dinner, and asked Laura if she was up for a walk; he suspected she might not be as she hadn't seemed to eat very much.

"No," she replied, "I'm still not feeling so well in my stomach. I must have a bug or something. If I don't feel much better by tomorrow morning, I suspect I will stay home from work."

Paul thought how odd it was to hear Laura consider staying home since she rarely missed work, no matter how sick she might be. "If you feel that bad, do you think we should take you to the emergency room?"

"No thanks," she said with a sarcastic laugh, "I would rather lie around here all night than spend five or six hours in a room full of sick and injured weekend people. You know how poor people always use the hospital emergency room for their medical needs. The last time we were there, many families seemed to know each other, like it was a party they all went to every weekend or something."

"Yes, I remember," Paul said, thinking about how he had cut his finger doing yard work about two months ago; Laura had to drive him to the hospital for stitches. It was a four-hour snore-fest before the physician's assistant even had an opportunity to look at his injury. "You're probably right."

"I think I'll just go in and lie down on the couch for a while and watch TV," Laura said.

"Would you mind if I took our 'Sawmill walk' alone?" he asked. Laura looked out the window and noticed the sun was beginning to set. "Are you sure you want to do that?" She suggested, feeling somewhat foolish, not wanting to express her apprehension too strongly.

"Sure," he said, "In fact, I might even run part of the way to make sure I get back before dark. Don't worry, I'll be fine."

"I suppose if you say so," Laura replied with discomfort. "Take your cell phone along with you in case you trip and fall or get hit by a car or something."

"I will," he said nervously as he held up his phone to show her he would be just a phone call away. He walked her to the couch and ensured she was comfortable before kissing her goodbye and leaving.

Paul walked out the front door of their home and strode briskly through the streets of the subdivision for about a mile until the cement sidewalks ended abruptly at Abington Lane. Checking for oncoming traffic, he crossed Abington to the right side of the road, walking steadily until he came to the intersection with Sawmill. "Saw Kill," a quiet, raspy voice echoed in his head, and he felt himself mouthing the words silently along with the thought. A cold chill ran down his spine.

As he turned right onto Sawmill Road, he felt a strange sensation, as if he was not just on another road but was entering another world. He looked out along the curves of the road, which seemed to take on a dreamlike, surrealistic appearance, knowing that around the farthest turn in the road ahead, the ominous sawmill awaited like a hideous specter, hiding in anticipation of his arrival.

He thought perhaps he should simply turn around, head home, and call it quits. He could always tell Laura he was too tired or say he got a cramp in his leg or some other excuse. But he knew if he did, she'd suspect why he didn't want to walk by the mill. Although Paul was certain that Laura would understand completely and not think less of him, he didn't like her knowing he had backed out; she would always know he could not bring himself to walk by the mill alone at dusk.

Paul decided; instead, he'd walk at a deliberate pace up Sawmill Road with his head focused on the highway and do his best not to change the direction of his vision until he was well past the mill. He considered jogging past the mill to get it over with more quickly but felt that doing so might be akin to a cowardly act, the same as if he had turned around and gone home. So, instead, he walked with his eyes focused on the blacktop, purposefully moving up Sawmill Road. "Saw Kill," he again heard a strange voice whisper in his mind. He tried desperately to ignore the strange voice, blaming it on an overactive imagination.

As he approached the mill area, he heard the voice in his head grow stronger, taking on a tone that sounded eerily insane. "Saw Kill," the voice said repeatedly, slowly growing louder and more frantic with each utterance; "Saw Kill, Saw Kill, Saw Kill" repeatedly. Paul stopped in the middle of the road and slowly raised his head, turning it cautiously to the right, where the decaying sawmill stood. Instantly, the voice assaulting him in his mind stopped and was replaced by blessed silence as he looked at the opening where the front door of the mill once stood: a cavern of darkness resembling the gaping maw of some hideous demonic creature.

Paul realized the apprehension he had previously felt about the mill was completely gone. In fact, he felt foolish for having the feelings in the first place. He suddenly realized the mill was an abandoned building, a run-down wreck, nothing more. He felt an incredible exhilaration flow through him as he stood in the waning sunlight of dusk in front of the sight of the community's most feared legend, and he didn't feel anything but pity for the unfortunate, uneducated locals who allowed themselves to fall prey to such wild imaginings.

Before he realized he was doing so, Paul stepped off the roadway, through the tall weeds and wild grass, directly toward the front of the building. He stood momentarily, looking up at the precarious structure as if defying it to collapse, which it didn't.

He walked slowly around the left side of the building and saw the dirt driveway and large opening where once two barn doors stood. He walked up the pathway to the entrance and was surprised to see the mill floor, which was still fairly intact and structurally sound, obviously constructed of thick wooden beams. He also noted a fair amount of light in the mill entering through the broken western windowpanes from the bright setting sun.

Paul stepped cautiously onto the floor, testing to ensure the structure was as sturdy as it appeared. Before he realized it, he took several steps inside the mill and turned to look down the length of the building. To his surprise, several hundred feet ahead, he saw a large worktable, above which hung the rusted, pitted blade of the notorious saw. Looking up toward the ceiling, he saw where once the huge canvas drive belts, used to power the saw, had hung, now were dry-rotted strips hanging limply like giant pieces of pasta, useless for powering anything any longer.

He approached the table and noticed a dark brown stain soaked into the wooden slab. Looking closely at the rusted circular blade, he saw a similar dark color. "Blood," Paul thought, "A bloodstain from the last night the saw was ever used." Once again, the shiver returned, and Paul started to feel a pang of apprehension and the resurgence of his earlier fears.

As Paul stared in amazement at the useless, rusted blade, he noticed it began to change. Before his eyes, the rust started flaking off in thousands of bits of falling debris and orange dust, revealing a shiny metal blade below. The dark area encircling the teeth of the blade was now bright red, and drips of blood began to fall from the teeth to the bench below. Above him, the rotted, sagging canvas belts began to regain their luster and seemed to climb upward, knitting themselves miraculously back together, repairing themselves, looking as good as new.

Paul tried to turn and run but was unable to move. Suddenly, he felt someone grab him from behind. He turned to see who held him and saw the unthinkable: a translucent being stood behind him, holding him securely, preventing him from escaping. Paul felt the impossible pressure of its icy death grip. He couldn't make out the thing's appearance but sensed it must be hideous. He felt his heart begin to pound violently in his chest.

Then he heard the same familiar voice in his mind saying "Saw Kill, Saw Kill" repeatedly. He looked in the sound's direction and saw a specter slowly walking from the darkness toward him. It appeared to be a man dressed in early twentieth-century clothing, a business suit that seemed stained with blood. As Paul looked closer, he could see the right side of the man's skull was missing, and his face was splattered with chunks of skin and blood.

Behind the specter, another creature came lumbering out of the darkness. It appeared to have once been a man, but now was something hideous. This poor creature stood naked, with no visible genitalia. From where its crotch should have been, a long line of awkwardly sewn stitching worked its way up along the stomach area, the chest, the neck, and even the center of its face and skull. Paul understood what he was seeing had once been one of the unfortunate workers that Hanson had cut in two on the very saw before him.

He assumed the creature holding him from behind must be the second of Hanson's victims. Paul tried to scream but found himself unable to utter a sound. The shambling creature beside Hanson came forward and grabbed Paul's legs, lifting them upward and placing them on the saw table. Unable to move, he was helpless to fight or escape.

Within a few moments, the saw blade started to rotate slowly, and then it began to spin madly, spraying droplets of blood down upon him. Soon, the edge moved slowly down toward Paul's chest, as his mind screamed "Saw Kill, Saw Kill" just before everything went black.

* * *

Laura stood silently at the gravesite of her dead husband, dressed in widow's black, surrounded by friends and relatives. One by one, the mourners approached her to offer their condolences until soon all were gone, and she found herself alone. That was, except for one lone man standing next to the grave. She recognized him immediately as the local medical examiner. He had told Laura he would tell her of his final determination of the cause of death as soon as he was ready.

The man approached Laura and said, "Once again, Mrs. Simmons, I am very sorry for your loss."

"Thank you, Doctor Johnson. I appreciate it very much," she replied. Then, wanting to get the unpleasantness over with, she asked, "I was wondering . . . did you finalize your report . . . you know . . . on Paul's cause of death? Was it . . . was it a heart attack?"

"Yes, my dear. That was the cause. Again, I am so sorry," the doctor replied.

Laura's face took on the appearance of resignation, which often accompanies the feeling of closure in such situations. "Thank you for all you've done, Doctor," Laura replied as the doctor turned to leave.

Walking slowly back to his car, the doctor saw his assistant waiting by his car to drive him back to the office.

"Did you tell her?" The assistant inquired.

"I told her what she needed to hear," the doctor replied, "Her husband had a heart attack, and that is why he died. End of story."

"But what about . . . ?" The young assistant asked curiously, stopping short of completing his question.

The doctor stared at him sternly and insisted, "I told her nothing. As far as you and I are concerned, there is nothing else. And since you and I are the only ones who know any differently, I had better not hear anyone else around this township repeating the story back to me, or I will know exactly where it came from. Do I make myself perfectly clear?"

"Clear as can be," The assistant replied. "I swear, I won't say a word."

The doctor and his assistant got into their car and silently drove away. The doctor was going over the incredibly impossible results of his examination in his mind. It was beyond his understanding, beyond his comprehension. When he autopsied Paul Simmons, he never expected to discover what he saw upon cracking open the man's chest cavity. No one ever expected to find the dead man's heart sawed cleanly in two.

DEATH CYCLE

/ 1 /

It seemed to appear mysteriously out of nowhere, and it sat parked in front of old Mrs. Fenwick's house that autumn evening. There was a chill in the air, somewhat colder than was normal for that late September night. None of the neighbors who saw the bizarre motorcycle sitting by the curb knew who it belonged to or why it was there.

The bike was painted a flat black from front to back. It had a long, extended, forked front tire configuration. Only a few accessories on the black motorcycle were chrome: the handlebars, the braided trim around the seat, the front fork extension, and the spoked wheels. Its most bizarre and notable feature was the shining chrome skull with ruby-colored eyes mounted at the base of the handlebars. The motorcycle had no lights of any kind, nor any reflectors.

"So, who do you think it belongs to?" Henry Walker asked. He was a slightly overweight man in his late 50s. He wore carpenter-style blue jeans, a red and black checkered flannel shirt tucked below his ample midsection, and work boots. Henry still had a good crop of salt and pepper hair, matching furry eyebrows, and a bushy mustache. His piercing dark eyes bore a look of serious concern. Henry was heavily involved with the neighborhood crime watch organization, so being suspicious was beneficial, especially since it came naturally to him.

"I'm sure it's just some young guy's bike. Probably some kid staying over with a friend in the neighborhood," Jim Goldman added. He was a younger man of about thirty-six, dressed in jeans, a Penn State sweatshirt, and sneakers. Unlike Henry Walker, Jim was not one to be suspicious or find some work of evil lurking around every corner. As an engineer, he thought logically and, as a result, deduced the young friend theory.

"What, young friend, Jim? There aren't that many teenage kids around here anymore," Henry said. "We've practically become a fifty-five and older community by natural attrition."

Jim said, "Well, the Johnsons have several older kids, including a boy, Chaz, who I believe is seventeen. I suppose the bike may belong to one of his friends."

"Or to young Charles himself," Miss Emma Hinkle, a retired schoolteacher, interjected. She approached the group looking curious, with her walking stick, her gray hair tied back in a bun, and her reading glasses resting low on her slim nose. "I taught young Charles in seventh grade, and he has always been interested in motorcycles. Perhaps his parents bought him one."

Emma was also the neighborhood busybody who knew most of the neighbors, having taught many of them in junior high before retiring several years earlier. It seemed like she was a walking encyclopedia of personal information about almost everyone in town and the neighborhood. Because of her bank of knowledge, she already knew Chaz's father would never have bought him a motorcycle, but she was just stirring the pot to see what floated to the top, as she always seemed to do.

"Sorry, Miss Hinkle, I hate to argue with you, but I know Chaz's dad really well. He hates motorcycles and would never buy one for Chaz," Bill McCarthy said.

"Yes, William. I know you and Wayne Johnson have been friends for a long time. Or did you forget how many hours the two of you spent in my detention hall after school?"

Bill McCarthy was momentarily caught off guard as Miss Hinkle had a way of always doing to him. He blushed slightly, then agreed, "True, Miss Hinkle. I remember those times very well. Still, I doubt Wayne would ever buy any of his kids a motorcycle or allow them to have a friend who had one. Wayne always calls them 'Donor Cycles' for obvious reasons."

Miss Hinkle added, "Well, William, I see Wayne still has the dark sense of humor and sharp tongue he frequently used in school to secure himself a place in detention."

"Yes, Miss Hinkle," Bill conceded, blushing again.

Henry suggested, "I'll bet whoever owns this bike is staying over with that young Jill Maxwell." Everyone in the neighborhood knew Jill Maxwell or, more importantly, knew of her reputation for being somewhat promiscuous. Perhaps "somewhat" does not give Jill's reputation full acknowledgment. She was considered by most to be the neighborhood slut. Jill was in her early twenties, the youngest of three kids and the only sibling still living at home. She had two illegitimate children before she was twenty from two different men, and both babies had been given up for adoption. Jill's parents were out of town as they often were, and it wouldn't have surprised any neighbors if she had a "friend" sleeping over. Based on the undesirable types of friends she tended to have, the idea of one owning such a dark and strange motorcycle would not be out of the question.

Miss Hinkle faked a sigh of sad understanding and said, "Oh yes. Poor Jill. I remember her well. From what I've heard, she has apparently continued cultivating the negative reputation she acquired in high school."

Henry said, "Well, Emma. From what I've heard, 'Apparently' doesn't even begin to cover what the young lady has supposedly been up to. She's known all around the county for . . . well, for things best not discussed in mixed company."

Now, it was Jim's turn to feel embarrassed about the direction this conversation was taking. Truth be told, Jim had 'known' Jill in the biblical sense a time or two himself despite being a so-called happily married man with two young children. Jim figured now might be the best time to keep the conversation from heading further down the road of Jill Maxwell. This was especially important because of the suspicious way nosey Emma Hinkle was eyeballing him.

Jim said, "Well, I suppose none of that is really any of our business. Jill is an adult and is free to do as she pleases. The motorcycle is parked legally, so I suppose it doesn't matter who it belongs to."

Emma Hinkle cheerfully added while still giving him the hairy eyeball, "Of course, you're correct, James, but you must admit, the mystery is quite interesting, especially if Jill is involved."

Jim decided it was time for him to beat feet and head home. He returned Emma's glare and said, "I can't speak for the rest of you, but motorcycle or no motorcycle, it's getting late, and those of us still in the workforce have to get up early tomorrow, so I'll say my good night to you all and be on my way." Then he turned and made a hasty retreat away from any further discussions about Jill Maxwell.

Soon, each member of the impromptu gathering began walking away, seeing no other reason to continue worrying about the motorcycle. Miss Hinkle wore a strange grin as she headed home, fairly certain she had just confirmed a rumor she had heard about Jim Goldman, something she would tuck away in her memory for use some other day. As Henry walked away, he occasionally gave a nasty glance back at the weird motorcycle. Something about it bothered him.

/ 2 /

Mrs. Fenwick was a widow and had been for more than a decade. She and her late husband, Clyde, had never had any children, so she lived alone in her modest Cape Cod-style home. At eighty-nine years old, she could no longer do many of the daily chores required to maintain her home, inside or out. Some of her younger neighbors took turns doing various tasks for her. For example, Jim Goldman often mowed her lawn and took her trash cans to the curb for pick-up.

Many other neighborhood wives would stop by her home to make her meals and clean her house. Mrs. Fenwick could still wash and bathe herself, but hauling laundry had become a chore beyond her capabilities. As a result, one of the neighbors would also pitch in and assist.

Maggie Dawson was a thirty-two-year-old woman who worked remotely from her home office. She would stop by Mrs. Fenwick's home around seven o'clock every morning to make breakfast. On Monday morning, the day after the odd motorcycle sighting, Henry Walker was out in front of his home loading his lunch box into his truck when he heard a horrible scream coming up the street at Mrs. Fenwick's house.

Henry dropped his box onto the front seat of the truck and ran as fast as his age and weight would allow toward the sound of the scream. When he arrived at Mrs. Fenwick's house, he noticed two things. The first thing he saw immediately. Maggie Dawson was running down the front porch toward him, waving her arms and screaming madly, "She's dead. She's dead. Mrs. Fenwick is dead."

Maggie threw her arms around Henry's neck and sobbed into his shirt. Henry gently patted her back, saying, "There, there, Maggie. Calm down now and tell me what happened."

Maggie pulled herself away and explained, "I came over to make Mrs. Fenwick her breakfast like I do every day. I noticed she hadn't come downstairs yet. So, I went upstairs and found her in bed, and she was dead."

But Henry only heard a small portion of what she was saying as his attention was focused on the street. The strange motorcycle was gone. It might have been a coincidence, but Henry was suspicious and didn't believe in coincidence. Sure, Mrs. Fenwick was old, frail, and more than likely had simply died of natural causes in her sleep, but something felt off or wrong with this situation.

Maggie interrupted his thoughts and asked, "Aren't you listening to me, Henry?"

"Um, yes. I'm sorry, this is all so shocking. What did you say?"

"I said somebody should call the cops or an ambulance or something. Do you know what to do, Henry? Because I have no idea."

"Um, ah, I suppose I should call someone in authority and let them tell us what to do." So Henry took out his cell phone, and instead of dialing 911, he speed-dialed the police department. As a member of the neighborhood crime watch, he always had the number handy. Local police often wished he didn't have the number, as Henry called them more often than they wanted.

Police Sergeant Joe Daniels was on the desk. He was a kindly old fellow who probably should have retired years earlier, but things in the peaceful town made his job essentially stress-free, save for the occasional calls from local busybodies and neighborhood crime watch organizations. Reluctant to have his quiet morning disrupted, Joe nonetheless answered the phone.

"Police department, Sergeant Daniels speaking. How can I help you?"

"Joe, this is Henry Walker of the neighborhood crime watch out in Riverview Estates."

"Of course it is."

"Excuse me?" Henry asked.

"Nothing, never mind. What can I do for you this time, Henry?"

"Joe, we have a problem. Mrs. Fenwick is dead."

"She is? Old Mrs. Fenwick? I thought she died a long time ago."

"No, Joe. She just died this morning. One of the neighborhood ladies, Maggie Dawson, who helps take care of her, found her a few minutes ago."

"That's Bob Dawson's wife, ain't it?"

"Um . . . yes, yes, I suppose it is," Henry said distractedly.

"Young Bob's a good fella. I went to school with his dad, Bob senior."

"That's all well and good, Joe, but what are we going to do about Mrs. Fenwick?"

"What's there to do, Henry? She's dead. That means she's probably not going anywhere anytime soon. Why don't you just call Jake McDoogle over at the funeral parlor and tell him to come and get her."

"But there might be a problem, Joe."

"What sort of problem, Henry?" Joe waited for Henry to exaggerate the situation, which he always did since he liked to make a mountain out of a molehill.

"Well, Joe. I think there might be foul play afoot."

"Did you just say afoot?"

"What?"

"Nothing, Henry. Why do you suspect foul play? Mrs. Fenwick was like a thousand years old. Don't you think maybe she just, you know, kicked the proverbial bucket with no outside assistance?"

"Well, Joe. There might be extenuating circumstances."

"What? What sort of extenuating circumstances, Henry?"

"Last night, a weird black and chrome motorcycle was parked outside Mrs. Fenwick's house. None of us knew who owned the bike as we had never seen it before. This morning, it's gone, and she's dead."

"And?"

"And, maybe whoever owns that motorcycle murdered Mrs. Fenwick."

"Why do you believe Mrs. Fenwick was murdered? Have you looked at the body yet, Henry? Was there a sign of a struggle? Does her body appear to have been beaten or violated?"

"No, I haven't even been in the house yet. You know I wouldn't risk disturbing a crime scene. I'm far too well-trained for that. You may recall I graduated from the Citizen's Crimewatch Training Academy night school at the top of my class."

"Yes, Henry, I recall. And if I didn't, I can guarantee you will remind me every time you call. You said Maggie found the body, right?"

"Yes, that's right."

"Can you put her on the phone?"

"Well, she's kind of upset after finding Mrs. Fenwick and all."

"Put her on the phone, Henry," Joe said in his best serious cop voice. A moment later, Maggie Dawson came on the line.

"Sergeant Daniels, this is Maggie Dawson."

"How are you doing, Maggie? I know you've been through a bit of trauma this morning."

"Yes, Sir. I never seen a dead person before like that, you know, dead in bed. I seen them at McDoogle's funeral parlor, all dolled up but never like that . . . it was horrible."

"You can relax now, Maggie. A patrol car is on the way, and you can tell the officers all about it when they get there. But in the meantime, I'd like to get some preliminary information if you don't mind."

"It's ok, Sergeant. Go ahead," Maggie said.

"Can you briefly run through this morning and tell me what happened?"

"Um, ok. I went in the front door like always; Mrs. Fenwick never locked her doors. I noticed she wasn't downstairs yet, so I called out for her. When she didn't answer, I walked upstairs to see if she was alright. That's when I found her . . . Oh God, it was horrible."

"You're doing great, Maggie. Now, can you tell me a bit about the condition of her body?"

"Her body? Well, um, she looked normal, peaceful, like she was still sleeping. In fact, I called to her several times before I realized she was gone."

"Did her body appear . . . um, damaged in any way?"

"Oh no, Sir. She looked like an angel sleeping there in her bed. Nothing was out of the ordinary at all."

"Tell me, Maggie. Did you touch the body or move it at all?"

"Heavens no. I ain't never touched no dead body in my life and don't plan on starting now. Dead stuff gives me the creeps."

"Ok, Maggie. Now, here's what I want you to do. Wait right there with Mr. Walker and when the patrol car gets there, you be sure to tell the officer everything you just told me."

"I will, Sergeant."

"Now, do me a favor and put Henry back on the line."

Maggie handed the phone to Henry, who said, "Joe? You still there?"

"Of course, I'm here, Henry. Where the Hell else would I be? I just told Maggie that a patrol car is on the way. When it gets there, you stay with her while she is being questioned. The boys will go in and check out the body, but from what Maggie tells me, it looks like Mrs. Fenwick might have passed on naturally."

"But what about the bike?"

"What about the bike? Some kid probably was visiting a buddy and left sometime in the night."

"But . . ."

"No buts, Henry. Let my men check out the situation; they'll call the coroner if they need to. But I'll bet dollars to donuts the old lady just bought the farm naturally, and there is no need to turn this into one of your whodunnits."

"Well, if you say so. You're the police."

"That's right, Henry. We are the police, and we'll handle it," Joe said, reusing his most authoritative cop voice again.

Henry knew he had no choice but to let the police do their job, and maybe Mrs. Fenwick's death was natural after all. Still, that strange motorcycle troubled him, and he hoped he never saw it again.

/ 3 /

Two weeks later, after all the excitement from Mrs. Fenwick's passing had calmed down and the speculation about the mysterious motorcycle had become forgotten, the horrible thing appeared again. The bike sat parked on the street, but now it was in front of the Lawson's house.

Pete Lawson was another neighborhood octogenarian who lived with his wife, Grace, in a split-level home on a corner property. Unlike Mrs. Fenwick, Pete and Grace were both in great physical condition for their ages. Pete took immaculate care of the outside of the property, and Grace had no trouble handling the inside responsibilities.

Henry Walker, Jim Goldman, and Emma Hinkle stood beside the motorcycle, studying it with great interest. During the first few days after Mrs. Fenwick's death, Henry wouldn't let go of the idea that the appearance of this strange motorcycle was somehow responsible for her dying.

"Well, it's here again. And you know what that means," Henry insisted.

Jim said, " Come on, Henry. Don't tell me you're going to start that again. You know Mrs. Fenwick died of natural causes. The coroner proved that."

"I must correct you on that, Jim. It was the coroner's determination. I don't know if that is the same as proof. He's not a medical examiner."

Jim said with frustration, "All the parties in authority determined that there was no need for an autopsy by a medical examiner. She was old and sickly. People like that die every day."

"Maybe so, but this motorcycle being here really bugs me," Henry said.

Miss Hinkle added, "We're all bothered by the infernal thing, but there's apparently no reason for us to do anything but ignore it."

"But how can we ignore it, Emma? You know what it means with this motorcycle being here?"

Jim said, "We know no such thing, Henry. You have no proof that this bike has anything to do with Mrs. Fenwick's passing. It's all conjecture on your part."

"He's right about that, Henry. Without proof, Sergeant Daniels won't give you the time of day, let alone open an investigation," Emma offered.

Henry insisted, "If either Pete or Grace Lawson passes away tonight, then I'll have my proof."

"I hate to have to play the Devil's advocate, Henry," Jim said, "But both of the Lawsons are in their late eighties. One of them passing away is not something terribly unexpected. Even both of them dying could be explained naturally. It's happened to other close couples before."

Henry chuffed, "But the motorcycle is here. That should be proof enough."

Then Emma said, "I don't think anything short of photographic or video proof would be enough to convince Joe Daniels to start an investigation. He was another of my junior high boys, and I remember him as being ornery and downright cantankerous. He's a number of years older than you, Henry, so you wouldn't remember him from school. I was only teaching for a few years when he was my student. Actually, I was surprised to hear when he became a police officer. I always figured him to end up on the opposite side of the legal system."

One of the automatic streetlights came to life. Jim said, "Well, it's getting late, and morning comes early, so I must be heading home."

Emma waved as he turned to leave and said, "Give that lovely wife of yours my best, James. And give your little ones a hug for me. I hope you appreciate how lucky you are to have them." She was staring at Jim with eyes that seemed to penetrate his very soul. He reddened with embarrassment at the idea that the old woman might have suspected about his extramarital dalliances with Jill Maxwell.

"I will," Jim said brusquely, not turning to make eye contact with Emma but raising his hand to acknowledge her comment.

"Goodnight, Henry," Emma said, "It's time for me to be going as well."

"That sounds like a plan," Henry replied as Emma walked away. But that was not part of Henry's plan at all. He intended to wait in the shadows to see who came to claim the motorcycle. Then, he would find out what was really going on, once and for all.

/ 4 /

Henry Walker sat in the darkness behind an oak tree. The night's dew on the damp grass did nothing to help his arthritic hip, but Henry endured the pain because solving this mystery had become paramount to him. After several hours of squirming and repositioning to get comfortable, Henry's determination paid off.

In the shadows cast by the small roof over the Lawson's front entrance, Henry saw a tall, thin, hooded figure slowly coming down their sidewalk in the direction of the motorcycle. It wore a long, dark, hooded coat that reached all the way to the ground, making it appear as if the person was not so much walking as floating along the stone pavement. The figure held something in its right hand that seemed to be a walking stick or perhaps some sort of farm implement like a scythe.

As the figure approached the motorcycle, it placed the stick into a holder that allowed it to rest horizontally along the length of the bike. Then, the mysterious figure threw a leg over the side of the bike and mounted it. With great effort, Henry stood up from his hiding place and approached the motorcycle and its hooded driver. Before the person could start the bike, Henry grabbed the man's coat sleeve and shouted, "Hold it right there, buddy. You're not going anywhere."

Henry was certain that whoever this character was, the man had just done something to kill either one or both Lawsons. He was shocked that he dared to approach the man unarmed, but Henry supposed it was pure outrage that allowed him to do so.

The man turned, and Henry saw the face under the hood in the glow of a nearby streetlight. In the seconds that followed, Henry wished he had not been so bold that he had listened to Jim Goldman and had left this all alone because the face that stared out at him from under that hood was the face of no living man.

The creature inside the hood looked like the essence of death. Its face was a blackened and yellowed skull with patches of gray, mottled skin clinging randomly about it. At first, Henry thought it might be a Halloween mask, but far too quickly, he saw it was real. Yellow, squirming maggots crawled in and out of black, empty eye sockets and fell like drool from the creature's mouth of rotten tombstone teeth. A foul stench of rotting meat and feces surrounded whatever was inside the hood.

A moment later, the creature slowly raised its free arm and extended a skeletal hand with a bony index finger pointing at Henry. In a voice as unhuman as was imaginable, the thing said, "You are Henry Walker. I have come for you."

Henry stepped back and stammered, "But . . . but . . . I thought you were here . . . for . . . for the Lawsons."

"Ah, yes. The old bait and switch. That's exactly what I wanted you to think. It appears, Mr. Walker, you are too suspicious and too nosey for your own good. Well, now you've got your answers. Climb on board, and we'll be on our way."

Henry resisted as best as he could but had no choice but to climb on the motorcycle behind the hideous creature. As he did, he looked back to the sidewalk where he had stood only a few seconds earlier and saw his dead, crumpled body lying prone on the concrete. That was when his questions were answered, and he understood.

EDGE OF THE WORLD

"*Coincidence is God's way of remaining anonymous.*"
—ALBERT EINSTEIN

"*What God intended for you goes far beyond
anything you can imagine.*"
—OPRAH WINFREY

"*I believe in God, but not as one thing, not as an old man in the sky.
I believe that what people call God is something in all of us.
I believe that what Jesus and Mohammed and Buddha and all the
rest said was right. It's just that the translations have gone wrong.*"
—JOHN LENNON

It was January 1965. The ten-year-old boy tossed and turned restlessly in his bed. Young Jack Dawkins had been feeling ill for several days, and now his fever was at its highest. He wanted to awaken, but try as he might, he was unable to do so. He found himself trapped in a dream. When he finally awoke, Jack couldn't accurately describe what he had seen because of his young age and limited vocabulary. However, he would remember every detail of his dream and often replay it for the rest of his life. Jack hoped that one day, he would find a way to pass on an accurate description of everything he had seen in the dream, hoping that perhaps he or someone else would someday be able to make sense of it.

* * *

Jack's field of vision appeared oddly obstructed, much like the view one might have when looking through the distorted plastic face of a cheap rubber diving mask underwater after it had fogged around the outer edges. The lack of visual clarity was causing the young boy a significant amount of frustration. To make matters worse, the scene unfolding before him seemed to flow and shift continuously, as if the image was struggling to maintain its cohesiveness, shimmering in and out of existence.

It was almost as if reality might suddenly transform into something quite different, unexpected, and frightening. Deep down in his stomach, Jack experienced what he thought of as a "knowing." Something was telling him the fear, which he might normally consider irrational, was actually something to seriously concern him. His stomach began to knot and turn over in anticipation of the potential unknown events that might follow. His head hurt, his eyes burned, and a feeling of dread filled him with incredible trepidation.

As he focused his foggy vision to the best of his ability, Jack noticed his gaze was concentrated downward toward the ground below him. Through the haziness, he could see two feet, his feet, which appeared to be wearing a pair of shabby non-descript canvas sneakers, walking steadily forward, leading him to some unknown destination, yet one he somehow anticipated.

Jack watched each step he took and realized that although he knew he was walking, it didn't seem like it because he couldn't feel the impact of the ground beneath his feet. He should have felt every step but didn't, even though he could see he was moving steadily forward. Despite his frustration with the restricted vision and the strangeness of not feeling his footsteps, the sight of those beat-up old sneakers helped calm him. Those sneakers had seen him through many adventures in his young life, and apparently, we're about to lead him toward yet another one.

His mother had picked up the cheap canvas slip-ons from the bargain bin of their local thrift shop. Jack's family could never afford the high-priced sneakers the more affluent kids at school wore. Although his father worked hard to support his family, there was never enough money for such frivolous items. He had heard the phrase "money is tight" more times than he cared to remember.

As he examined his feet, Jack noticed he wasn't wearing socks. This was his typical style of dress for summer, although he was uncertain for some reason what season of the year it was. He was confused because he felt he should know this, and he was certain his last memory might have been of ice and winter. Yet now, Jack walked without socks and felt no cold. Come to think of it, he felt nothing whatsoever, as if he were watching a movie of his feet walking. Jack was aware and able to comprehend what was happening to him, yet he couldn't determine why it was occurring. He understood the particular season of the year was irrelevant to where this journey was taking him.

Jack tried to lift his head but was unable to do so. It was as if some supernatural force held his head downward and tilted slightly to the right as he walked onward. This caused a dull ache in his neck and severe pain in his head. However, he could do nothing to stop it. He discovered that his pain subsided somewhat if he didn't resist the pressure forcing him to look in that direction.

As a result, he tried his best not to put any resistance to the mysterious force. Yet still, somehow, in the back of his mind, he again felt the uneasy "knowing." It was a fear of what might be awaiting him at the end of this long walk. Young Jack Dawkins found it very disturbing not to know what was coming, yet to feel that he actually did know but couldn't put it into clear or concise thoughts. It was as if his thoughts had become as blurred as his foggy vision seemed to be. It was like a memory that refused to come to the forefront of his mind; it was almost there, but not quite.

Then he realized he wasn't in control of the motion of his legs either. They were walking at a steady pace, yet he could do nothing to control them any more than he could break the paralysis that forced his head downward. The more he struggled to control his body, the more it resisted, and the more he began to feel the pain.

Despite his forced position, Jack discovered that if he used his peripheral vision, he could somewhat increase his awareness of his surroundings, so he did his best to investigate. He felt as though he were walking on an upwardly sloping path, which wound in a clockwise helical direction around what must have been an extremely high, centrally located mountain. This sensation only helped to increase his uneasiness since Jack had an extreme fear of high places. Thinking about where he might be going immediately produced a feeling of vertigo in him, even though he couldn't see just how high he was climbing.

Jack couldn't tell how wide the path he walked was but suspected it might be quite narrow. That was either an accurate assumption or simply his fear of heights rearing its ugly head. It was causing him to imagine that just off to his left was a high, unprotected drop-off and that he might lose his footing and fall to his death at any moment.

His only salvation was that he was walking along the far-right side of the path, essentially hugging the mountain around which the trail seemed to wind. This was a small blessing because at least he couldn't see the open side of the path and couldn't tell how high above the ground he might be. As he climbed higher, he understood that the view from the left edge of the track might be more than he could tolerate.

He believed that whatever power forced him to plod onward might be aware of his phobia. If that were the case, it might explain why he walked on the right side of the path and why his vision was controlled. The portion of the way he could see passing beneath him was flat and brown, consisting of a soft, compacted substance, making walking easy.

Jack listened carefully for sounds around him. He could hear nothing except the steady rhythm of his steps, finding it strange that he couldn't feel his footsteps but could hear the gentle tread of each one. Interestingly, there were no plants, trees, bushes, grass, moss, or weeds along this trail. No smells of any kind were present either. He had never experienced this type of climbing path before, with such a narrow walkway spiraling along the side of a mountain.

He found that if he strained his vision to look as far to the right as possible, he could almost make out the mountain's surface, especially the portion of the hill that intersected with the path near his feet. It appeared to be unnaturally smooth. It, too, was brown in appearance and seemed constructed of the same densely packed dirt-like material on which he walked. It created an extremely smooth-faced solid surface.

It seemed as if someone had fashioned this mountain in the same way a child might make a sandcastle. However, he believed the words fashioned or formed might not exactly be the right words. On the other hand, maybe they were the right words but not the right tense of the words. Perhaps fashioning or forming was a more correct tense of the words.

"Forming. Yes," he thought. The word came instantly into his head, and he suddenly knew he was right. As he listened more intently, he heard what sounded like the distant pouring of sand through a funnel. It was faint and almost indistinguishable, yet it was still there. It was a nearly silent whooshing sound. He momentarily thought of a tagline at the beginning of one of his mother's favorite soap operas, "Like sand through an hourglass, so are the days of our lives."

He realized someone or something was creating the mountain as he walked. "How could that be?" he thought. He began to imagine that if somehow, he could break free of the controlling force and look up, he might not see anything higher than maybe two or three feet above the top of his head. Likewise, he believed if he could run around the next turn, he would likely fall off the end of the mountain since the next portion of the path and the mountain might not exist yet either.

How strange this was all becoming. What manner of being could control his every movement and create a mountain out of loose dirt on the fly as he walked upon it? With sudden assumption, he believed he might know, but the very thought filled him with such an overwhelming fear that he quickly tried to force the notion out of his mind that simply dwelling on the idea might make it a reality.

As Jack walked, he noticed a slight change in the path's appearance. Along the brown dirt path and the mountainside, he saw the occasional splotch of white start to appear. Seeing this dark path littered with these occasional white patches was unusual indeed. The spots resembled patches of snow, yet they were so much more.

Jack realized that the patches were unlike anything he had ever seen. They projected a glowing iridescence whiter than any white he had ever experienced, and they appeared to be void of any texture. The best way to describe them was to say they were simply the presence of ultimate whiteness.

When he took his gaze away from the white patches and again concentrated on his feet, he noticed his sneakers were gone and that he was now barefoot. Strangely, Jack still couldn't feel the surface nor see any change in texture when his feet passed over one of the ever-increasing white patches. He believed these patches might feel smooth or cool, perhaps even ice cold, but he felt nothing. It was almost as if he was still walking slightly above the path and the patches on a cushion of air.

He also noticed the legs of his jeans were no longer visible, just his naked legs and feet. He was surprised to see that his feet appeared to have grown larger and were those of a young adult. They seemed to grow older as he walked. At first, they resembled his father's feet, then appeared more like a much older man's.

He suddenly wondered with some embarrassment if he were completely naked. He believed that he might actually be the case. He was apparently walking along a path to who-knew-where, against his own will, naked as the day he was born, but now he was an old man. He wondered if perhaps he might simply be dreaming. Surely, he had to be.

Yet this was unlike any dream he had ever had where he either ended up in his underwear or naked. In this dream, he wasn't at school, standing in the classroom in front of his friends, trying to read a report buck-naked or clad in his underpants. In addition, for some reason, he was suddenly no longer embarrassed with his nudity. It was as though naked was the way he was supposed to be in this place. Nothing seemed strange or dirty about this either; it felt as natural to him as breathing.

His aging legs carried him onward and steadily upward. After a time, He noticed this glowing white substance had replaced almost all of the brown soil. Using his peripheral vision again, he saw that the sidewall of this mountain pathway had also changed to a glowing white surface.

Soon, he became aware he was approaching the top of the path and the end of his journey. He didn't understand how he knew this, but somehow, he just understood, and knowing this terrified him.

Jack tried to listen once again to the noises around him. The sounds of the path under his feet and the mountain formation had stopped. He was now on a plateau surface constructed of complete whiteness, and all around him. He was starting to feel like his control was returning to his muscles. Jack noticed the white path ended about three feet in front of him. From there, it seemed to drop into some vast dark chasm.

His vertigo began to kick in immediately. Even though he was not yet viewing what he believed to be a massive drop-off, Jack could imagine what it might look like, and his legs became weak. He could feel his balls start to tighten up and begin to crawl back inside his body like they did every time he fought his fear of heights. He didn't want to look because he somehow sensed what lay before him was something no man should see.

Then, without warning, every muscle in his body was back in his control as the force that held them in check released him. He stood naked at the top of some tremendously high glowing white mountain on a path that ended just a few feet before him and dropped off into some vast unknown and unseen void.

Slowly, keeping his eyes cast downward, he moved his head slightly to the left just enough to see that his path had widened to form a shelf that extended about twenty feet to his left before dropping off apparently into oblivion. Cautiously, he moved his head back to the downward position and then slowly to the right. Again, he saw the path wrapped around the mountainside and ended about twenty feet to his right. It also seemed to end abruptly and drop off into blackness.

The previous "knowing," haunting him throughout his journey, had become stronger. He knew what he must do next but didn't want to with all of his heart and soul. Yet he understood he had to raise his head and face what lay before him. He lifted his head cautiously, slowly allowing his eyes to follow the path in front of him, leading to the sharp drop-off into blackness.

Then, with an overwhelming clarity of vision, he saw everything at once. It was almost more than his mind could comprehend. He instantly saw everything in front of him, behind, below, above, and all around him simultaneously. It was impossible, yet he saw it, nonetheless. He saw himself standing on the edge of a precipice from a distance high above as if he were part of the event, and yet he was also watching it in a movie. He was no longer the young boy of ten, but somehow, he was impossibly an older man, perhaps in his late seventies or eighties.

"How could this be?" He thought.

The area directly in front of him was suddenly illuminated with incredible light, and he heard what sounded like a choir singing as one all around him. The voices were initially quiet, but then their volume gradually increased.

He saw he was standing on a shelf on the highest mountain that he could have ever possibly imagined. Spread out below him was the entire world. He could see towns, cities, farms, and countryside, everything laid out like tiny fixtures on a model railroad platform. He was so high that he could hardly recognize huge skyscrapers as more than miniature models that were part of some incredible diorama.

His eyes went back and forth, repeatedly scanning and rescanning the view before him, never wanting to look up above the horizon line because Jack sensed what might be awaiting him there. The chorus around him continued to swell as thousands of beautiful-sounding voices joined the others.

Finally, when the chorus sounds were so loud that he could barely stand it, he looked first out over the vast abyss before him. Then he finally looked up into the clouds above him and saw what he was destined to see, what he feared seeing more than he could express.

Jack's eyes immediately focused on an enormous face forming in the clouds off to his right side. It had to be huge because, although it was apparently very far away from him, it still appeared massive. He guessed it had to be many miles across and many miles high. The clouds in the sky had merged to make up a young man's face. Yet it was not just comprised of clouds alone. The vision seemed to have molded and solidified. The face looked off to his right. It looked down at the world spread out below and appeared extremely sad. Jack could see a teardrop form in the corner of the vision's eye and slowly roll down its cheek. He wondered if this might be some sort of heavenly being, perhaps an angel, maybe the archangel Gabriel himself. Jack attended Sunday School and church regularly, and he knew much about such things.

Before he could further think about the sight, something forced his head sharply to the left. Jack saw another formation take shape in the clouds, equally as large as the first one, if not larger. He knew immediately that this was not just another angel but a face he had seen depicted in countless paintings, a face he knew from church. It was the face he recognized as Jesus Christ.

Now he started to think he must be dead. He remembered he had been very sick and feverish. Maybe he had died in his sleep, and this was his judgment day. Why else had he been alone on his journey up the amazing mountain to the highest of high places? Why else would he be standing at the edge of the world facing the Lord himself?

He now saw the face of Christ also looking down in sorrow at the world below. Then, as with the other angelic figure in the clouds, a tear formed in the corner of the Christ figure's eye and trickled down his cheek.

Suddenly, the singing chorus got louder than ever, and Jack thought his ears would rupture from the incredible volume. His skull began to pound with agony that he had never experienced, and he began to fear that his brain might explode.

The part of Jack that simultaneously floated high above the spectacle could see everything as he looked down from on high. He could see the clouds with the image of the angel and that of Christ off in the distance with a jumble of swirling clouds between them. He could still see himself as an old man on his knees, weeping in supplication at the edge of the world.

Jack wanted the vision to end so he could walk back down the path to his family. Surely, his mother must be worried sick about him by now. However, his mind was suddenly filled with the images of hundreds of thousands of newsreels flashing by simultaneously, showing the most horrible examples of atrocities man had committed upon his fellow man. He had seen many of these in history class and believed that by the time he reached the age of the old man on the ledge, he would see many more. That was assuming he ever did get to that age.

That old man version of himself had fallen to his knees and was obviously overflowing with shame and sorrow, apparent in the way he was pressing his head down against the glowing white ground. Jack knew this terrible event would not end until he again looked up and saw the final image he was required to witness. Knowing what that image would be, Jack simply didn't believe he could bear to look upon it. Old Jack cried and sobbed aloud, ashamed and not wanting to face what might be his ultimate judgment.

Once again, the mysterious power controlling him forced his head to rise, and his eyes looked skyward. From his position, bent on his naked knees, Jack saw the swirling mass of clouds between the two heavenly images begin to take a human-like form.

He instantly understood what he was about to see was only what his mind could tolerate without driving him insane. The swirling clouds formed a face he had seen in many paintings, television shows, and movies. It was the face of Neptune, Zeus, and Santa Claus, an image from the ceiling of the Sistine Chapel, a face representing the image of God.

The swirling clouds formed a massive, bearded face larger than the other two images. It had great, bushy eyebrows above a pair of angry eyes that seemed to stare right through him to his soul. He felt as if he were not just physically naked but spiritually exposed to the piercing gaze. When he could no longer bear the shame of those soul-searching eyes, Jack found himself again able to move, and instead of attempting to flee, he bowed his aching head, folded his hands, and began praying not only for himself but for all of mankind.

* * *

Jack awoke in a cold sweat in his bed. It was the middle of the day, and he was terrified. He reached up and felt tears coursing down his cheeks. He could recall every detail of his dream and went over it as he would countlessly for the rest of his life.

He had sensed a message in that dream, although he had no more idea what it was as an adult than he did as a boy. And if there was a message, why send it to him? He was no one special. He had only been a typical kid when the vision came to him. Then, he had grown into a man, led a normal life, and was now an older and wiser man. Yet the dream still haunted him, and its meaning still eluded him.

He could only hope that the event someday might make more sense to him. Then Jack realized that the term event was a more accurate description of what he had experienced. He had always considered it more than a dream or a vision. But maybe that was wrong. Had it been an actual event? Had it actually happened?

Had he been more ill on that fateful day than he had known? Had he been so close to death that he had seen into the future, his future? When his time to die came, would he have to walk the same path he had walked in his vision all those years ago? Would he see his life symbolized by the steady plodding up a narrow mountain path? Would the mountain form as he progressed, or would it be finished? He suspected the latter since it would be as complete as his own life had been.

Perhaps that was the answer. The mountain he walked as a child represented the life he had yet to live, symbolically forming as he walked. When Jack's time came to walk the path again, would the mountain, like his life, be finished? When he reached the summit, would he face judgment for his life, good or bad? Perhaps so.

Then again, maybe this vision was nothing more than a hallucinogenic dream brought on by his high fever and medication. Did the teachings of his Sunday school classes creep into his dreams and affect them? Yet why had that dream been so real and so detailed? Why did the vision affect him so intently that it haunted his thoughts all these decades afterward? Jack wondered if he would ever comprehend the true meaning of this elusive dream.

He supposed he wouldn't know until he knew. Thinking for a moment, Jack realized how oversimplified and perhaps idiotic that statement sounded. Yet he also understood how profoundly accurate it was. Jack wouldn't know, he couldn't know, any more than any of us can know what, if anything, awaits us after death. Jack understood that he and everyone, unfortunately, must accept their ignorance and wait. Jack believed that everyone may have to walk a similar path on some fateful day.